Raven

Raven Dane is the author of the Dark Fantasy series, The Legacy of the Dark Kind with Blood Tears, Blood Lament and Blood Alliance already published. The series has already gained an enthusiastic and growing international following; the next eagerly awaited books will be Blood Legend and her first steampunk novel, Cyrus Darian and the Technomicron.

The manic world of Fuggis Mire first started as a creative exercise to beat a crippling writer's block. Now this scurrilous, irreverent and most definitely adult fable has a life and following of its own after Raven posted a few sample chapters online. The story was an instant hit with readers clamouring to read more of her wicked sense of humour. Now they can.

As Raven says, 'It may be a parody of High Fantasy clichés but it is a most affectionate parody, written with due reverence to much loved conventions and tropes.'

Or as her bad boy character Zaff would scoff, 'Yeah, right!'

The Unwise Woman
of Fuggis Mire

RAVEN DANE

First Edition published 2010
by Prosochi, an imprint of
Endaxi Press, 2nd Floor, 145-157 St John Street, London EC1V 4PY

ISBN 978-1-907375-99-6

British Library Cataloguing in Publication Data.
A catalogue record for this book is available from the British
Library.

Printed by Lightning Source, Kiln Farm, Milton Keynes.

Dedicated to Lee and Lyndsey Done, 'Neets' and my many dear friends who have loved and supported this book from its inception, including the Authonomy gang.

The Prologue From Hell

Even a prince of the underworld could have vocational problems. Rafial certainly did as he approached the Boss's audience chamber, a booming cavern of infinite size and crazed dimensions, grandiose in its demonic décor and impressive perma-flames. Rafial was different to the other devils working in the Deadly Sins department of Hell, he had brains, he had ambition. He was sick to death of his job for eternity, in charge of tormenting the souls of the greedy. How tedious was dangling scrummy food at the end of long poles above the heads of the forever hungry? Beyond words. Rafial had an escape plan, during his off duty breaks, he created *The Book*.

As he wished it to be real, it had sprung into existence fully formed and entirely complete. A unique entity with only one purpose: to spread discord, disorganization and ultimately destruction. The Boss would love it, he would then love Rafial enough to promote him up to Research and Development of Evil Ideas. Gathering together his courage, he entered the booming cavern.

Within what passed for minutes in Hades, Rafial was on the ground cowering from Satan's fury.

'A book?' the Boss howled in derision, 'You waste my time bringing me a book! Are there not a new group of food critics just arrived for you to torment? The ones poisoned by a starter of wheatgrass foam on pork belly jus.'

He picked up the offending item by the tips of his talons, 'If I wanted a book, I'd call up Dan Brown or Jordan!'

Rafial did his best to swing the situation in his favour, he'd seen it work sometimes on Dragon's Den; 'Sir, this book becomes whatever the reader wishes it to become. It finds the hidden desires of the person who holds it and it gives them exactly what they seek... They won't be able to put it down.'

'I have already invented the Argos catalogue,' seethed the Devil, who loathed dissension in any form.

'You have wasted my time and tested my patience with this nonsense ... this is what I think of your book...'

He tore it into pieces. Not cross ways, the Boss wasn't that physically strong; more brain than brawn.

'And this is what I think of you.'

The Boss sent Rafial flying out of the cavern onto a jet of hot air powered by the Pit of Politicians which threw him upwards into a tear in reality and out of Hell with the pieces of book swirling around him. As is often the way with rips in the time space continuum, when the demon landed the pieces of book were scattered far and wide. To his relief, Rafial had arrived in the mortal world and a new life. One where he called the shots and didn't have to torment another soul. Unless he wanted to.

The pieces of book were not so blasé. They had been torn asunder. They felt pain. They felt incomplete. Each section knew it must rejoin with the others. This gave them purpose, which gave them power. Though weakened, they still contained the magicke with which Rafial had imbued them. This caused them to be like magnets, to be irresistibly drawn to each other.

One day the parts would re-unite and The Book would be whole again. Then terrible things would be wrought. The parts of the whole had no idea what terrible things, but they knew that as an entirety The Book would have no similar difficulty. They didn't need Rafial to reconstitute them, they would do it themselves, if it took millennia. Time and space presented no serious problems, not as long as they knew they had each other – somewhere. Until then they went undercover and waited to be found by enquiring minds.

Part One
The Feast of St Epiligia

Morven Moonraven

Mrs Morven Moonraven

Mrs Jed Moonraven

Mr Jed and Mrs Morven
Moonraven

The Moonraven Family

The Unwise Woman chewed the soggy end of her green biro as she paused from doodling in a well-thumbed Book of Shadows. The words were not details of a love spell but wishful thinking. She couldn't make things happen against someone's free will, sooo against the rules. It was the sort of thing that would come back and bite her on the bum three fold.

She dropped the biro with a sigh of self-disgust, she was not some drippy loved up teenager but an on duty witch with an important job to do. It was the first morn of the week long Feast of St Epiligia. Throughout the realm people would be rising early, making preparations for the marathon of merry making to come. Except the St Epiligia Pedants who were readying themselves to get really riled in public which would end in tears. Always just theirs.

As Morven wandered outside to gather mireberries for her breakfast, her attention was caught by a small blue bird carolling its delight at a new day dawning, flying high in the rosy sky above the malodorous and dangerous region where she dwelled, the Bog of Fuggis Mire, home of strange creatures and lurking mysteries. As the bird headed towards the Land of Goodness and Light she knew that below its wings spread a deceptively slumbering landscape.

In the meadows and along riverbanks, the official highly skilled Catchers were diligently at work finding small furry creatures for the feast days, to be caught but strictly not harmed. Indeed all would be released back where they came from at the end of the festival. Though sometimes the original locations got mixed up. No one knew if they ever found their true homes or settled in the wrong ones. To date there had been no complaints.

At the farthest borders of this blessed land was a vile hinterland of bleak plains scoured by howling winds that in turn led to the Land of Darkness and Despair.

Far to the north were the majestic snow-capped Mountains of Adventures Yet Untold and beyond them a barren desert that stretched to the vast, wild Ocean of Dreams Undreamt. And beyond that was Basingstoke.

None of this concerned the happy little bird as it dipped and soared in the cool early morning breeze, singing its full repertoire of lilting song. It flew low across cornfields slowly ripening into a rippling sea of gold, high above orchards where branches were already overladen with fruit, across a wide, sparkling river where silver shoals of fish glinted beneath the fast moving clear water. With its nest in sight, the bird quickened its pace, approaching a tall, graceful oak tree where generations of its kind had raised and fledged their young. Where its own mate and newly hatched chicks waited.

With one swift grab, a plummeting hawk grabbed the bird and took it home to its own ravenous brood. It was the Feast of St Epiligia but shit still happened.

'Lucky little wotsit,' murmured a hard labouring serf as he watched a small blue bird flit above his head in the pre dawn twilight. With its mouth crammed full, it was indeed the early bird that got the worm. Envious, the peasant's stomach grumbled, reminding him that in his liege's crazy rush to beat all the others, he had gone without any breakfast. Not that this fact would have bothered the armour plated pillock he served. Ahead of him, trudged his lord and master, only two hours into their journey and whingeing already.

'Suede boots!' Prince Pravis muttered with dour bad grace as he sunk lower into the stinking bog, 'What low bred varlet decided that suede thigh boots was de rigueur for handsome heroes on noble quests?'

His serf, dragging their unwilling and increasingly surly horses by the ends of the reins did not answer.

Squarf was tough and muscular but vertically challenged. The fetid bog ooze had long since splurged over the top of his boots and he now trudged behind his master with his socks sodden with freezing squelching mire.

'And why do wise crones always have to always live in filthy bogs?' continued Pravis, 'What is wrong with a little bijou cottage in a neat flower strewn meadow? Preferably close to my castle.'

The prince threw back his long mane of golden hair in a dramatic gesture of pique, startling a carrion crow which in turn spooked the horses. The animals spun around, pulling the reins from the serf's hands. As Squarf fell face down into the bog, the animals laden with all their spare weapons and supplies galloped off, kicking up a flurry of stinking silt with more than a suggestion of equine smirks.

'By Odin's Armpit!' cursed Pravis balefully glaring after the swiftly disappearing rumps of the horses, 'If I thought I'd end up in this dreadful mire, I would never have agreed to go on the quest for the Chalice of Untold Delights.

'Now the bugger tells me,' Squarf muttered under his breath. He would have spoken it out loud, risking a kicking from his master, but his mouth was still full of black, foul tasting ooze complete with twigs and wriggling bugs. He fished the debris out of his mouth and sorting out the insects, stuffed them in a pouch strung from his leather belt. Well, he had to eat something that morning.

Within an hour of exhausting struggle through the mud and mire they came across a bizarre dwelling built on a small hillock of grass and trees that rose above the swamp.

With objects hanging from every branch of the tall Snivelling Willow that draped wistfully over her hovel, the wise woman's home was at first glance everything Prince

Pravis and his manservant Squarf had expected. Even the deafening sound of bleating goats and croaking toads triggered by their arrival was weird but a normal and expected weird. This thought changed as they approached to within touching distance. Instead of the regulation shamanic objects; bones, rune stones, raven feathers, unidentified bits of animal, the crone had tied up a colander, a fluffy toy duckling wearing wellingtons and a sailor's hat and pictures cut out of cereal packets.

Higher up the branches she had displayed a hideous retro orange lampshade and a cat basket. From the lower branches of the tree, dangled a hideous pair of fading-once-multi-coloured stripy-socks, some knickers, a red bra and three red plastic spoons and at least twenty banana skins ranging from fresh yellow to malodorous and rotting black.

'We'll be ok for bananas then,' quipped Squarf, still hungry from his meagre breakfast of bug sushi.

From her medicinal herb garden, Morven watched the clumsy progress of two men approaching her hovel. She swore under her breath. Visitors! And so early, that was all she needed. Unseen by the newcomers, she ran into her back yard to get ready. A noble knight or a prince with his servant on a quest. Rats. Why did they always turn up when she planned a lazy day snuggling under the duvet with a good book? Sighing, she mussed up her tumbling auburn locks, stuck a few twigs and feathers in for good measure and grabbing handfuls of bog mud, rubbed it into her clothes and her face. Princes on quests had high expectations. She would not disappoint. She then ran back into her hovel using the back door, hitching up her long trailing gown, once a delightful shade of sea-green velvet trimmed with gold lace. It now looked like it had been dragged through a hedge and dunked in the bog. Which it had; once a week whether it needed it or not. Morven was nothing less then a true professional.

By the time the visitors reached the outer gate, she had perfected her fey, mysterious slow walk, her direct stare making full use of her beautiful dark green eyes. She was only twenty, a long way off full wise crone status. But travellers through the bog expected a wise woman, not a maiden. Well, tough, she was the nearest bog dwelling seer for forty miles, since Angharad the Extremely Knowledgeable Unless it was Questions about the Weather, retired to go to live with her sister Maud in Penge.

Mindful things had also to be right inside her hovel, Morven ran about spraying instant mysterious incense to cover up the fresh summer flowers she'd had to dump out of the window into the surrounding bog. Expectations again. Daisies and cornflowers weren't mysterious. She threw the can behind an ethnic patchwork cushion and stood proudly, her head high as she went to greet her visitors. One was a regulation tall, handsome prince with a fine head of long golden hair. The other, an equally regulation sidekick; a dumpy but burly peasant stinking of cabbages and stale vomit. A routine visit then.

Puzzled by the array of odd objects, the prince and Squarf dodged their way around an eclectic collection of footstools in various stages of decrepitude arranged in clumps around the seer's hovel. There only purpose seemed to be to provide comfy seating for the many loud, croaking toads. Pravis shoved the serf in front of him to make a grand announcement of his princely arrival. Before Squarf could open his mouth, a melodic voice called out from the murky shanty.

'Welcome noble traveller, seeker of answers.'

'She's good,' ventured Squarf, 'she sensed our approach and knew why we are here.'

Pravis sighed, deeply unimpressed. 'Who else would be up to their backsides in filth but a noble knight on a quest?'

'Tourists?' Squarf pondered aloud, 'Ramblers? Particularly ardent Jehovah's Witnesses?'

He wanted to add 'morons on quests' but didn't want to risk another routine kicking.

The young woman ushered them in with an enigmatic smile and bade them make themselves comfortable then pottered around gathering salves and potions, rune stones and crystals, ready to do her best as the on duty seer for the holiday weekend. Her gaze caught a nasty graze on the servant's forehead. 'I have just the thing for that,' she murmured before disappearing behind a curtain to seek an ointment.

'Corrrr...' leered Squarf, 'She's a bit of all right. Very tasty.'

Pravis growled his disapproval at such base behaviour. Though indeed the weird wench was comely, more than that, a curvy figure, a gorgeous face with creamy pale skin and a merry smile. But he was royalty and could only date princesses.

'She'd scrub up well, that one,' continued the serf ignoring his master's displeasure. The prince's discomfort with Squarf's leering was aggravated by his own imagination running riot, in his mind he could see the young woman emerging from a bath, her long titian locks all wet, draping around her shapely shoulders and down to a pair of ripe, pert... ...Damn it! These witches could mind read! Or so he had been told. Pravis forced himself to concentrate on un-arousing thoughts, the hairy wart on his

Aunt Prudence's chin, the bollocky backside of an incontinent male pig, butterbeans, Squarf eating live bugs.

'Forgive me, My Lady of the Swamp,' Pravis bowed low, very low hoping to hide his swift rising interest in her, grateful when she turned her back to him to attend to Squarf's wound.

'But I could not help noticing the strange collection of objects you have around your home.'

Morven wrinkled her nose in puzzlement. 'What strange objects...there is nothing out there but my totems to ward off evil and my toadstools.' She concentrated hard, shrugged. 'No, nothing much but the toadstools. I bought them from a wandering piddler.'

'You mean peddler,' corrected the prince.

'I was right the first time,' countered an affronted Morven, what did this prat know about the ways of the bog?

'Saw you coming,' sniggered Squarf ducking a swipe from the prince's chain metal gauntlet.

'And the significance of the strange objects hanging in the tree?'

'What strange objects?' Morven wrinkled her nose in puzzlement. 'They are but totems to ward off evil.' She made a couple of last finishing touches to her ministrations and stood back from the serf fully satisfied she had done her best work on him.

'And what manner of evil might the collection of garments in the lower branches protect against?' asked the prince trying to appear intelligently interested.

'The evil of dirty underwear,' retorted the witch. 'That's my laundry hanging up to dry.'

Squarf sniggered at this exchange from his doubly safe position as both temporary invalid and protected due to

Epiligia's traditions. Irritated, the prince gave vent to his temper.

'Look, as you can see, I am a noble prince and a mighty warrior, so I have to be chivalrous etc etc to ladies. But you don't seem very wise to me.'

Morven bit her tongue as she fought to be polite, the customer is always right and so forth, 'That's why I call myself the Unwise Woman of Fuggis Mire. To avoid falling foul of the trades description act. And no one can sue me if I get it wrong. The ultimate get out clause.'

'That seems very wise to me,' smirked Squarf, enjoying his master's confusion. It didn't take much to confuse Pravis.

'All this way, through a stinking bog, losing two horses! And you have no words of wisdom for me?' The prince's chiselled face turned puce with the effort of remaining valiant. He wanted to swear, kick a few footstools, startle the toads. But that would have wrecked his hero cred. Big time.

Picking up her dignity along with the ends of her trailing dress, the Unwise Woman, her hospitality fading fast, poured herself a stiff drink, what was it with these Knights Errant? Quibble, quibble, quibble. 'I am sworn to do no harm. And I never will. Nothing I recommend will hurt anyone seeking my aid.'

'And nothing will work either!' guffawed Squarf, forgetting he had dutifully applied one of her mango yoghourt, bluebottle and bourbon biscuit salves to his forehead. It was difficult not to agree with the malodorous oaf, mused Pravis. The prince had gazed at the rows of jars on a nearby shelf, reading the labels in rising incredulity. **'Yellow Fingers of Marigold - extra large,' 'Dried Lumps,' 'Assorted Sploins,' 'Naval Fluff,' 'Unused Meefles.'** And a big, black jar with a leering skull and crossbones labelled '**Extremely Dangerous**' that appeared to contain Mars bars.

'At least tell me why you live in this dreadful place?' Pravis demanded. He had to find one reason to justify his horrible, futile journey through the mire.

Her eyes opened wide with surprise, 'I have to,' she replied, 'this is where you quest seekers expect to find wise women and seers. I'd much rather live in a bijou cottage in a neat, flower strewn meadow.'

'Near a castle?'

'Yep, why not? You can get the best seats for the jousting tournaments and outlaw hangings.'

Squarf laughed again. Outlaw hangings? That was the best joke he'd heard all week, even better than the one about a nun, three bandicoots and a packet of blancmange. With one notable exception, no outlaw had been hanged for decades. Oh, they'd captured many, got them as far as the scaffold. Even managed to plonk a noose around a few necks. But there was always a cohort or three in the crowds. The condemned always managed to get their noose shot down and escape in the following confusion. It was expected. It didn't happen once though. The villain in question was Duncan 'Pigshit Breath' Stott. A man with precious few cohorts and no feisty female lovers. The crowd waited, expecting the fun of a dramatic escape but after ten minutes of faffing about, with the executioner running out of stalling tactics and with no sign of imminent rescue, the crowd began to boo.

And thus the unfortunate Duncan was the one exception.

Built high in a distant desolate land, where mountains ceased to resemble toblerones but became twisted malevolent shards of stone, where eerie winds moaned through bone strewn valleys, was a black fortress. It had many names, Allhopes End, The Hall of Despair, Deathskull Palace. Which made it hellish for postmen.

Darkness reigned supreme in this place, called the Land of Darkness and Despair or Land of Hackneyed Clichés to the more worldly wise of its night-bred inhabitants. A greenish-yellow sulphurous mist swirled through the forests and around the base of the fortress. Large bats permanently flitted around the turrets in a dizzying whirl. Obviously in shifts except at weekends when the skeleton crew took over.

The moon was always full and often blood red when it felt the need for added melodrama. And whenever anyone or anything approached the fortress, a violent thunderstorm would strake the night sky, a sort of paranormal intruder alarm. The worse offenders for setting it off were the werewolves using the storm as an impromptu bath when their coats became too manky. The evil minion guards of the castle had become accustomed to so many false alarms and now ignored them, a case of crying werewolf.

Despite this, the demon that lived there called it home. A reluctant dweller on Earth, he had been kicked out of Hell for the heinous crime of dissension and creativity. To Rafial, all that prodding with pitchforks had seemed so petty, so pointless. An eternity living in sulphur scented darkness with no reality TV and soaps was surely punishment enough for the souls of the damned? What was the point of having devilish powers and a fallen angel's beauty just to dangle food on long poles in front of the eternally hungry? And do all that annoying maniacal

17

laughter. It was so trivial and tedious. His dissent and ambition had led to banishment, condemned to live amongst humans for eternity. It could have been worse. Living with lemmings or wombats would have been far more problematical.

With a huge, gloomy castle to roam in and plenty to read, Rafial was content. Unlike his daughter Demonica. Born from a brief but tempestuous relationship with a human woman, she was desperate to create merry hell on earth. Bored and restless, she frequently railed at her father to go out and wreak some satanic havoc, to corrupt souls and torment people. But Rafial was adamant. He would leave humans alone if they didn't bother him. They had enough misery in their lives already...clip on ties, verrucas, puberty, gangsta rap, piccalilli, spam emails selling shlong enlarging cream...the list was endless.

In her spacious, cobweb draped quarters, Demonica stood in front of a suitably gothic mirror, black glass, dark pewter surround decorated with skulls, dragon claws and bats. A click of her fingers and the mirror cleared. She was darkly glamorous like her human mother, tall, with long slim legs, an ample bosom and a tiny waist. The tumble of her raven locks down her back hid two neat horns, courtesy of her father's side of the family as were her neat yet sharp fangs. Her eyes were jet black and would flare into flame when angry - which was often. Long, blood red painted talons completed her look. To her dismay she had not inherited her father's impressive black wings. Wasted on him of course, another sore point, Rafial never flew anywhere.

Unlike the contents of her chambers. The demon's daughter stepped back from her mirror and kicked a childhood favourite toy, her scarebear flying across the room to bounce off the furthest wall. It waited, crumpled into a heap on the flagstones until her attention was drawn to a pile of magazines by her bed before wisely slinking into the shadows. Around Demonica agitated by her fury and frustration spun a dizzying tornado of **'Succubus'** and **'Lilith'** and other teenage girly demonic magazines as well as a copy of **'Not Ok'** featuring hot gossip from the damned in Hell. What was the point of them all anyway? Alone in the castle with her demon father and his slug-like minions, she had no friends to gossip with or boys to gossip about. Therefore she dismissed it now as time wasting trivia, she had no intention of becoming trapped in perpetual ennui like her pathetic, list making father.

'It's not fair!' she howled, 'I am nineteen today. Nineteen and not one birthday card or present.'

She sank down on her impressively gothic bed and sulked. 'It is so unfair, nineteen, no birthday party and no boyfriend. I wish we had never left Hell.'

Demonica had a point, there was a dearth of suitable suitors in the Land of Darkness and Despair. They were all either too ugly, hairy or diaphanous. The evil minions were globular warty creatures oozing pus with zero personality and off puttingly squat. At least Hell had many fit looking fallen angels to date. If only her mother was still here, Demonica sighed but Pashmina had found guilt and religion and had run away to join an order of the Nuns of St Repressia. After this, her father Rafial began to make his endless, pointless and obsessive lists and all but forgotten he had a daughter.

Time for action, with a flash of fire from her eyes, she incinerated the still flying flock of magazines and all of her toys, save the cowering hidden scarebear.

Dressing in her favourite skintight black leather cat suit decorated with vicious looking stud and spikes and arming herself with various weapons of mass destruction, Demonica was ready. Watch out world, the Daughter of Darkness was on her way, ready to kick some weakling human backsides and find love. Whatever that meant.

Deep in the shadowed depths of the town's most disreputable bawdy tavern, a lean, dark clad figure sat alone. His long legs wearing battered and filthy thigh boots were crossed and resting on the table, his face hidden by the brim of an equally shabby tricorne hat. The more clued up drinkers in The Vexed Hamster Inn left him alone, assuming his hidden but watchful eyes scanned for danger, cocked and loaded pistols at the ready beneath his caped riding coat. He was Jed Moonraven, the most notorious and ruthless highwayman to gallop the moonlit roads of the land. A handsome young rogue with a ready merry quip and a long overdue date with the gallows.

Most of the tales of his notorious exploits were wildly exaggerated as was the manner for folk anti-heroes. Jed never contradicted the stories, he enjoyed watching the price on his head rise as a matter of pride and when the inevitable day came when he would feel the hemp noose tighten around his neck, at least he could guarantee a good turn out for his grand exit.

Though the rowdy crowd of drinkers appeared to be ignoring Jed, many shifty eyes watched him warily. The highwayman was the instant passport to riches, dob him in to the militia and you could clear the mortgage on your fleapit, upgrade your clapped out mule and buy a little holiday hovel on the Costa Lotte. And still have enough change to buy the latest must have fashion accessory...shoes with really, really long pointy toes. All the nobility sported them. Even the Town Crier had worn a natty pair in eau de nil leather until he tripped over them and knocked himself unconscious on his bell.

The inn fell to instant expectant silence as a loud snore reverberated from beneath the lowered tricorne. Was it a ruse? Was he really awake? Or sleeping off a night of heavy drinking and debauchery? Who had the balls to risk making a move against the leading scourge of the highways? An 'A' lister among the land's villains and malcontents?

'Idiot.'

Jed sprang awake as someone kicked his feet off the table.

'If you are so keen to take that short walk to a long drop, you do it alone!'

Rubbing his bleary, now bloodshot, dark blue eyes, drawing a hand across the black stubble on his chin, Jed nodded his gratitude to the bear like man joining him at the table. Oakham Strang, the brawn and the brains behind Jed's nefarious career. Many men as big and burly as Oakham were really softies at heart, giants with hearts of gold who bred budgies or rescued kittens. Not Oakham Strang. He was a nasty bastard who'd eat a budgie whole for the hell of it, finished off with a dessert of freshly strangled kittens in custard. The only reason he tolerated the handsome but feckless Moonraven was he needed a good frontman. One that kept the coach loads of titled ladies giggling and blushing while engaging in threatening roguish banter with the furious men while Strang got on with the serious business of robbing them blind.

Raising his hand to call over the nearest serving wench, Jed did his best to force aside the effects of a heavy night's carousing. His mind a blur on how much ale he'd sunk, how many wenches he'd had, how much money he'd lost on the gaming tables.

Strang waved the woman away with a growl of displeasure and focused on the hung-over fool now slumped across the table. 'You've had a skinful already. Another one of your damned all nighters! Don't you know what day it is? The first day of the Feast of St Epiligia! The questing season is officially open. The sun has hardly risen but already the moors and swamps will be overrun with well-bred young fools starting their pointless noble journeys. Rich and easy pickings.'

The highwayman groaned. He just wanted to find a warm, safe place to sleep off the hangover from hell. His head was full of devilish imps armed with blunt pickaxes. Others inhabited his bowels, forcing up the contents of his stomach higher and higher...He needed a drink.... Now! Hair of the dog to drown the little buggers in his gut.

'Sod you, Strang!' he moaned, 'I need a drink. And I am having one.'

The big man stood up. 'I'll wait for you by the horses. You have exactly three minutes. Then I will be gone and so will Milady.'

The thought of losing the best mare he'd ever stolen sobered Jed instantly. He leapt to his feet and pushed through the crowd, cheekily taking a long draught from a meek little man's liquid breakfast - a freshly drawn tankard of frothy ale.

'You young blaggard! To Hell with you!' the man cursed, not knowing who the tall young scoundrel was.

'Sorry old chap,' Jed countered, with a low mocking bow, 'The Devil had to barricade Hell to stop me getting in. Frightened I'll take over!'

He strode through the inn, helping himself to a bite of someone's bread roll crammed full of Wensleydale and cranberry cheese on the way out, thoroughly enjoying the outrage he left in his wake. With an impudent bow he bade farewell to the furious mob of drinkers and leapt into the saddle of his ugly mare...

'Ten seconds more and I would have gone,' grumbled Strang.

Jed believed him. His partner was a nasty bastard after all.

Ignoring the wooden steps wobbling beneath his boots, Durgin the baker resignedly climbed to the attic above his home. Wheatley, his apprentice lived there. And once again the master was hoping the straw pallets were unoccupied. He was wrong. Slumbering and noisily breaking wind lay the trainee baker, oversleeping like every other morning.

'Boy, wake up!' Durgin hated to do this, but being mean to your apprentice was part of the contract, it had to be done. As gently as he could get away with, Durgin used a long pole to nudge him awake. Correctly performed, it should have produced bruises but the baker was too soft-hearted. Maybe that was the problem.

'Do you know what day it is?' Durgin asked, averting his eyes as the apprentice rose to his feet, yawning and sleepily scratching his nether regions.

'You've forgotten haven't you? It is the first day of the Feast of St Epiligia of the Blessed Vole, Patron Saint of Pointless Journeys and er.... voles...The official start of the questing season. And you are still here.'

Maybe if the baker had not been so kindly, had beaten and kicked, insulted and berated the apprentice when he was still a young boy, he would not still be living above the bakery. Wheatley was forty-nine. It was getting a bit late for him to run away and discover his true destiny. A remorseful Durgin accepted it was long overdue time to take positive and direct action. It was just that Wheatley was such a good employee, working seven day weeks in return for the attic room and all the stale buns he could eat, it had been so easy to let year after year slip by.

By the time Wheatley was ready to start work, the delicious smells of fresh cake mix and bread dough wafted up into his attic room. The warmth from the lit ovens rose like a welcoming hug. All this preparation was his job of course, as an apprentice. But Wheatley was a useless baker. Never got the amounts right. Eccles cakes with glace cherries instead of currants were a great disappointment to the customers. But he was good at selling, a born salesman. He could even shift those stodgy square pastry cakes with a thin filling of unknown sweet stuff that always got left at the end of the day. Wheatley loved his life, his job and he loved old Master Durgin as the father he never had.

So it was a shock to find the kitchen empty. On the table where the baking trays should have been lay a long pole with a large red, spotted bundle tied to the end. And a note from his master.

'Sorry Wheatley, you are like a son to me. But you are an orphaned apprentice with an unknown past. Therefore by law, you must go out and seek your destiny. Somewhere out there is a kingdom under a terrible curse, a sword that needs shifting from a stone, a maiden princess trapped in a high tower. Go out in the world my boy and learn what your fate will be.'

'But I know my fate,' cried a desolate Wheatley, 'I want to sell cakes. buns, cheese straws and biscuits! And those triangular sponge things covered in jam and shredded coconut.'

It was no use. He was an apprentice; he had to obey his master. With a sorrowing heart, Wheatley took up the pole and without a backward glance made his way to the outside world.

He kept his head down, unwilling to take in the merriment around him. The Feast of St Epiligia was at hand, a busy time for the cake business and he so loved being diligent. Later today, queues would build up all morning outside the bakery, waiting for the annual treat of vole shaped lardy cakes with real vole droppings as eyes. A traditional touch. Perhaps the peasants thought they were exotic dried fruit? Wheatley didn't have the heart to tell them the truth; they loved the cakes so much. Soon there would be peasant women clutching their hard earned groats and money off coupons from Ye Toile and Grubbinge magazine, the one with pictures only, which showed the best way to make a pot of gruel for a family of fourteen last a week and the latest fashions for the turnip harvest. Why spoil their pleasure?

But what pleasure would he have this day? None. A hard road and a dangerous, unknown future was all that stretched before him, with not even a beady-eyed vole cake for company.

Being hit on the head with an air filled badger bladder was not the best start to the day. Waking up, full stop, was not the best start of the day. Robard groaned and wriggled further into the musty darkness of his cover of goatskin rugs. Darkness was his friend, his lover, his Muse.

'Oi, emu boy...Shake a leg! We still face a long journey across the swamp to make that St Epiligia gig at the castle.'

Salatious Prink, the leader of the band of roaming troubadours and mummers was nothing but determined. His protégé teenager Robard was once the most promising and talented troubadour ever to don the motley. The beauty of his voice could turn the hardest homicidal maniac of a warlord to maudlin tears. Maidens would faint away delirious with excitement as he hit the high notes. And most importantly, Robard had made the troupe shedloads of dosh, enough to get them through the lean times of winter and wet bank holiday weekends.

All was well until Robard, wandering through a Newe Ayge Paigan Fayre had discovered ...The Book!!! Bound in black, written in red/brown ink to suggest dried blood, the book was a collection of poems by some obscure scribe who wrote under the penname Draven Dea'th. Once his fingers touched the tome, Robard's fate had been sealed, unable to put the gloom-laden tome down, endless dirges mainly about suicide and haunted graveyards. By the morning he was a changed boy. He had thrown away all his vivid, multicoloured, ribbon trimmed garb, the gaudy silks and satins of his trade. He'd bought a new wardrobe of all black clothes and found a wandering and suspiciously convenient pedlar to sell him black hair dye and kohl. Robard was deliriously happy in his newfound misery. This was the real him, he'd released his inner self, one desperate to emerge like a black winged butterfly. No, more accurately a melancholic night dwelling moth.

Pulling the rugs off the boy, Prink grabbed his arm and pulled him to his feet. 'Listen lad, St Epiligia is the biggest festival in these parts for three months. We are down on takings, especially since the last fiasco.' He threw Robard a long frock coat made of patches of turquoise, purple, day-glo green and orange velvet. Multicoloured silken ribbons hung from the shoulders. Tiny silver bells trimmed the hem and the end of the sleeves. It was magnificent in its unique gaudiness. Robard recognised it and groaned.

'Yes, laddie. The coat that once belonged to Stanley Egbert Thrubb. The greatest troubadour ever to tread the boards. Who now has his own castle on his own island on his own lake.'

Prink wiped copious fake tears from his eyes. 'I loved that boy as one of my own. And you are far better then he ever was. You could dazzle the world with those looks, that voice.'

Struggling to his feet, Robard picked up the flashy coat and reverentially handed it back to his boss. He gestured to his black garb and added, 'This is who I am. I must be true to my soul.'

'What a load of old bollocks.' Prink muttered darkly. There had to be someone out there who could rid his irritating songbird of this gloomy and pretentious pose. The bog should contain at least one official wise woman. Maybe the troupe's luck was about to change, they were heading in the right direction to take a short detour and find a crazy old crone with a book of spells or dusty cabinets full of weird potions. And a ready supply of newts and toads, for some reason, their magic always involved amphibians.

A fact not lost on the squadron of security toads that protected the hovel of the Unwise Woman of Fuggis Mire. Not now they had an unexpected visitation from a militant arm of the Society for Cold-Blooded Amphibious Beings - or SCABS for short. Passively they sat in a damp, mossy hollow as the leader of the deputation gave vent to its emotions. It was one angry newt.

'Eye of Newt!!! Toe of Frog!!! It is an outrage!!!'

'An outrage!' echoed the other pond life in ribbetting unison.

The leader, a Great Crested Newt paced around the hollow, fixing the toads with its glassy yellow-eyed glare. 'Why must they use our body parts in their vile potions? Why not eye of stoat? Toe of wildebeest...or why not bits of their own anatomy? It will all grow back.'

One of the Unwise Woman's toads raised a tentative hand. The Great Cresteds were strictly protected by law, a fact that had long gone to their heads. This one's warty skin had grown a shade darker in its righteous fury. The toad was wary of angering it further in case the myth of exploding amphibians was true, but his unswerving loyalty was to Morven.

'Er, excuse me, but our kindly witch never uses any animal bits, she is sworn to harm none. Apart from a few bluebottles...'

'Aha!' shouted the newt in triumph. 'That's how it starts. Bluebottles, then comrades, it will be your turn soon. Mark my words.'

'Well, I'm not bothered,' announced another one of the security toads, 'humans only lick us toads to cure their sore throats. I don't mind that.'

'Actually, I'd quite like that,' added another with a knowing smirk and a wink, 'especially if I'm being licked by some gorgeous page three stunna.'

Shocked at the lack of solidarity and unseemly inter-species lewdness emitting from the complacent toads, the newts began to wave anti-human placards and swish their long tails in fury, looking for backup from the frogs. It was not forthcoming.

'I've been kissed three times,' ribbeted a small green frog, 'by a desperate princess too dim to realise she kept picking the same one from the pond.'

'I can better that!' added a larger gold frog puffing out its throat proudly. 'Make that a hundred times, I lived in an ornamental pool at a finishing school for princesses.'

The Great Crested could feel the mood within his troops evaporate from indignant fervour to embarrassed unease. The proposed picket of Morven's hovel in the swamp was rapidly deteriorating into a fiasco. Abandoning the guffawing frogs and toads swapping princess stories, he gathered together all of the efts, including a confused exchange axylotl from Mexico and stomped off in a huff. Nothing got as pissed as a newt.

Except perhaps for a demon...

Creeping and grovelling in full evil minion mode, one sidled anxiously up to the demon prince. He probably could have walked straight up to Lord Rafial, who easy going as demons went but it was always best to be cautious. It had been years since Rafial smited a hapless minion. An accident, a mishap triggered by the lackey's unfortunate nervous habit of sneezing with a curious noise that sounded like 'cheesus.' After reducing him to a pile of ash stinking of brimstone, Rafial had even politely apologised to the smouldering pile. So that was all right then.

Rafial was still listing off all the ills that beset mankind. 'Junk mail, guilt-inducing beggars with patient dogs on a string, rubbery Edam cheese, that shouting man with his cleaning stuff....'

'My Lord, I have some news,' the minion ventured, his voice tremulous.

'Butterbeans, zits on chins on first dates, Bratz dolls...'

'My Lord, it is important!' The minion dared to raise his voice.

'Children eating bogies, door to door gas salesmen, running out of toilet roll while sitting on the toilet.'

'MY LORD!'

Startled, Rafial blasted the underling into a pile of ash stinking of brimstone.

'Where was I? Oh yes, tights, snarky bus drivers, zits on the end of noses on a second date, did I say butterbeans?'

Five piles of ash later, the demon prince finally got the message that his daughter had helped herself to the coach pulled by four high-spirited, pedigree Pookas and driven by the headless coachman. Rafial was not worried, Demonica would not get far. The driver was a reckless idiot who obviously couldn't see where he was going. The coach was probably wrapped around the first tree it encountered. A miffed, dishevelled and bruised Demonica would soon be back in the castle. No doubt to berate him for being such a useless prince of darkness. He still had time to continue his list. 'Old potatoes with hideous sprouting bits lurking at the back of cupboards, young women in white Mercedes parking in supermarket disabled zones, slugs....

Oblivious to the amphibian angst agitating on the perimeter of Morven's bog side home, an uneasy concord festered within.

'Was there any point in asking?' Prince Pravis mused to himself as he wiggled his toes in a warm footbath of mulched marigolds, tealeaves, pulverised cheese and onion crisps and fizzy cream soda. He and Squarf had taken up the Unwise Woman's offer of a brief rest in her hovel. Well, he was in the hovel, Squarf as a mere serf stayed outside with the seer's goats and toads.

Though hardly a palace, it still felt good to dry his clothes out and sit somewhere warm after so many predawn hours spent wandering aimlessly through the vile morass. Though he would never admit it, even to himself, the prince's brainwave to have an extra early start had backfired spectacularly. He glanced up at Morven, busying herself preparing salves and ventured a query, not really expecting a sensible answer.

'So, Lady of the Swamp, how exactly do we proceed with our mission?'

'On foot,' Morven replied simply. 'How else?'

The prince sighed. His hope that some honest bog dweller would find his steeds and return them for scant reward had not happened. No doubt that appalling reprobate Jed Moonraven had stolen the animals. Word was the notorious highwayman frequented this area in the questing season. Pravis looked forward to encountering the villain, to have the glory of running Moonraven through with his trusty broadsword. Gathering together the last shredded threads of his patience, he continued to question the witch.

'I meant my good woman, what signs should I look for in my search for the Chalice of Untold Delights?'

Morven shrugged. She hadn't a clue. But this was a paying customer, she didn't like to disappoint. So she sought out her crystal bowl, removed the fruit from it and looked intently into its depths. Pravis bit back the urge to ask her why she didn't use a crystal ball like other seers, but what did he know? His world was all macho stuff, jousting tournaments, smiting varlets, slaying dragons, eating the hottest curries with a side order of raw chillies when out with his knightly followers.

'I am seeing something coming through the mysterious mists of what yet will be...'

The prince nearly spilt the contents of his footbath onto the rush flooring, actually it was shredded copies of Hamster and Sock magazine but it served the same purpose. Could this comely but bizarre female actually have real powers? 'Tell me, what do you see? Death or glory for me? The chalice raised high in triumph as I ride back through the castle gates?'

'Er......No chalices. Cakes...? Yes, I see cakes and buns.' Morven stared into the bowl intently, 'There's more. I see cheese straws, cream horns and jam tarts. Iced cinnamon whirls on Wednesdays.'

She looked at the royal face and accurately read the mood thereupon. 'Tell you what, I've got an ancient old pamphlet of maps of the area, tucked away somewhere - I'll throw that in as a free gift with the price of the Spa treatment shall I? Can't do any harm can it?'

She didn't notice the slight frisson as she slipped the thin volume from the pile of old books she had inherited with the hovel from the previous incumbent. Goodness knew how long it had waited there. But evil had even more of an idea.

'Give it to my serf, he can study it while I finish up in here. You wouldn't have some chamomile tea would you? Mama makes a mug for me when I'm feeling a bit stressed and it always helps.'

Morven raised a delicate eyebrow but said nothing, just nodded and went to do her royal visitor's bidding. He who pays the piper calls the tune. Or should have done, the growing number of rats around here was shocking.

'I won't do it!'

Robard was in full teenage rebellious mode. Surrounded by the rest of the troupe already dressed in full motley, he stubbornly refused to don the harlequin coat of many bright and gaudy colours.

'I have to be true to the darkness of my soul. Cutting my wrists with rusty barbed wire would give me more pleasure then the pain of betraying my true pre-ordained destiny.'

'It's just a gig...a highly lucrative gig. And we all have to eat!' huffed Muriel, who played all the female roles in their productions. He wore a white gown covered in red dots in honour of the saint, a pointless exercise if they didn't get their backsides into gear and back on the road to the castle.

Pushing through the muttering, surly mummers, Prink arrived with a sly grin across his thin, cadaverous features. He was not a bad person but keeping the troupe together and making money was his life's obsession.

Something one snot nosed, black clad songbird was not going to wreck. He waved something in his hand over the campfire, perilously close to the flames still lively from cooking the morning's breakfasts. 'Look what I've got in my hand!' he taunted melodramatically. 'And the only way you are going to get it back is to cooperate with us. Your friends. Your family.'

Growling in fury, Robard considered rushing his boss and snatching The Book before his boss had time to hurl it into the blaze but Prink for all his spindly height and age was sprightly and fast. And determined. Sighing with the burden of martyrdom, the humiliation and suffering he was prepared to endure for his fight for individuality and freedom of expression, Robard agreed. 'Just one more time,' he muttered.

'I'll keep the Book safe,' smirked Prink. 'Dangerous places these bogs, highwaymen, boggarts and all sorts of deadly dangers.'

'As opposed to undeadly dangers,' retorted a furious Robard, stomping back to his tent. Adults were such losers, no one understood him, he didn't ask to be born and it was all sooo unfair.

Prink watched the retreating stroppy teenager with a twinge of unease. His bony fingers tingled and a creeping feeling of dread spread along his spine, there was something evil about The Book and not just the dire poetry.

With a sigh of relief, Morven watched the prince and his manservant trudge off into the swamp, now draped in soft wafts of ethereal mist that glowed in the early sunshine. A fragile beauty that hid the true nature of the morass, though not its stench, not even an explosion in a deodorant factory could quell that. When Vinny Grimes's personal hygiene plant erupted in a rain of multiple fragrances including '**Eau de Neil**' and '**Extortion**', the bog stayed true to its self, shrugging of the posh pong with smelly pride.

The mist drew a fleeting gossamer veil over the slime, the slugs, the crack of human bones underfoot. One thing about human devouring boggarts was they never cleaned up after a meal. Even meals that came in tins like the knight errant, Prince Pravis. Morven's heart had hardened against that particular visitor after he had bragged about all the things he would do to Jed Moonraven. All the different ways he could kill him, all brutal. All fatal to Morven's wayward lover. Yes, she knew all too well that he was as faithful as a tomcat on Viagra. Morven didn't care, she loved him. After all she was the Unwise Woman and though a bit older, not any bit wiser than she had been as a teenager when her heart was stolen by the gangly youthful Jed with his roguish smile and mischievous dark blue eyes. She found this exciting newcomer's thieving ways to be no detraction from his charms, especially once she worked out the best way to hide her lunch money and new pencils.

The other kids had not been so welcoming to the new boy and for a while she had been his only friend. Maybe that was why he had been so kind when her mother Rowena, Druidess to the Stars – glamour puss and local celebrity, had run off with Dutchman Knight Sir Phil Aan De Rhur. Sadly her clueless father Aedric, had been so engrossed in his extensive garden rake collection that he failed to respond to his daughter's distress. It was ten years after the event that he even showed any signs of noticing his wife's absence from the home.

Jed had officially become Morven's boyfriend one moonlit night after many evenings allowing her to sob into his boyish, dampened but still manly chest. On high school graduation day, they stood side by side at the Giving of the Rolls Ceremony – eager to find out what career path they had been assigned. She had been given cheese and tomato and details of her future as a trainee witch and Jed, tuna mayonnaise and the address of the Federation of Arsonists, Rogues and Thieves.

She would never forget watching as her beloved rode off on the headmaster's horse, school trophies clanking away in a burlap bag dangling from the saddle, with some other girl's lipstick on his cheek.

He had promised he would find her again, that he would love her until the end of time, and the unwise teenager had believed everything he said.

Morven pulled herself with a jolt back into the present day. This was no time for daydreaming. It was the start of the questing season. Which meant Jed would soon be in the area seeking easy pickings. This thought sent her into an excited fluster, simultaneously trying to tidy the hovel, have a bath and de-tangle her hair. She also made sure every object that had any value to her was well hidden away. Her favourite crystals, spell candles, rare unguents and expensive exotic herbs. All easy things for Jed to pocket during his visit. She didn't bother hiding any of the jewellery he had brought her. It was all stolen and she never dared get fond of it. It never lasted long in her home.

The last thing she wanted was more customers which she accepted was a frankly unrealistic hope what with battalions of metal clad inbreds invading the bogs, bleak forests and blasted heaths of the land in their lemming like rush for fame and glory and probably non-existent holy chalices.

The bleating of her guard goats and croaking of her security toads brought the bad news she had dreaded. It couldn't be the highwayman; Jed could always slip past the loyal creatures undetected. Ever since he bribed them with a curiously ready supply of mango yoghurt, bourbon biscuits and bluebottles. She never needed to stock up on those particular ingredients. Damn. More visitors. There was nothing for it but to return to full seer of the swamp mode as her latest clients arrived outside, a group of travelling mummers...at least that made an interesting change from clanking knights and their malodorous hangers on.

Three stepped forward from the merry cavalcade gathered on the perimeter, to approach her hovel. A very tall, spindly middle-aged man with a wonky purple top hat trimmed with a pheasant feather which added to his ludicrous height, a fair maiden in a St Epiligia white spotty dress and impressive five o'clock shadow and the most miserable looking black clad teenager she'd ever seen. He'd apparently rubbed flour onto his face to increase his pallor but the steamy heat from the swamp had made it clump to look like badly applied porridge. And his hair dye was overdue a touch up, dark blonde roots appeared from his central parting.

Definitely more interesting visitors then noble quest bound knights, but why today, why now! Still, despite her true feelings she welcomed her three newest guests inside. Duty was duty and fulfilling it diligently, greetings and names were exchanged. Then she followed Robard's long tale of woe with growing disbelief and compassion. As he gave full vent to the outpourings of his tortured, embattled, soul she was stirred to greater and greater depths of sympathy.

Such misunderstanding, such a battle to be recognised. Poor Mr Prink! How could he have endured such self-pitying whining for so long? She'd have hit the sullen Robard with something much heavier than an air filled badger bladder by now.

'I don't have much time to sort this out, my gracious Lady of the Swamp, we need to be at the castle for the St Epiligia festivities.' Prink's anguish was pitiful and seemingly genuine. 'I love this boy as a son. Robard has the voice of an angel but he ruined our last show in Swillington-on-Sea to celebrate the Feast of St Hupert.'

Undecided which was the most convincing voice, Muriel started in a high trilling falsetto, then gave up and continued in his normal gruff bass. 'It was awful. Just the worst day of my life. We were half way through a well received rendition of our recreation of St Hupert's rescue of the sacrificial virgin of Thebes. One of my most successful roles.'

Stifling a giggle and biting her tongue at the thought of the deep voiced, stubble chinned Muriel as a simpering virgin about to be eaten by a giant hell spawned centipede. Morven struggled to look serious and concerned.

Unaware of her difficulty, he continued. 'It was to be the highlight of the play. St Hupert is doubting his own courage, could he really take on such a huge, vile beast? Robard was supposed to be lowered on stage from above, dressed as an angel to sing an inspiring, stirring song to give the saint hope and courage.'

Muriel shuddered at the memory, held his hand to his forehead in distress and couldn't continue. Prink took up the woeful tale, 'The long pole came down but without the angel! Instead there was a hideous scarecrow with a noose around its neck dangling from it.'

He paused for dramatic effect. 'Then Robard slouched onto the stage and began to wail a dirge about graveyards and a lover's cruel betrayal. Maybe alright for the Pagan Feast of Wolfsbane in October I suppose but St Hupert's?'

Shuddering as the memories crowded back, he continued, 'The crowd went crazy, started lobbing old tomatoes, potato peelings, tramps' used underwear at us.'

'And far, far worse...' whimpered Muriel as he reluctantly recalled the full horror of that day, 'don't forget the butterbeans....Cold. Straight out of their tins.'

'And the tins,' added Prink dourly. He still had the bruises to prove it.

Morven realised the teenager had been silent all through this sorry tale. She turned around to speak to him and realised the reason for the lack of input. He was not there.

Wheatley made slow progress out of the town and into the vast unknown that were the outskirts. He knew that convention demanded that he should be stepping out into a world of adventures with an optimistic tune on his lips or at the very least a cheery whistle and a jaunty stride. It was no use. He couldn't or wouldn't sing or whistle. His heart was too heavy; already missing the cosy, safe haven of the bakery and yearning for the racks of freshly baked, still warm rolls and buns. His feet ached and the delaying tactic of having a hearty breakfast had backfired as it lay like a lump of clay in his stomach.

How long would it be before he met with the required travelling companions for a seeker of true destiny? A peculiar, gruff old man who turned out to be a wise, fatherly wizard, a mysterious and suspiciously curvaceous young man who turned out to be an elven princess in disguise. Maybe a dashing rascal of a thief with a heart of gold. Or a grumpy gnome also with a heart of gold. A talking animal? He didn't like the sound of any of those. Could he be allowed to find his destiny alone? Was there a get out clause for shy or anti-social apprentices seeking their hidden, true destiny? Something that allowed him to be free of irksome sidekicks, some of whom would be required to die heroically in a selfless act of sacrifice?

Wheatley wished he had bothered to read the rules, his complacency at the bakery had backfired as badly as had the bacon and eggs which now threatened to come back up to rejoin the outside world, a sensation deepening with every step towards his unwanted future.

After a couple of hours dejected trudging with not a soul in sight, Wheatley began to regret his earlier outburst. Even a grumpy gnome would be an improvement on this solitude. It was a big scary world beyond the protective wattle and daub walls of the bakery in the heart of the city. Passing dragons had twice shadowed the morning sun. They were apparently not hungry and had ignored him, perhaps late for some fire breathing contest somewhere - appalling show offs dragons. But they were also creatures that could have had him for a well-roasted light snack should they have chosen to.

He came to a crossroads. The four fingerboards could well have pointed to 'Certain Death', 'Excruciating Torture then Death', 'Nasty Jibes and Sarcasm then Death' and 'Staines.'

Instead they read, 'The Bog of Fuggis Mire', 'The Land of Darkness and Despair' under which someone had scribbled in orange crayon 'Land of Hackneyed Clichés', 'The Enchanted Wood of Mhmin,' and 'Staines.' What a dilemma. Wheatley could not turn back but none of the destinations appealed, especially Staines. He decided to head for the vile morass, the stinking swamp, the baleful bog of Fuggis Mire. At least he could find the services of a Wise Woman there - according to the crossed broomsticks icon on the fingerboard. He would search her out to see if he could glean some clues to his true destiny. More importantly he would be able to use her privy. There were limits to Wheatley's sense of adventure.

His Demonic Highness, Prince Rafial was nearly right. His wayward and impulsive daughter did soon realise the folly of her choice of transport. Of all the things she could have stolen from the fortress's huge stables, four high-spirited pedigree Irish Pookas driven by a headless coachman was the worst possible choice. The carriage careered through the swirling, sulphurous mist, accompanied by a dark cloud of bats coming off their night shift and looking for some after work fun. Totally out of control, the carriage narrowly missed some malevolent haunted trees, a pack of manky werewolves heading for the fortress to have a shower and a particularly surly ogre taking a leak against a rock.

Never one to be a passive victim of circumstance, Demonica agilely climbed out of the coach and up onto its roof, clinging hard with her long talons digging into the ruby incrusted and gilded wood. She crawled across to the driver, plonked herself down beside him and grabbing the reins off him hauled the bolting Pookas to a bone shuddering halt.

'You...off!' she growled at the wretched driver who held up his hands in protestation. Of course he could not answer back. 'Now!' She helped him on his way off the side of the coach with a well-aimed kick of her black stiletto boots. 'If you want to get on in this life, my friend, you must get ahead.' Demonica chuckled, mightily pleased by her joke.

Jed Moonraven had but one thought on his mind. Not a coach packed with rich folk dripping with jewels, with their luggage of trunks crammed full of gold pieces strapped to the back, not even a night of debauchery at his favourite tavern. He was riding along the narrow path winding through the bog and that meant Morven. The one woman he would have considered becoming law abiding for. Well, considered anyway. Briefly. Very briefly. For a fleeting nano-second.

He had once nearly come to blows with Strang by making the mistake of mentioning this momentary lapse of faith to his partner in crime.

'I'm glad you eventually listened to what passes for your brain instead of what you use to pass water,' Strang had sneered. 'You were born to the outlaw life, it's what you do best, turning your back on it would be a tragic loss.'

Of course the most tragic loss would be to Strang's purse.

'The start of the questing season means rich pickings; the market for 'second hand' armour is at an all time high at the moment what with so many commoners trying to pass themselves off as toffs.'

'Idiots, all of them,' Jed replied, taking a swig from a leather bottle of brandy and slinging it over to Strang. 'Just because one young penniless goat herder succeeded to win the heart of some royal tottie, there's an insane rush to do the same thing. And the whole thing turned out to be a con all along, he was really a handsome prince of royal blood under a curse!'

Shaking his head, 'What some people will do for publicity!'

Exactly! thought Strang draining the brandy and pondering what Jed wouldn't do for infamy? The feckless fool couldn't be content to be anything but the most notorious, most wanted villain in the land with the highest price on his head. In the brief reign of Duncan Pig-shit Breath Stott, the young highwayman had been furious when the price on Stott's head rose above his. To fix this outrage, Moonraven had gone on a dangerous spree of reckless high profile thievery. He'd even gatecrashed the king's birthday bash up at the castle and had it off with two of the monarch's daughters before narrowly escaping with half the crown jewels.

There was no way Stott could have competed with that, well, bonking the royal women bit...not with his unfortunate acne, the virulent halitosis and the severe weight problem. Jed was once more the king of the outlaws. But just to make sure, Strang being a nasty bastard had shopped Stott to the militia. Jed's extraordinary run of lucky escapes could not last forever.

Despite the curiously eerie pamphlet of maps Morven had given them Prince Pravis and Squarf knew they were hopelessly lost by the time they reached a gnarled spinney of witch hazel for the fourth time.

But both being of the male persuasion, chose not to admit it openly. Indeed, they couldn't articulate anything much as colony of boggarts lived beyond the pitiful attempt at a forest. And it was definitely the same one they had passed four times already. The mounds were uniformly disgusting, piles of silt coated bog peat, greened over with algae and strewn with the festering remains of many meals. None vegetarian. Except one mound that was covered in recently rendered stone cladding. No doubt a fellow boggart or two may have tried to dissuade him or her of this decorating disaster, that it would knock off value from the boggart hole. But then twenty percent off bugger all was not a lot, even in this desirable regions for discerning boggarts.

The prince needed to sit down, his armour felt like solid lead, he'd tripped up over his metal, long pointy shoes many times but with nothing in sight, he signalled Squarf to crouch down and serve as a chair.

'In your dreams!' shouted the serf beyond caring. He was cold, exhausted and hungry and sick to death of trudging through a swamp with this titled prick. He folded his arms, spread his stumpy legs apart and refused to get down on his knees. Pravis's eyes widened with horror, not at the act of rebellion, he could give Squarf a good kicking anytime but at the unwelcome loud noise so close to the boggart colony.

Drawing his sword and standing in a valiant pose, Pravis waited for the inevitable. He heard the slobbering wheeze of an approaching boggart and prepared to do battle. 'Er, my Lord Prince,' ventured Squarf helpfully, 'we could still run away.'

'Never, you cowardly varlet!' Pravis replied, not totally convincingly, but standing up to a boggart or two was less embarrassing then tripping up over his pointy toes in headlong flight through the morass. He proudly sported his valour badges from knight school on his chain mail clad chest, time to prove they were well earned.

The boggart approached out of the murk and stood before them. By the vile creatures' standards he was quite dapper, his warty green skin covered festering sores and draping of slime looked neatly arranged, his slab like yellow teeth had minimal rotting flesh trapped between the many gaps. Squarf rightly deduced this was the boggart with the stone clad dwelling.

'Piss off.'

Tightening his grip around his sword hilt, the prince looked puzzled at the unexpected curt address. 'What did you say?'

'You heard me the first time, you metal-clad toffee-nosed ponce. Piss off!'

'That is no way to address a noble prince of royal blood,' Pravis retorted, noting in his mental notebook of things that require a good kicking that Squarf was sniggering.

'Prepare to do battle!' Pravis commanded. 'You need to be put in your place you slimy cur!'

The boggart dragged his trailing, calloused knuckles off the ground and stood to his full impressive ten foot height, the full dramatic effect somewhat lessened by a loud, squelchy fart.

'My place? *My* place? Look around you little tin man...This is a boggart colony in the centre of a bog. This *is* my place. And we are sick to death of having titled morons tramping all over our lands and homes every year. I've eaten one already this morning and my hand aches from having to use a tin opener to get at me breakfast. So, piss off!'

Tugging at the prince's arm, Squarf whispered anxiously, 'I think we should do what the fellow says.'

'Nonsense!' shouted the prince in high dudgeon. 'No grubby slime-dweller insults a prince of the realm and lives!'

Squarf was determined to defuse this unnecessary standoff. 'My lord, maybe we could use this fine, upstanding and intelligent boggart to guide us out of the bog - for a price of course!'

'We are not lost!' thundered Pravis turning an unflattering shade of puce.

'Oh yes you are, sunshine!' snortled the Boggart. 'You have passed my stone clad mound four times already this morning!'

'Have not!'

'Have so!'

While they argued, a devious plan leapt fully formed from nowhere and unfolded in Squarf's fevered brain. He tucked the pamphlet into his belt and, as prince and boggart gave each other their full attention, surreptitiously drew his crossbow and released the safety catch.

How easy it would be to leave the royal corpse here and just say the boggarts got him. By the time anyone came to check the story – the evidence would be no longer useful having passed through a few boggart digestive tracts. Highly efficient digestive tracts, boggarts always started the day with big bowls of AllGruel.

'Look, you vile grotbag, I'm a bloody prince, I know what I am doing!'

'And I'm a grotbag who isn't lost in a bog!'

'I am *not* lost in this bog!'

'Oh yes you are, the stupid princey wincey is going around in circles!'

At this cutting remark Pravis was goaded into moving suddenly, and tripped headlong over his long pointy metal shoes. Almost simultaneously the boggart fell over backwards, a bolt through his forehead. Stone dead. The prince looked up to see the serf putting his crossbow away.

'It would have ended in tears one way or another,' Squarf said with deceptive calmness. 'Now let's get the hell out of here before any more boggarts turn up.'

Squarf's mind was in turmoil. The prince's sudden fall had happened exactly at the wrong moment for his plan. What bad luck! Not just for him but even more so for the boggart.

The next section of this tale was removed on the instructions of lawyers representing the Boggart Unified Movement. BUM maintains that the acts of cannibalism described in gross detail in the offending paragraphs when the other boggarts returned home to discover one of their own slain, is a heinous slander on the nature of all boggarts and all other slime-covered swamp dwellers. Unless they

dwell in the Louisiana bayous...they have their own representation.

Demonica saw the sign post and bracing herself against the coach's driving seat, hauled the tireless and squabbling Pookas to a sudden halt, no mean feat when you held the reins with fingers tipped by long talons and were wearing stiletto heels. But her mother had not raised her to be a weakling. Her mother, now Sister Penitencia had not raised her at all. A fact born out by the sorry trail of burnt out villages and scorched woodlands she'd left in her wake. Silencing the Pookas with a stern growl, she studied the signpost. They obeyed with a series of whispered surly mutters. The creatures were used to terrorizing country folk on rural lanes – but always working their devilment alone. Being harnessed together was bound to be problematical.

Squinting, Demonica was too vain to wear glasses, she studied the signpost. The route through the bog was an obvious no-no. Apart from being an unsavoury place fit only for boggarts and hippy dippy wise women, the wheels of the coach would be mired down within seconds. As it would do within the tangled woods of Mhmin, it was nearly impossible to walk through that let alone drive a coach and four.

That left The Land of Darkness and Despair where she had just fled from and Staines. Her useless demon of a father would have said the inhabitants had suffered enough just by living there. Demonica threw back her raven locks and gave a demoniacal laugh, worthy of... er...a demon and slapping the reins onto the Pookas' rumps hauled them around towards the hapless town. Her plans to wreak diabolical havoc and rule the Land of Goodness and Light had to start somewhere, why not Staines?

She was having fun with her plans to wreak diabolical havoc and she wasn't going to stop until she'd had enough. It was just tough luck on everyone else that she had a high threshold for fun and was a long way from having had enough. And she hadn't found a boyfriend yet.

Wheatley had had enough and he wasn't having fun. With feet stinging and ankles rubbed raw, he sat down on a soggy but almost solid mound, unaware it was a boggart's home, pulled off his boots and sunk his feet into the squelching ground. A black cloud of tiny annoying flies arose where his feet had sunken in, the mud stunk to high heaven but at least it was soft and cooling. It was nearly midday and despite hours of lone trudging, he had made little progress on his quest to find his destiny.

'If the boggarts don't get you, septicaemia or swamp fever will...Or creeping toe nail phage.'

Wheatley spun around at the sound of a young and thankfully human sounding voice. A black clad teenager stood a few feet away, black kohl from his eyeliner smearing his flour caked face. He had been crying. Was this the sidekick the apprentice had been waiting for to join his mission? Wheatley sincerely hope so. In fact his heart leapt with joy. So much flour must indicate a shared love of baking, at last someone Wheatley could share hilarious anecdotes and swap recipes about cakes and buns.

'Crumbs! Fondant Fancy meeting you!' chortled Wheatley with a broad smile of relief and welcome, extending a hand of friendship that was ignored.

'Eh?'

'Crumbs? Fondant Fancy?' Wheatley repeated with less enthusiasm, the boy had not responded with the correct secret greeting response of the Bakemeister's Union.

'Sorry, dude...you lost me with the fondant wotsits...'

It was then Wheatley could see the newcomer for what he was, a pathetic looking youngster using flour as a poor excuse for makeup. His dreams of jolly companionship dissolved like swamp mist in the sun. The pain from his feet did not and came back to remind the apprentice of his dire situation. Taking the lad's advice about avoiding boggarts, the ex-baker's apprentice dried his feet and wincing, gingerly replaced the boots. Instantly regretting it, his feet had swollen and the pain was excruciating. The thought of walking anywhere was unbearable.

The lad spoke again with his irritating whiney voice, 'If you retrace my steps down this track, you will come across a wise woman's hovel. She will be able to fix those sore feet in no time. It is not far.'

Scrutinising the young man's face for signs of guile, the bogs were rampant with tricksters, shape shifters, wraiths and timeshare salesmen. But he only saw abject misery and a shameful misuse of good quality flour. There was enough smeared on his face to make an almond slice!

'Where are you going?' Wheatley enquired, fighting his prejudice against cake abusers, 'This is no place to wander alone.'

Sighing, the teenager forgot his own advice and sat on the boggart mound, head in hands. 'My destiny is to wander this cruel world alone...my soul mourns from the depth of the abyss of misery. My life is worthless...

pointless. A mean-spirited joke played on me by powerful demons from an eternal dimension of torture and infernal despair...'

By the time he raised his head, Wheatley was long gone.

Morven was glad to see the back of the mummers. As well as leaving Robard's grimoire with her, they hadn't coughed up for any potions, unguents or spells.

'I expect a book like this might be worth a bit to someone of your persuasion Mistress Morven,' Prink had said tapping the side of his long nose and winking. 'But seeing as you have been so helpful to us, I won't ask any payment from you – No don't trouble to thank me. We'll be getting off now. Can't spend any more time waiting for the lad.'

Prink and Muriel rather harshly decided to leave their young errant songbird to his fate in the swamp. 'He knows where to find us,' growled Muriel, puffing on a large, stinky cigar, 'should he ever come to his senses.'

'Loved him like a son,' wailed Prink before bowing low to the Unwise Woman and rejoining his troupe to head off away from the swamp and from the hapless Robard.

Holding the Book under her arm, Morven decided there was nothing she could do for the lad now, his fate was sealed as boggart fodder. She watched them from the doorway of her hovel, just to make sure the whole damn lot had gone, put the Book down then rushed back to her preparations for a wild night of unbridled passion, should Jed find his way to her home.

With a sigh of delight, she hung up a gorgeous green velvet gown trimmed with real gold. A gift from her wayward lover obviously stolen, no doubt some posh woman travelling by coach across the countryside would have ended up shivering in her lacy undies as Jed relieved her of this fine robe. Probably had it off with her too, knowing Jed.

Morven carefully ensured that any valuable items she owned were well hidden. Crystals, spell candles, rare unguents, expensive exotic herbs; in other words anything small, easy to pocket and saleable enough to tempt a habitual pilferer. Jed couldn't read and books were too large to hide, so it was safe to leave lying any around so the grimoire stayed on the sideboard where she had placed it with a shiver of unease. She didn't bother hiding any of the jewellery Jed had given her either. It was all stolen anyway. Jewellery led a revolving-door kind of existence in her home. Easy come, easy go. The Unwise Woman knew what she was letting herself in for with a nefarious rogue like Jed but it was worth it. Sort of.

Morven boiled up as much hot water as her hearth could cope with, scented her tin hipbath with essence of flowers - ultra full strength to hide the all pervasive pong of Muriel's cigar and the surrounding swamp and wrapped only in a towel, put one toe in the bath...

The shadow of a man darkened the room. She turned with an expectant, loving smile. 'Aaaaarghh!' With a shriek of alarm she realised it wasn't her handsome highwayman.

'How the hell did you get past my guard goats and security toads?' an embarrassed and disappointed Morven yelled, wrapping herself tightly with her towel.

A far more embarrassed Wheatley, stepped back and turning around, sheepishly introduced himself.

'Stay there while I get dressed,' Morven muttered. Another damned visitor. Was it all some sort of official quality control test by the authorities...to make sure she was fulfilling her seer duty? Or some prudish deity punishing her for lusting after the country's most notorious bad boy? Or just sod's law? Whatever, she threw on her weird woman clothes and did her best to make the gangly man nervously waiting on the doorstep feel welcome.

'Dandruff, crazy frog ringtones, bunions...'

'MY LORD...' The evil minions had wised up and were using a megaphone from the farthest reaches of Rafial's audience hall. 'MY LORD...WE BRING YOU NEWS OF YOUR DAUGHTER!'

Pausing from his list, the demon prince glanced across to where the evil minions lurked, quivering fearfully. He beckoned them over with a sigh of weary impatience. Whatever game they were playing, it was beyond tiresome. At first none moved, then the others booted one forward. Out in the open and in plain sight of his fearsome master, he had no choice but to snivel his way up to Rafial's throne, a wondrously gothic extravagance of gilded and jewel encrusted dragon skulls, bats, spider's webs and bones. The other dogsbodies skulked behind the chosen victim, the smuggest being last in line.

'I don't have time for this,' Rafial growled, 'it had better be good.'

'It's your daughter Demonica, She of the Fiery Gaze, the Soul of Hopelessness, Princess of the Darkest Dominions...'

'I know who my own daughter is,' Rafial snapped, holding up his hand which terrified all the evil minions who dropped onto the floor and quivered. There was the inevitable resulting wet steaming puddle. Or two. Demonica's official titles were many, five hundred at the last count, being only half demon. He, as a royal prince of darkness had three thousand. At least that's how many he counted last time he listed them.

'The princess is laying waste to vast tracts of the neighbouring kingdom,' the bravest muttered.

Rafial shrugged, unconcerned. It was about time Demonica got a hobby and stopped stomping about the fortress having tantrums.

'But sir, it will trigger a whacking great war,' the underling snivelled on.

Again the demon prince seemed unbothered, causing misery and despair was what demons were supposed to do. It had been many centuries since the last war between the forces of good and evil. That had ended in a draw which meant the forces of good were two games up. Time to organise a replay, a whacking great war might be fun.

'Leave me...I have an Armageddon to plan.'

Relieved at their survival at bringing what they thought was bad news, the cronies filed out. The smug one at the back bringing up the rear. He slipped on a golden puddle, coughed with a noise that sounded like 'ghhdd.' Another pile of ash smelling like brimstone smouldered on the floor.

'Sorry!' Muttered the demon prince absentmindedly, his mind already on listing armaments and troop numbers for the conflagration to come.

'Now that's a sight you don't see every day!' mused Jed Moonraven to his sidekick the nasty bastard Strang as they controlled their shying horses, preventing them from dropping off the narrow path into the treacherous mire. Forty or more voles scampered towards them, scurrying through their startled steeds' legs. Despite the horses whirling and stamping in alarm, none of the tiny beasts was trampled. Truly a miracle for St Epiligia's Day. The fleeing rodents were followed by a mixed bag of mice, shrews and rats. A tumult of rabbits, badgers and wallabies. Then stoats, foxes, ferrets and weasels. By now the highwaymen's horses were spinning and rearing in panic. And by the time whole herds of deer and bog-dwelling wombats had hurtled past in a tsunami of brown fur and antlers, the horses were nearly out of their minds.

Logic said give into this warning from the wildlife, let the horses turn and flee away along the same path. But what had logic ever had to do with human curiosity? Why else would people go down into cellars when they heard spooky noises? Or walk at night in a group through haunted forests and at the first suggestion of creepiness split up to walk alone? Or believe a Nigerian diplomat's son needed their help claiming a thirty million dollar fortune? Well, maybe not the last one - that was old-fashioned plain stupidity and greed.

Using all their equestrian skills and persuasion, they pushed their balking horses forward into a nervous, snorting, high stepping walk. As they turned the corner of a narrow path winding through some wilting and canker ridden Snivelling Willows, they saw a coach mired deeply into the bog. The four creatures that strained in vain to haul it out looked at first like ordinary large black horses, but their eyes were huge and glowed fiercely like yellow lanterns.

The two men quickly reined in their own mounts and hid in the stand of snivelling willows to assess the perfect prey; a coach unable to flee from the highwaymen. Unsettled by the baleful yellow eyes of the horses, Jed fished out a little book from an inside pocket of his greatcoat that his beloved Morven had given him. After all knowledge was power in a world of uncertainty. Fading and well worn, it was a wayward little book which appeared to have a mind of its own. Why else would it always fall open on the well-read rude entries such as succubae and sirens?

Jed thumbed through the 'Ye Olde Gyuide to Magicke Folke.' Pausing briefly to glance at a picture of an exceptionally well-upholstered mermaid, he finally found a reference to spectral horses where he came across the entry for Pooka.

'The Pooka appears in the form of a tall dark horse with huge sulphurous yellow eyes. It rampages across large areas of countryside at night, smashing down fences and gates, scattering livestock in terror, trampling crops and being an all round damn nuisance around farms. It is the curse of all late night travellers, throwing them into muddy ditches or bog holes. The Pooka sometimes has the power of human speech and it has been known to stop in front of certain houses and call out the names of those it wants to piss off. If that person refuses to respond, the Pooka will wreck their property because it is a very vindictive gobshite of a creature.'

'They are Pookas,' ventured Jed, but his burly sidekick had no interest in the animals or the ornate high gothic and rather camp coach. He only had eyes for the glorious ruby encrusted golden coach and the expensive looking beasts that pulled it. So blinded by the glistening mobile treasure, he almost overlooked the fact there was an outrageously evil female in tight black, studded leather lashing at the Pookas' rounded backsides with a whip. What a terrifying obstacle to so much ill gotten gains. Even more so when she began berate the 'Useless nags...I will barbeque you where you stand! Obey your princess! I am heir to the Land of Darkness and Despair, you must do my will!'

'Aha!' Strang cried, his view on the female instantly changing to more mercenary ideals, an heiress at last! No more skulking around the countryside with the feckless Moonraven. No more watching out for their enemies while Jed had it off with all the best-looking trollopes. Winning the heart of an heiress was worth more than a handful of rubies and four peculiar almost equines.

Before Jed could stop him, his companion nudged his horse slowly forward out of the willows and approached the ferocious female.

'May I be of service, your most beauteous Highness?'

The ferocious female spun around, her eyes flaring with hellfire, which beyond a nervous gulp and trembling knees, did not stop Strang in his suicidal tracks. For the first time in his heinous life, he tried to emulate Jed and be raffish and charming.

'Oakham Strang at your service, Ma'am,' he gave a sweeping, theatrical bow, 'it is clear My Dear Young Lady of the Realm of Darkness and Despair that your beasts cannot haul your carriage out of the bog without help. I have a strong horse of my own that can assist them.'

With no other means of extricating the coach, the demon princess nodded a terse agreement and watched with an expression of imperious disdain as the burly human dragged over a nervous horse and lashed up a makeshift harness from the reins and saddle.

The lead Pooka began to protest loudly in a strange accent no one understood, a complaint taken up by its companion and the one behind it, both equally difficult to understand. The remaining Pooka spoke with a soft Southern Irish lilt. 'Me fellows are from North Dublin and Belfast. The eejit beside me comes from Kerry. None of us can understand *him.*'

Seething with impatience, Demonica fixed the Pooka with a fiery glare, 'Then you will have to translate!'

The Pooka was too canny to argue and continued,

'He says, how do you expect me to pull your coach when I have to look at a horse's huge hairy, farting arse in front of me?'

'Well, I have to!' interrupted the Pooka harnessed directly behind him triggering a furious row amongst the Pookas which further frightened Strang's horse, a situation rapidly deteriorating into equine related chaos.

Jed was delighted. Like Strang, his eyes glowed with greed at the sight of the coach decorated with many carved bizarre beasts, griffons, basilisks, gargoyles, bog chavs; their eyes made from a tempting adornment of inlaid rubies. With all the fuss created by the Pookas refusal to have an ordinary horse harnessed in front of them, Jed took his chance to help himself to some loot. He sneaked out of the wood, crept behind the coach and taking a sharp knife began to dig out the rubies and stuff them in an inside coat pocket.

A sudden pause in the argument could have led to his potential discovery. Jed cussed under his breath and hoped the creatures would continue to whinge to Strang and Demonica long enough to prize the last remaining rubies from the coach. Just a few more...

'So what exactly is the problem now?' growled a dangerously impatient Demonica, she had an overdue appointment with the unsuspecting people of Staines.

'We are on strike,' muttered the Pookas' spokeshorse.

'The only strike they will receive is from my whip!' screamed Demonica, 'before I turn you all into piles of ash stinking of brimstone!'

'But the filthy nag just did a huge stinking dump! Inches from our sensitive, well bred noses! This is no way to treat pedigree Pookas! Your father would be furious.'

Nearly giving away his thievery by sniggering, Jed bit his tongue and swiftly levered out the remaining ruby. With the coach still mired in, it was time to make a rapid getaway. But he'd forgotten about Strang being a nasty bastard.

'My Princess, to save your beasts' fine sensibilities, we need to get this coach out of the mire as swiftly as possible. I have another horse. With that I will surely set you free in no time.'

Cursing, Jed slunk back into the willows, unable to stop his now former companion hauling away an unwilling Milady and harnessing her in front of the Pookas. Brave and reckless as he was, there was no way he was going to challenge a demonic princess with a penchant for setting people alight. Not over a stolen horse, even one as useful as the grey mare. He watched in futile fury as the Pookas became visibly excited at the prospect of some equine tottie's rear end in front of them, that Milady was as ugly as any mare foaled on this earth apparently mattered naught. And she was exactly the incentive needed to entice the creatures to put in that extra effort to haul the coach, now minus its ruby inlay, out of the bog.

Demonica whirled the whip around her head and as one the equines, both supernatural and natural reared and pawed the air. Jed winced, praying the sadistic bitch wouldn't hurt his mare and grew angry as Strang pleaded with her,

'Take me with you. I know this land well, I can be your guide, your minion,' and with an unsubtle leer added, '*anything* you want me to be.'

Glaring with her firebrand eyes, Demonica considered blasting him for the impudence of addressing her. 'Why shouldn't I turn you into a pile of ash stinking of brimstone?'

'Because I am a nasty bastard. And I have nine inches.'

Demonica had no idea what that meant, but this was a human male and therefore a possible boyfriend. There was no time to play all of the flirting games suggested by the teen magazines to keep a boy interested. With nothing to lose, she pointed to the coach.

'Fair enough. Hop on board.'

Adding with a curious mixture of command and entreaty...

'You are my boyfriend now.'

For the umpteenth time that day, Morven mixed up another potion. At least this sorry looking man had paid up front. That showed either great honesty or overwhelming naivety, either way it was cash in hand. She threw together an interesting concoction of crushed peanuts, lemon fresh washing up liquid and aerosol cheese.

'Will that help?' muttered the exhausted Wheatley.

'Can't harm...' Replied Morven truthfully. There was an innocence about this visitor, a total lack of guile, his large brown eyes stared up at her from beneath a thick, unruly thatch of reddish brown hair. She would have taken him for an apprentice out to find his hidden destiny, if it wasn't for his age. It was also clear he had reached the end of his day's journey. He was totally done in. *Bugger it,* thought Morven, if she chucked this man out, it would be detrimental to his welfare and therefore the unkind act would come back three times stronger to haunt her. Why had she picked that particular course at the academy of mystic skills? She could just have easily chosen the black arts. Then she could have slung him out with a few caustic curses and had the whole day free to prepare herself for her Jed. And she could have put a fidelity spell on her lover too, to bind him to her and curb his notorious philandering.

In truth, she had chosen the only path for a woman of her caring nature. And her dashing highwayman would not be the same man if tamed and chained to her. But she still wished the unwelcome visitor would piss off. And if the morning continued in the same vein, there would be more out there seeking her counsel.

Unprompted, Wheatley introduced himself and told his story, the words tumbling out of his mouth in a flood of misery. There was something about this beautiful woman's warm green eyes that triggered a need to unburden. That the wondrous green eyes had glazed over completely escaped him.

Many years ago Morven had perfected the skill of feigning interest. She had developed this talent during many tedious one-sided conversations with her father Aedric the Toad Flanger, who had eon's worth of not-very-fascinating tidbits to share about his life's endeavour to create the definitive garden rake collection. It was characterised by a slight smile and the occasional nod.

Done properly it enabled her to go wandering in her head to more absorbing places. It was also a vital tool in self-protection against terminal boredom. A condition she was dangerously close to by the time Wheatley got to the point of explaining the precise differences between Bath buns and Chelsea buns.

Far from wandering aimlessly through the perilous mire, Robard had thought up a cunning plan. He hid in a nearby grove of bog oaks and waited. Any minute now, the troupe of mummers would come looking for him. A search party would desperately scour the area, crying out his name plaintively. When they found him, after a joyous celebration at his safekeeping and reunion, they would realise how much he meant to them. They would know how much he was prepared to sacrifice for the purity of his art. They would respect him for the unique individual he was. And would never force him to wear the motley again. Or make him sing jolly upbeat songs about buxom milkmaids and lusty young swains. Or voles.

While he waited, Robard passed the time exploring the bog oak grove. At first he attributed the strange markings carved on the trees to bog chav vandals, their grannies were deemed the worst offenders. But on closer inspection rather then the usual 'Shardonay is a toofless slag.' And 'Dwayne fancies Shazza,' Robard could make out ritualistic symbols and with a sinking heart, he recognised many from illustrations in Draven De'ath's grimoire. He tried not to panic, it was still broad daylight. For he had discovered irrefutable evidence that someone else claimed this woodland as their own. Satanists! Or to be exact, a sect of Vegetarian Satanists. Robard searched further and discovered amongst the trees with symbols painted on their trunks, were the remains of a recent ritual. A virgin red cabbage had been sacrificed to their demonic deity. He knew it was best not to touch it, but it was still fresh and he was so hungry. Glancing around to make sure this desecration was not being watched, Robard tucked in, hoping his troupe would find him before the crazed devil worshiping veggies returned.

Three hours passed, the morning drifted onto a hazy late morning where a weak, hazy sun managed to agitate some mosquitoes and particularly vicious midges. These had a severe attitude problem. Always playing third place in the biting order of the bog's most annoying insects, with the mozzies first and leeches a close second, the midges had thought up a well planned campaign to raise their profile and standing in the official Nasty Bug League. Robard would have voted them number one, such was the hell they were putting him through now, he was covered with furiously itchy bites. As well as being unbearably uncomfortable, all the red blotches were a bad look for him. Though it did fit in with the bloody feast of bloody St bloody Epiligia! He could endure no more. With no sign of his troupe and the danger of discovery from furious veggie Satanists, Robard had no choice but to leave his hiding place. It was back to the Unwise Woman's hovel for some soothing salves. And to make his peace with the mummers.

With Squarf keeping a wary watch out for pursuing hordes of vengeful boggarts, he and the prince began another dejected trudge through the mire. The Quest for the Chalice of Untold Delights was becoming the Quest to get out of this Damned Bog with a Single Shred of Dignity Left.

'By Odin's bum fluff! Its all your fault, serf!' grumbled Prince Pravis. 'We could have used that boggart as a native guide to get us out of this mess. But instead you shot the creature and now we will have all its horrible slimy relatives after our blood.'

Squarf seethed, the desire to push his master off the path into the bog to disappear forever beneath the stinking ooze had never been so strong. 'And what exactly would you have paid the fellow to act as a guide?' Squarf queried. 'They don't use cash. Or collect supermarket school vouchers.'

'You...' replied the prince with dangerous candour, unaware how close he was to ending up in a peaty grave. 'Wait!' He held up a gauntleted hand and pointed to a signpost at a crossroads down a narrow, winding path. Unaware, like Demonica hours before, that a gang of bored bog-chavs had switched it around, there was sod all else for them to do. The noble questers' low spirits finally rising, Squarf postponed his heinous but well justified act of princicide and hobbled towards the sign.

'Well, there's nothing very inspiring there,' the prince muttered, visibly disappointed. 'What does it say in the pamphlet Squarf?'

Still fuming with resentment the serf flicked through the maps and to his amazement found a picture of the signpost and a write-up of the paths indicated by it. He showed the prince.

64

'My Liege the signpost seems to have changed since the picture was drawn, the fingerboards are pointing in different directions now.'

'I expect the artist got it wrong. You know what these painter chappies are like.' Pravis spoke from bitter experience, his mother Queen Hemelda was a patron of the arts and fan of interior design and garden makeover programs.

'There is some writing to go with the picture my Liege, maybe that will explain it.'

'Well read it out man, read it out, we haven't got all year.'

Squarf began to read;

'Warning to Travellers,

'The Forest of Mhmin is a large area of tangled, haunted trees, a place where some of the most irksome dwellers of this world live. Everything that inhabits the forest tries a bit too hard to be fey and mysterious. It is highly competitive. The result is that it is impossible for a visiting stranger to have the simplest conversation.

'For instance, if you are forced by circumstance to ask a tall, elegant elven warrior the time, he will lean on his bow or staff and glance meaningfully into the distance for at least twenty minutes before fixing you with the full force of his wondrous shimmering eyes and in a voice full of portent and meaning, declare;

'The shining golden orb that brightens the azure heavens hath made but a small passage of his eternal celestial pilgrimage. The haunting beauty of the silver lady is still a slumber in her star-strewn chamber and will not grace us with her gentle presence, we must bide our time to seek audience with her....

'By that time the traveller may have lost the will to live. As they will if they turn back towards Staines. The Land of Darkness and Despair is an obvious no-no being inhabited by unmitigated and relentless evil, though it does have attractions for those unwilling to risk a sun tan or who actively enjoy pain and humiliation.'

Squarf stopped reading, aware that the prince wasn't listening anymore.

'No more of that twaddle,' Pravis declared, 'that pamphlet is a total waste of paper. I'd tell you to throw it away but I might use it later if I can't find the right sort of leaves. I'll make the choice without it. Just let me think a while.'

'Oh look, a snowball has just flown out of hell to join a squadron of airborne pigs on a fly past,' is what Squarf wanted to say about their chances of getting out of the swamp alive with Pravis and what passed for a royal brain in control. Instead he held his tongue and stuffed the pamphlet away as he fumed silently.

Prince Pravis was hungry for valiant adventure, itching to do some serious smiting and everything that lived in that baleful, night-cloaked region was fair game. It was the realm of evil, ruled by a demon, populated by werewolves, zombies, spammers. A haven for all manner of vileness and depravity. Pravis could have some suitably heroic exploits there and it was as good a place as any to hide the Chalice of Untold Delights.

'At last, a ray of hope in our noble venture.'

Squarf's heart dropped to his boots. Or would have done if it hadn't been well attached in his chest.

'I will gather up every ounce of courage and fortitude and march with my head high into the depths of hell itself.

Face down Rafial's demonic hordes and seek the Chalice to return it to the Land of Goodness and Light.'

Shuffling his sodden boots in the squelch, Squarf coughed to interrupt the flow of heroic bollocks from his master.

'There was something I was meaning to talk to you about. My leave?'

It was too late, a new shining light of valour gleamed from Prince Pravis's contact lenses to give his eyes a more heroic shade of blue and he strode away towards what he believed to be the Land of Darkness and Despair.

'Come on serf, you are holding up my voyage to destiny and glory.'

'I wish,' muttered Squarf, remembering Destiny and Glory were too delightfully unpicky and accommodating trollopes in Madam Providence's house of ill repute and bicycle repair shop. It paid to diversify.

The sun had set and so had Squarf's hopes for a well-earned kip.

Grateful for the cover of deepening darkness and leaning against a mildew encrusted bog oak, Jed Moonraven felt a strange new feeling course through him - self-pity. He didn't like it, it didn't suit his devil-take-the hindmost attitude to life. But what a pathetic and vulnerable position to be in, a highwayman without a fast horse, marooned alone in a bog with only a bag of rubies stolen from under the nose of a demon princess. One that could turn people into a pile of ash stinking of brimstone at a whim. And what a treacherous nasty bastard Strang had turned out to be, leaving his partner in crime to go chasing after a bit of demonic tottie with a fortune, a massive castle and a whole kingdom to inherit. Ok, so maybe not such a bad move after all.

But that still left Jed on foot in a mire full of danger. The price on his head, once a sign of great pride now felt as choking as the noose around his neck it represented. questing knights would be everywhere, setting out on this auspicious day for pointless but heroic journeys. The tin-plated fools who recently were his prey now became his enemies. As was every man, woman and child wanting to buy fashionable pointy shoes. And tins of butterbeans to chuck at mummers and mimes. Bugger! This was not how he wanted to end his career. He removed his tricorne hat and ran his fingers through his long hair, coal black with streaks of very dark red as if it couldn't decide what colour to be and ended up with both.

At least his career and life would end as the undisputed top highwayman of the realm. A thief renowned for his charm and success in relieving travellers of their wealth. The hated epithet of 'dandy highwayman' would never be used for him. Jed dressed well but in sober coloured and tough garb made for a life on the road on horseback. No flounces or frills. Unlike 'Gentleman' Toby Mulch. By the time the militia had finally caught up with him, Mulch actually believed his own hype and wore outrageous garb, exaggeratedly long baby-blue lace cuffs, a pompadoured lilac powdered wig, over the top day-glo blue glitter on his tricorne hat and his name spelt out with flashing neon lights on the back of his white caped coat. Jed's only thought had been why the silly sod hadn't been caught years earlier.

There were problems at Mulch's execution. At the sight of his garb, the crowds had bayed with laughter, the official executioner got hopeless fits of the giggles and couldn't perform, his whole body shaking, tears of hysterical laughter streaming from his eyes. In the end they had dragged a dour old git out from retirement. So miserable that he silenced the hysterical laughter in the crowds with one baleful glare. Stepping forward, he had been so overcome by Gentleman Toby Mulch's aftershave that he dropped dead on the spot.

'It's a sign!' shouted the gleeful crowd. And so Mulch ended up retiring from thievery and had turned to a career selling timeshares for holiday hovels in the Costa Lotte. So not that much a change of career then. The recalling of this tale did nothing to help Jed's uncharacteristic depressed mood. But he couldn't waste time moping. Keeping a watchful eye all around him, Jed Moonraven took to the road, gritting his teeth against the ignominy of being on foot with no sign of a horse to steal anywhere.

But all this reminiscing was doing nothing to help lift Jed's uncharacteristic depressed mood. He had to stop wasting time moping. He resolved to draw a line under what had happened for now and stop brooding.

Wary and alert, Jed Moonraven took to the road, gritting his teeth against the ignominy of being on foot and with no sign of a horse to steal anywhere. At least he was not walking aimlessly.

There was one place of sanctuary left if he could reach it unseen. The Unwise Woman's cottage and the welcoming arms of his beloved. Hiding his black scarf, the most obvious sign of his gentleman-of-the-road status — he didn't bother using a black mask, an ugly, restricting thing — Jed made his way towards Morven's home.

It never crossed his mind even for a second that she wouldn't protect him. He had been certain of her loyalty since their first school day together, when he stole her ruler and eraser and she didn't run to Sister Mortadella to tell on him.

He'd loved her ever since then. Won over by her magical green-gold eyes and generous compassionate heart. He adored how she readily accepted his explanation for his thieving nature – that he had been born under the star sign of Klepto. And the explanation for his roving eye – that he was born on the day of the popular pagan feast of unbridled lust and fertility; Tumescentide. Those excuses would never work with anyone but lovely trusting Morven.

He wondered if the indulgently tolerant blind-spot she looked at him through was something to do with the fact that she had nobody left to call kin, since her last distant auntie had passed on three years ago. The smudged badly written parchment had been so hard to read, bearing as it did the sad news that her aunt had died in a tragic accident involving a shovel, three beetroots and a runaway rhino. But the last bit was possibly wrong. The smudged parchment had been very hard to read after all.

Night had fallen. Sinking back onto the plush purple velvet seats of Demonica's coach, Strang, the nasty bastard attempted a weak smile. He was nearly naked, completely exhausted, drained by his demon mistress's insatiable demands. She had never experienced sex with a human before and her curiosity had to be sated.

It had all begun so well for Strang. With Moonraven's thrice stolen mare swishing her tail flirtatiously at the Pookas, the nasty bastard had successful hauled out the mired down coach. With her mission to cause hellish mayhem and create her own demonic realm back on track again, Demonica had been well pleased with her first ever boyfriend. Even allowing him to drive the vehicle so she could return to being a princess and sit with icy hauteur in the comfy seats. But shortly after heading for what they believed to be Staines, she had demanded he pull over and join her in the back. Strang had been proud of his achievement; she was so ferocious, so dangerous yet so desirable. He'd somehow managed to erect a proud, upstanding example of human manhood only for Demonica to fall about laughing. 'What do you call *that*?' she guffawed, 'and why is it shrivelling?'

A bizarre mixture of her threats and his heroic victory of mind over matter had finally enabled Strang to perform. And perform. And perform again - sort of. Fortunately Demonica eventually enjoyed his efforts, preventing her human beau and his hard working appendage from becoming a pile of ash stinking of brimstone. It was a brief reprieve. Strang knew if she wanted any more, he would be finished. He suspected no one said 'sorry, luv but not right now' to Demonica and lived and there was no way he could satisfy her again. But the terrifying princess from the Land of Darkness and Despair had other things on her mind.

'Are there any gloomy, brooding castles or mighty baleful fortresses in Staines?'

Strang thought carefully. There was a town hall, a leisure centre and a great many hovels. That was about it really. He shook his head.

'What about creepy gothic abbeys or mysterious ancient temples with a curse on them? After all I am a princess of Hell, I need a suitably regal but foreboding looking residence to start my reign of darkness and despair over this soon to be blighted land. Any suggestions, evil minion?'

71

'My Lady there is none in Staines. But I know somewhere else that has a castle ripe for redevelopment...'

A delighted Strang told her about the one on the other side of the bog. The one Moonraven had recently gate crashed and pillaged. It was a bog-standard edifice, not remotely scary looking but nothing a bit of DIY couldn't fix. It was amazing what could be done with MDF and a few scatter cushions these days. And she had called him her boyfriend...he liked the sound of that. It had a certain cache to it. But not as much as King Strang, Lord of the Dark Dominion of Despair and Anguish. From wandering highwayman, to evil minion/boyfriend, to Demonica's husband was quite a leap of status but Strang was nothing but ambitious. Him being a nasty bastard and all.

The Pookas cantered on through the night, their huge yellow lantern eyes illuminated the road ahead like headlights. Strang was able to recover his strength and dream of future evil glory.

Having emerged from the forest canopy and still leading the stampeding woodland creatures the voles suddenly diverted off the trajectory they had previously been vectoring on like speeding furry bullets.

The other fire-spooked creatures kept going on the original path, but the voles were marching to different drumbeat now. They had no idea why, but for some strange reason they were inexorably drawn. A new compelling fate, a new destiny called out to them and they had no inclination to deny that call.

Maybe one or two had a vague unease, having had cousins who were lemmings they were aware of the possible implications of giving in to irrational compulsions.

But what the heck - it was the Feast of St Epiligia - what could possibly go wrong?

In her delicate gossamer gown dyed with forest violets, sparkling with moon crystals, Cylphie was as enchanting as any elven maiden in the Forest of Mhmin. That the flowing garb was long enough to hide a pair of brand new lace up Dr Marten boots was a bonus. Cylphie sat on a log - a dead piece of ordinary tree, an enchanted one would not put up with anyone's bottom even a pretty elf maiden's trim backside. (Well, actually, there was one particular enchanted oak that wouldn't have minded.)

As the new morning droned on, she began to drum her boots against the side of the unprotesting log, startling a family of piskies who lived inside the hollowed trunk. She ignored their berating, pretending not to hear them, which was easy to do, what with elves being tall and slender and piskies being irritating little short arses.

What a dreary start to the day. The wood looked ethereal, mysterious and beautiful, it always did. How it remained so green and lush, strewn with so many wild flowers when it never rained was beyond anyone's comprehension. But there was the one great cop out that could explain everything that happened in the wood. Magic. It didn't matter whether it was a stolen pie or a vexing boil in an awkward place, every unexplained or annoying event in Mhmin was put down to magic. Which was handy for Cylphie. She could explain why she wasn't wearing butterfly silk shoes trimmed with dew diamonds but was sporting whacking great boots by blaming magic. It was obvious, her feet were under a dark enchantment.

And nothing to do with a mail order delivery from Twee Bay earlier that morning. There were many advantages to living in the forest. Listening to elven poetry for bloody hours was not.

Her vantage point on the log was perched on the top of a natural amphitheatre of soft grass, a silver birch lined, sun-dappled glade where the ever present wafts of pollen and drifts of glistening gossamer filled the air. Also glittering bits of sparkly stuff. Hay fever was a constant drawback to living on Mhmin, no 'magic' ever solved that. Many of the forest dwellers had permanently runny eyes and red noses...not a good look for a graceful dryad or willowy elf. Bizarrely, the only beings immune from the hay fever were the wood gnomes who could have carried off the red nose look with aplomb.

The next performer stepped into the centre of the grassy arena to rapturous applause. Her cousin, Devin. Or the 'Utterly Divine Devin' as his swooning underage followers called him. Cylphie thought he was a prat, a pompous one who insisted in reciting his long, dreary verse sagas in archaic Elvish that no one spoke any more. A pretentious, pompous pillock. But he was glorious to look at. Like her, he had long silver-blonde hair and lustrous dark violet eyes. His voice was hypnotic, which was clearly part of his success. Why else would crowds gather to listen to long-winded drivel in a language nobody understood? They had been brainwashed. Possibly by magic. Whatever other conclusion could anyone reach?

Bored rigid, Cylphie picked a piece of bark from the old log, again only possible with a non-enchanted tree. The only thing she annoyed this time were some woodlice, glistening in the sunlight with their silver and green enamelled backs - everything in Mhmin had to look beautiful or enchanted - even things that lived under stones and in rotting wood bark. Absentmindedly, she flicked the scrap of bark, which flew and spun across the glade like a miniature Frisbee. It was the nearest to amusement she would get that morning, so Cylphie pulled off another piece and sent that flying too. So engrossed in Devin's great opus, no one seemed to notice the whirling scraps of wood. A sense of mischief overcame her; if anything went wrong she could always blame some dark enchantment, the same spell that changed her delicate slippers for clumping great boots.

The elf maiden began to target some of the rapt and respectfully silent audience. A sliver of wood bounced off the nose of the Queen of the Water Nymphs. Another landed in the lap of a particularly surly gnome. A third clipped the ear of an elven warrior she once had a crush on. Till she found out he was in love with Devin. Which was a waste as her cousin was too much in love with himself to notice any would-be suitor. Another knocked a packet of biscuits from the hands of a Hobnob goblin sending a cloud of crumbs to join the sparkling miasma.

Gradually the mood of the crowd changed. Concentration on the saga switched to discomfort, then suspicion. Angry looks were exchanged across the glade. Looks that became words which in turn ended in pandemonium and an all-out fist fight between a burly centaur and a flower fairy. Cylphie's money was on the flower fairy, most had vicious tempers beneath the saccharine smiles and fey mannerisms.

In all it was the perfect end to a morning of poetry.

With a hammer in one hand and a fat, malodorous cigar in the other, Muriel stepped back to admire his handiwork, narrowly avoiding stepping on the trailing hem of his white chiffon and voile gown, tastefully embroidered with red dots, in honour of the blessed saint. He was an expert at erecting the mummer troupe's stage in record speed and had made up for the time wasted wallowing around the wretched bog, humouring the now missing Robard.

He had worked all through dawn and breakfast and soon the great hall of the castle would be full of nobles and their families, all excited and expecting to be entertained. A long hollow pipe had been set up from the stage, across the high vaulted roof, out a window and down into the courtyard. The assembled grovelling peasants and serfs in the courtyard could not see the performance but would at least be able to hear it.

Admiring the decoration, a relieved Salatious Prink wandered around the hall. They had made it! The show that could change his fortune was about to begin. He glanced up at the dramatically long white pennants decorated with red spots or the images of voles hung from the massive overhead oak beams. As was a vast net crammed with hundreds of highly inflated pigs bladders, a new innovation to this year's festivities suggested by the Queen. At the end of the festivities, the bladders would be released to bob and bounce about gaily amongst the celebrating crowd. This was more like it; the nobility knew how to celebrate in style - and how to spend money. No more villages knee deep in mire and pig shit for his troupe!

He was even more certain of success because he had tried something daring. The short time he had taken possession of Robard's grimoire had yielded him some useful information. For within its pages had been a short rhyming verse described by the author as guaranteed to draw a crowd *within a shorte time after itte hasse beene utterrede in lowdnesse to the winde.*

While in the Unwise Woman's hovel Prink had noted down the few short lines and just at the start of rehearsals had *utterrede in lowdnesse to the winde* each and every syllable with thespian aplomb. He had no idea if it would work but as Morven would say, it would do no harm.

With all being well, Prink rejoined his troupe dressing into their costumes behind a tapestry arras, helping lace Muriel tightly into his suitably solemn holy nun's gown. Prink needed to have words later with his leading lady. Too many lardy cakes and tankards of cider were taking a toll on his waistline. Gradually the hall began to fill up with the well-bred audience, a little noisier then usual as many tripped over their modish shoes with long pointy toes. At one point a tripping baronet caused a toppling domino effect, felling three arch dukes, their ladies and a visiting high-ranking Viking berserker. Thankfully the festive spirit of the feast day prevailed and no one was cut down by a Norse blood axe.

The audience seated, hushed with anticipation and a gerbil-driven winch pulled the curtains back. Staging the play was a traditional St Epiligia custom, performed every year at the castle though this was the first time Prink's troupe had been booked. Despite the familiarity, all the audience suspended doubt and disbelief as the age-old but still stirring take of how a simple nun takes on a terrible, bloodthirsty pagan king and wins him over to the true faith was told in a mixture of song, dance, drama and puppets. There used to be a long mime section too but this was dropped due to the performers' complaints about being pelted with old shoes, rotting melons and butterbeans.

Unknown to the ardent performers on their Muriel built wooden stage, a distraction was losing the audience's attention. It began with a rustling, scratching noise above their heads, a sound growing louder and more insistent. Hearing the sound and sensing the audience's disquiet, Muriel did his best to captivate them in his acclaimed performance as the beatific St Epiligia as she cured the world's worst case of acne plaguing the pagan king of the Vandals. A moving scene for once cured, the king falls at her feet and pleads to be converted. But by now no one was watching his showpiece performance. The audience's eyes were drawn inexorably up to the roof, to the sound pipe for the serfs and peasants. By now, there was not just a loud rusting and scratching sound but the whole pipe was bouncing up and down

Now the pipe above their heads transfixed everyone's full attention and an expectant silence fell across the hall. Muriel tried his hardest to regain the audience but it was futile. He hauled up his long trailing gown, exposing sturdy and very hairy legs and stomped off the stage muttering surly oaths and accusations that the audience were all inbred fools and over-privileged philistines. No one noticed.

Like a bomb bursting a hole in a dam, an explosion of small dark shapes shot out of the pipe to land on the heads and upturned faces of the audience creating a chaos of panic, a squeaking, screaming and shouting uproar. An appalled Prink watched as his dream of social climbing, of leaving behind performing to filthy oafs and proles in rancid villages knee-deep in muck and becoming adored entertainer to the nobility dissolved in a furry river of angry voles.

He plonked himself down on a chair, swiftly tucking his trousers into his socks to prevent the tiny rodents scurrying up his legs. Removing his tall, wonky hat, he rubbed his balding scalp in despair. Could this day get any worse? First there was the loss of his troubadour, now an invasion of voles? Obviously an act of sabotage by revolting peasants. Or maybe a militant section of the St Epiligia pedants. Prink received his answer by a heavy object falling on his head from a great height. It hurt. A lot.

So of course it could get worse, someone had foolishly released the bladders and far from bobbing and bouncing around gaily amongst the audience and rampaging voles, they landed with the force of leathery bombs. They had been mistakenly inflated with water not air. The pandemonium intensified as the vole-harassed audience now had to dodge the bladders, those that didn't get knocked out, were drenched by smelly water as they burst. It was too noisy to hear an ominous creaking. The sound of stressed wood breaking under strain. Built in a hurry, the stage began to lurch to one side at a drunken angle before collapsing in a huge pile of gaudily painted debris. It also ripped down the strings holding the pennants which fluttered prettily above the great hall before engulfing the beleaguered wet, vole dodging, pennant enwrapped and pointy toed shoes-hampered crowd. With an enraged, wet through Berserker with a deflated pig's bladder stuck on his helmet's horns, wielding a blood axe for good measure.

There couldn't be a worse end to the play designed to celebrate the supposedly joyous Feast of St Epiligia. Like all performers, Salatious Prink was a superstitious man. This was a bad omen. A portent of great doom. Something bad was going to happen. And for once it did not involve Robard.

Salatious Prink gazed in horror at a scene far beyond anything he had even contemplated in his wildest theatrical imaginings. How could this disaster have come about?

He'd been sure the spell he'd tried would bring good luck and success to the proceedings. The poem had been endorsed at the bottom of the page by someone who had waxed lyrical about its efficacy. But he had his doubts about that now. The poet had probably paid them to write that glowing review. Maybe the poet had even written it under a false identity? Come to think of it what sort of daft name was Piede Piperre?

As the new day dawned with birdsong, they were back.

'Why don't I just put up a bloody great sign,' moaned Morven whose dreams of a passionate tryst with Jed were rapidly fading away. 'To every traveller lost in the bog. Please come to the Unwise Woman's hovel. Free salves, all the free food you can eat and a comfy spot by the fire.'

'Wow, that's an amazing offer!' marvelled Squarf with a wide grin. 'Maybe there will be some poor, lost, fair maidens needing shelter. And a comforting hug from a big strong man.' He glanced at the raised eyebrows around the hovel. 'OK, from a small strong man.'

The prince kicked him in the shins, 'I believe the lady was being sarcastic,' he turned to the Unwise Woman, 'it's your own fault we ended up back here Mistress Morven. If the pamphlet of maps you'd given us had been any good we'd have been well on our way by now. As it is we've incurred the wrath of the boggart community and wasted a great deal of time.'

'Well if the maps were no good perhaps you'd like to give them back?' Morven asked not unreasonably, they were freely given after all.

'Certainly. Squarf - hand them over.'

As indicated by the witch, Squarf put the pamphlet on the sideboard next to the grimoire already there. Unnoticed by anyone but themselves a small tremor of recognition rippled through both of the printed objects. So close and yet so far. Energy levels rose and if anyone had looked they would have seen a shimmer above the rough piece of furniture, very like a heat haze. But a different radiation was causing the disturbance in the air as the magic tried its best to manipulate circumstances to bring the pieces together.

The lady was thoroughly pissed off. As if her overnight guests, poor disorientated Wheatley, still nursing his blisters wasn't bad enough - there was only so much discussion about cakes one woman could stand and the Goth lad with his midge bites, now she had the unexpected return of Prince Pravis and his oafish serf to contend with.

It seemed their idea to find some suitably valiant though pointless adventures had come unstuck when en route to seek the Chalice of Untold Delights in the Land of Darkness and Despair they had encountered a picket line, a hundred deep with angry boggarts egged on by their lawyers. A breakaway group from BUM, this lot called themselves BOGOFF. Which stood for Boggarts Offensive Group Of Fearsome Fiends. And therefore able to be featured in this story.

At one side of the road had been a gang of unruly bog chavs hoping the increasingly chaotic scene would be filmed by a news team and they could be on the telly. On the other side, a deputation of St Epiligia pedants also hoping that a news team would turn up, so they could get their point across. They were being kicked and bitten in the ankles by a small army of vexed voles unwilling to have their status as holy creatures demoted back to ordinary small, furry rodents. It would end in tears. Pravis and Squarf had turned back. Clearly an unseemly place for a noble prince on a serious and dignified quest to be seen, especially when it would inevitably degenerate into an inevitable riot. Voles were such vile little stirrers.

Outside, hastily feeding bourbon biscuits to the guard goats and a big, 'Value' bag of organic bluebottles to the security toads, a dismayed and anxious Jed peered through a gap in the daub and wattle to spy on the people crowding into Morven's hovel. The prince was really bad news. Jed had pleasured both the royal prat's pretty maiden sisters. Both now very much ex-maidens thanks to him. And stolen one of their gowns to give to Morven.

Though it was early in the morning, a fast-moving shroud of darkness hid the sun. A line of black smoke and the acrid smell of burning drifted towards them. Something very bad had happened and was coming their way. Jed could no longer hide, not when Morven was in danger. He stepped into her hovel, ignoring the startled gasps from the men or the furious growl of recognition from the right royal prat and Morven's exclamation of 'Jed you are an idiot!'

'Look, I know you all want to see me hang and claim the reward but that will have to wait. We have a more urgent problem to deal with first.'

'I will deal with it...you will be dead!' announced Prince Pravis aiming his sword at the highwayman's chest. Jed in return raised his two ornate pistols and took aim at the prince's head. 'Unlikely. I have the edge of better technology over you,' he replied, his voice glacier cool and steady. He also had the edge of ruthlessness and almost zero conscience unlike the prince who was raised to be chivalrous and law abiding.

Morven's hand went to her mouth in shock with the very real prospect of having both her lover and the prince lying dead on the floor of her hovel, which would be heartbreaking, inconvenient and messy in turn. Bloodstains were also nightmarish to get out of the earth floor and very off-putting for clients. She prayed nothing would happen yet, the stand-off was still at the macho posturing phrase. Yet she daren't move, though a strategically thrown jug of water might dowse down the testosterone overload. The problem was Jed had such fast reflexes and a hair trigger on both pistols, he might shoot instinctively if startled.

'This scoundrel is a foul, poxed cur that needs to be put out of its misery. The noose is too good for such a degenerate reprobate,' snarled Pravis. 'I am sorry to distress you, Lady, but this odious worm dishonoured two royal princesses and stole half the crown jewels!'

'I took nothing that wasn't freely offered up to me...apart from the jewels and they might as well have been, they were so badly guarded!' Jed answered with a humourless grin.

Morven shrugged with a sad attempt at a grin as all eyes other then Jed's turned to her, perhaps expecting her to be distraught at the revelation. What else could she do? Her highwayman's rampant womanising was hardly news. It wasn't his fault though. He couldn't chose the day of his birth. Her pain was not helped by Jed's taunting embellishment. 'In fact your luscious sisters were begging me for more when I tried to leave the bed.'

'Varlet! Scoundrel!' roared the prince, his face bright purple with outrage.

'A princess on each ankle, clinging onto my boots as I tried to walk across the bedroom floor...they were both absolutely gagging for it!'

Poor Morven was trying hard not to feel or show her discomfort at these public revelations. Nothing being said was news to her of course, but she would prefer not to have her nose rubbed in it publicly. Jed couldn't help his inclinations – given the extremely inauspicious portents and constellations surrounding his birth date. But a little more discretion would be nice. He was born on Tumescentide – not Blab it All to the World and His Wife Day after all. Meanwhile the name calling continued.

Vile, odious scum! By Odin's kneecap, I will see you beg for death!'

Morven began to think that if Pravis didn't calm down soon it was possible he could get stuck with a purple face forever and one day the people would be under the purple reign of a king formerly known as their prince.

'What a fine head of heroic hair, Pravis...who does it belong to?' queried a grim-faced Moonraven adding to the prince's furious colouring.

'Enough! Both of you! Stand down your weapons!'

The sound of a young male stranger's voice, commanding and resonant with authority made both protagonists spin around. Robard, the Goth lad had copied one of the actors in the mummer troupe. His impersonation of the mighty barbarian god Throd the Thunderer worked perfectly. Back in his ordinary voice, he walked to the hovel door and gestured outside.

'The highwayman was right. We do have a more urgent problem to deal with. May I respectfully suggest you two he-men postpone murdering each other till later?'

In the corner the meek baker's apprentice dropped his head into his hands. Adventures? Quests? Noble searches to find hidden destinies? Madness, complete madness. Why had he ever left the baker's shop?

Black, acrid smoke swirled around her, too feeble to be truly apocalyptical. It would not go down in the annals of Hell as a mighty blow against Mankind. More like a gentle, limp-wristed poke.

To Demonica's vexation, it was evident that her rampage of death and destruction was not going to plan. The princess was expecting weeping and screaming villagers to come pouring out of their flaming hovels to drop to their knees pleading and grovelling for her mercy. Instead they had run away with all their goods and livestock ahead of her Pooka-drawn coach leaving their villages empty. Not one stalwart but suicidal local hero staying behind to fight for their village. Where was the fun in torching empty villages? One hovel in flame looked much like another. A few scorched stray chickens did not make for much amusement for one so diabolically evil as Princess Demonica.

'Why are they fleeing?' She demanded of her boyfriend and evil minion, the worn out shadow of the man once known as nasty bastard Strang. She gave a violent tug on his chain, nearly breaking his neck. 'You are a human of this land. Why do they not try to defend their homes?'

'Insurance,' Strang managed to gasp as the leather spiky collar around his neck tightened, 'they all bought insurance policies from Vinny Grimes, cover for fire, theft, creeping magenta hovel rot, damage from stoat riots.... they are much richer now their hovels are toast.'

Strang was rapidly turning an unhealthy shade of crimson, 'You have done these peasants a big favour.'

'NOOOOOO!' screamed the demon princess, stamping both stiletto-heeled boots in her outrage. She did not do good deeds! She was evil, through and through! Making scabrous, filthy human peasants happy and richer! How ridiculous would that make her look? She cringed inwardly, thinking of the mileage her appalling half-brother would make of that.

Her eyes looked to the west, to the ever-nearing castle that should have been white and shiny but was a disappointing dull pale stone. An appallingly ugly pale beige stone. It was far more fun desecrating pure white. In fact a diabolical make over might be doing the place a favour. Again the irony of her situation swept over her in a wave of nausea. There must be something she could do of a suitably extravagant and downright evil nature. Flash-frying chickens was not that much needed grandiose gesture.

Demonica glanced around her, thinking of a new plan. Staines was too tedious to terrorize. And Vinny Grimes had probably beaten her to it with his insurance policies. The castle was too awful to conquer though she decided to burn it to the ground at a later date and make her new slaves, the entire population of this land build her a new one. That left the Forest of Mhmin! A delightful, peaceful paradise populated by gentle ethereal spiritual beings that meandered about in a gossamer-wafting warm breeze. A meeting place for the noble, elegant elves, the delicate, pretty flower fairies, nymphs and dryads and fauns. Magical unicorns, enchanted trees and sturdy honest wood gnomes. Talking squirrels and miming moles. Mischievous piskies and cheeky sprites. How she hated them all!

Now burning that lot up... how delightfully evil would that be! Even the big boss down below would be impressed by that, enough maybe to disinherit her disgrace of a half-brother. Demonica screamed at the Pookas to pay attention to her and not the enticing rumps of the horses in front of them.

'There is a change of plan. Turn around! I'm going to annihilate the Forest of Mhmin.' Then added unconvincingly, 'Honeybun.'

Relieved to being still alive and untoasted, Strang obeyed without question, if there were any perks to being Demonica's boyfriend, he was yet to experience them.

In time-honoured tradition, Cylphie had intended to dress as a young man and have many exciting adventures beyond the Forest of Mhmin. The boots were the first stage. Bit by bit her Twee Bay purchases would add up to a complete outfit including a large hooded cape to hide her delicate but unmistakable pointy elven ears. She had idly strolled to the edge of the woodland to escape the poetry and the inevitable blame for the fight and was startled to see a line of black smoke along the horizon, one that was so fast moving, it had already blotted out the sun with a heavy veil of acrid smoke. She smelt panic and burning on the air. The blaze was heading towards her. Soon there wouldn't be a Forest of Mhmin to escape from!

Stifling a shriek of alarm, Cylphie hitched up her long gossamer gown and hurtled back towards the poetry recital, knowing it would still be on. They usually lasted longer then an Eisteddfod and only two weeks had passed since the start. Thankful for the stout and comfortable boots, the elf maiden was able to cover the tangled ground in record time. She threw herself into the centre of the grassy amphitheatre and screamed 'Fire!' as loud as she could. Some of the startled audience thought it was performance art and began to applaud loudly. Others thought it was an act of jealous aggression against Devin and began to boo her. No one listened to her warning.

'I mean it! There's a bloody great fire on its way to destroy the Forest of Mhmin!!'

Her mother Syleste glided over in the serene, graceful manner of the elves in a flurry of floating, sparkling gossamer and pointed down to her daughter's footwear.

'Dark enchantment!' she shrieked in horror, 'My daughter is under an evil spell!'

'No I am not,' Cylphie replied witheringly, 'but who cares now...the forest is about to be engulfed in a raging inferno!'

'Nonsense, my dear child,' soothed her father Gryad, 'this is a magic forest. No harm can damage its beauty and serenity.'

'Apart from Mongolian Silver Birch pox,' shouted a nit-picking Hobnob Goblin.

'Or the dreaded Purple Spotted Mildew,' added a completist Centaur.

'And what about an attack of the Flange Moth, nasty little critters - causes havoc with elven gossamer garb,' chuckled a flower fairy at the thought of those toffee-nosed, condescending elves walking around naked.

The auditorium collapsed into pandemonium as other scourges of the enchanted woodland were brought up.

'Luminous Brain Scald! Blair Witch Disease!'

'Mungus!'

But Cylphie heard none of them. She strode off towards the edge of the forest, determined to seek urgent help

At the thought of a mighty demonic army threatening the realm, an excited, deranged gleam lit up Prince Pravis's ice blue eyes. In a dramatic gesture of heroism, he threw back his long blond hair, startling a flock of yet more gore-crows roosting on the hovel roof which in turn crapped all over Squarf. At last ...real danger! A valiant and righteous adventure against the forces of darkness and evil. This was far more worthy for a noble prince than chasing after some crusty old silverware which may or may not exist. There was no time to lose...he must return to the castle to a raise a great army, to start a crusade for the cause of justice and freedom. Every noble knight in the land would gladly join him to prove their valour. And all the peasant men folk would carry their weapons into battle to avoid a good kicking.

Watching the line of black smoke and flickering flames across the horizon, Jed was less convinced. It had been many centuries since the Demon Rafial and his evil horde fought and lost against the allied army of Goodness and Light. It took a hell of a lot to piss off such an easygoing demon as Rafial. Why was he attacking now? Jed was certain there was an alternative and more likely cause of the fiery horizon. Demonica!

Pravis spun around. 'You two, apprentice... er... boy and dark clad youth. You will assist me and my serf to escape this vile bog. You will be well rewarded. Alas, highwayman, you will not live to corrupt any more innocent maidens and steal from the good. You die now.'

Again Pravis raised his sword and again Jed raised his pistols.

'Not again!' Cried Morven in despair.

'Overpower and seize the scoundrel!' Shouted Pravis to Squarf, Wheatley and Robard who all pretended not to hear. 'I will run him through with my trusty sword and we will tie his body from the lightning tree by the crossroads to rot, a grisly reminder to all that pass of the fate that awaits all defilers and thieves!'

Shrugging Robard stepped back into the hovel. 'Heavy! Leave me out of all that negative shit!'

A hand-wringing Wheatley attempted a smile of reconciliation. 'I am sure the fellow understands the wrong direction he has taken. Perhaps he had a rotten childhood? Fell in with the wrong crowd as a teenager? Maybe he had a bad mead addiction to finance? We should give him another chance.'

A puce coloured Pravis turned towards his faithful serf for support, who had his back deliberately turned away from the prince and was cussing colourfully as he cleaned off the stinking gore-crow crap from his clothes. Before Pravis could explode with fury at such feebleness, he was knocked cold by a determined squelchy whack to the head.

Holding the bloated body of a large security toad that had died from eating too many bluebottles, Morven stood over the prone form of the prince with a smile of triumph.

'I don't care if they are a prince of the realm or emperor of the whole bloody galaxy. Nobody threatens my man.'

Jed tucked his pistols back into his belt and striding over to the Unwise Woman, swept her up into his arms and walked back towards the hovel, pausing to turn around to address the others, his face wreathed with a wide, delighted grin. 'Excuse us, gents. I have some long overdue business with the lady. Keep walking to the west and you will find safety. Take that pompous prat with you.'

She wanted him, really, really wanted him so badly her whole body quivered with desire but this was not the time...damn it! 'Jed, my love, put me down. You must get out of here, the prince will wake up any minute and will not rest until you are dead.'

The highwayman would not release his grip, he looked back at the unconscious form on the ground and gave a mischievous smile. 'Only time for a quickie then.'

Morven kissed him, how could she deny him anything? After all she was the Unwise Woman of Fuggis Mire.

A few x rated, steamy moments later...

With the prince still out cold, Jed buttoned up his breeches and taking her face in both hands kissed Morven passionately. 'I'd better scarper, my lovely. His royal homicidal pomposity will be back in the land of the living any minute.'

Delightfully sated, a rosy blush on her cheeks and cleavage, Morven adjusted her clothing and saw him to the door. 'What are you going to do, my love?' she murmured softly, already missing him terribly.

Jed shrugged. 'I am a dead man without a steed and your guard goats though no doubt valiant are not up to the job. I am going to get my mare back.'

Taking an amulet from around her neck, Morven placed it around his neck. It was only later that Jed realised it was fashioned from an old baked bean tin lid with a purple boiled sweet stuck on. 'Thank you my darling. Will this give me protection?'

Morven's eyes dropped to the ground, she had deliberately given him something worthless, an object he couldn't sell for tankards of ale and a wild night with a doxie. 'Well,' she paused, 'ahem...er... it will not harm you.'

The highwayman stepped into the smoke filled afternoon, turning darker by the minute from the ever-nearing hell fires. He smirked at the three men standing over the prostrate form of Prince Pravis; they must have heard every giggle, moan, groan and triumphal cry from his brief but explosive encounter with Morven. Embarrassment and envy was etched all over their faces. He swept them an extravagant bow and disappeared with a post-coital swagger into the smoky gloom.

With Moonraven gone, the rest of the unwanted visitors to Morven's hovel stood around the still prone form of the prince and anxiously wondered what to do next.

'Maybe he is dead.' Wailed a frightened Wheatley. If he had a hidden destiny, alas it wasn't to be a mage with the power of healing. He had laid his hand on Pravis's head just in case but nothing wondrous happened. He drew the line at attempting the kiss of life. One possibility struck off the official list of possible destinies. That still left dragon rider, first born royal son of a treacherously deposed king, various other forms of wizards and sorcerers and that old favourite the orphaned waif-like child that would save the world with a special power. Only he was too old for that.

'Nah!' grumbled Squarf, 'The silly sod is still out cold. He'll be well pissed off when he does come to. I'd scarper if I were you. Especially you, Mistress Morven.'

Unconcerned, the Unwise Woman shrugged with indifference, her whole body still brimming with pleasure, her heart aching for Jed. 'He won't know I whacked him with a rancid dead toad. Unless one of you lot tells him.'

She glanced around, fixing all three men in turn with a formidable look; they weren't to know she had never taken any classes in the Dark Arts. At the horrific thought of being turned into toads, rancid or otherwise, they hastily nodded and murmured they would never tell on her.

'A wise choice, gentlemen.' She added in suitable mysterious tones, 'We can say he was hit on the head by a dragon dropping.'

This would not have sounded far fetched as the darkened, smoke filled sky was filling with dragons, the evil ones heading towards the Land of Darkness and Despair and the good ones towards the rallying point for the Forces of Goodness and Light - Petunia (formally Valiant) Castle. Inevitably there would be mid-air clashes, vile name calling and unseemly squabbles, with the heightened emotions resulting in a rain of dragon poo. Made from an unpleasant solidified amalgam of their victim's bones and ashy slurry from their fire breathing, this was often lethal, especially when falling from a great height. The prince had been lucky to get off lightly with only being knocked out.

'I don't want to get caught up with a battle between Good and Evil!' announced Robard in full belligerent teenage mode, 'I belong to no side in this world of pain and despair. I don't know what I want, except to be accepted as the deep and troubled soul that I am, the lone poet, misunderstood and rejected by an uncaring world, to

be left alone to...' At the sight of Morven picking up the
dead toad again, he shut up with a sulky pout.

'Nor do I,' muttered Wheatley, 'I was so happy selling
cakes. If there is a hidden destiny out there for me, it can
go hang.' He blushed as he caught Morven's distressed
face at his unfortunate choice of expression in front of the
lover of a wanted highwayman. 'So sorry, Mistress
Morven.'

'And if that pillock kicks me one more time!' growled
Squarf, sorely tempted to grab the offending toad and
finish the job. 'But I am a serf, if I leave him I become an
outlaw, no more comfy, warm sleeping mat in the castle,
below the royal hounds. No more tasty though gnawed
leftovers from the hounds' dinners. A bath in the moat
once a year, even if I don't need it. Even my fleas and nits
are royal ones.'

Looking down at the prince with a sneer of total
derision, he continued, 'Actually, I do quite fancy being
caught up in a war. I may be small and squat but I am
tough and brave. I could earn my freedom, a pension and a
hovel of my own if I do something noticeably valiant. Like
saving Prince Bollock-face's life in battle. And I like the
sound of kicking those demon backsides right back to
hell.'

He sat down beside the prince. 'I will stay with him.
But with that accursed hellfire on the way, I suggest you
others make yourselves scarce. Especially you, Mistress
Morven. I don't think even his Royal Ignorance here will
believe the dragon shit story.'

Sadly, she had to concede he was right and nodded in
agreement. Morven had broken her vow to do no harm,
whacking a client with a rancid dead toad even if he was
threatening to kill her lover which was a definite no-no.
She untied her guard goats and shoed away the security

toads and after packing a large carpetbag with a few essential bits and pieces, she was ready to leave. She decided to join Wheatley and Robard both wisely heading in the opposite direction from the conflict to come.

'It's a shame,' noted Squarf as they said their farewells, 'you guys have all the makings of a classic Fellowship. The apprentice seeking his hidden destiny, a troubadour, a witch. All you need is a thief with a heart of gold, an elven princess disguised as a mysterious youth and a talking animal and eh voila – a full house.'

She was clearly heading in the wrong direction, Cylphie stood back to let a tumult of fleeing bog dwellers hurtle past, fleeing from the encroaching flames. One of the bog chavs had paused long enough to swap some flashy elven bling for a spare set of clothes. Now with a grey hooded top and matching baggy jogging bottoms, her long silken tresses hidden by a backwards baseball cap, Cylphie looked like a young man, a mysterious traveller seeking others to team up with and have an adventure, to join a quest. Well, only if a bog chav could ever be arsed to do such a thing. There was always a first time.

Cylphie had at least ensured the conventions of the land were being upheld. But her attempt to seek help to save the Forest of Mhmin were spectacularly unsuccessful. Every creature had but one thought - to save their own skins. The elf could not blame them. The stench from a nearby burning village on the edge of the swamp was over-whelming. The fear in the air was so tangible it felt like a ravening creature spreading panic and hysteria to all it touched.

The would-be saviour was desolate, knowing that the forest dwellers would carry on with their marathon poetry festival, while all around them burned, utterly deluded that magic would protect them.

Cylphie took a phial from her belt, expecting some refreshing elven tonic, an infusion of sweet herbs and aromatic petals. Instead a powerful liquid seared the back of her throat, sending her head into a spin. Then she remembered it was poteen. Some months before, she had bet some visiting leprechauns that she could drink a pint down in one after they suggested it was too strong for a delicate elven maiden. She had won the bet and was given a magic phial that never run out of the potent brew. Grateful for her bravado, she took another, deeper swig.

Following the acrid stench of scorched debris, Jed found the over the top, uber gothic coach parked above what was once a pretty village of thatched hovels situated on the edge of the bog. There were the team of Pookas, not arguing for a change. In fact all were looking smug as indeed was Jed's twice stolen mare, Milady. Though he had found what he was looking for, the highwayman was anxious, she could give him away with a welcoming whinny of recognition. Luckily her mind was more interested in her four Pooka suitors and Jed was able to back slowly away before being spotted by any of the equines.

Unfortunately, he backed straight into his former partner in crime, the now even more nasty bastard Strang. Jed didn't know whether to laugh or cry. Actually he did, Jed rather rashly in the circumstances laughed out loud. It was hard not to. Strang was virtually naked save for a studded black leather codpiece and horribly thin G-string that exposed his hairy behind and left nothing to the imagination. Unfortunately. He also wore long black, laced up boots with high heels and around his neck was a black leather collar with extremely long spikes. That was not all; he was also now bald apart from a thin Mohican of spiky purple hair. It had only been a day and a night since Strang teamed up with the demon princess, but he had lost a lot of weight and his bloodshot and dark-shadowed eyes were heavy-lidded with fatigue. Jed correctly deducted Demonica was literally bonking him to death.

'Bloody 'ell! What a sight!'

'Fuck off Moonraven!'

'And what are you going to do to me if I don't? Spike me to death with your collar? Strangle me with your G-string? On second thoughts, don't take it off, just use the spikes!'

Blushing bright red and growling with embarrassment, Strang wished he had a cloak to hide his hairy nakedness, especially in front of the fully clothed and smirking Moonraven. Hopefully the wondrously evil Demonica would be back soon from terrorising the village peasants and reduce the highwayman to a pile of ash stinking of brimstone. Or turn him into a toad, if she could do that. Then a truly horrific thought overcame him. What if his mistress decided she would rather have the undeniably handsome and legendarily rampant Moonraven as her boyfriend? It could happen! She had worn Strang out and there was no retirement plan for her employees.

'Jed, for pity's sake...she will be back soon. Tell me what you want?'

The highwayman leant against a tree and folded his arms. And waited long enough for Strang to hop up and down with frustration. Just when he thought the nasty bastard would explode, Jed answered.

'Firstly I want to know what your mistress's plans are.'

Strang was relieved, that was easy. Such was her power, there was no need to hide the truth. The entire land would be hers by the next dawn. 'She is going for all out dominion of this country, to become its queen and live in Valiant ... Er...Petunia Castle.'

'Thought as much,' nodded Jed. 'What else would a hell-born princess want?'

'Is that all?' demanded Strang, his mean little bloodshot eyes darting about in case Demonica returned. She was very close but as the surrounding fields were still burning and the Pookas refused to get their hooves singed, she was forced to walk the twenty yards or so into the heart of the smouldering village... 'Please leave...Now!'

'Such touching concern for your old partner in crime. I am deeply moved,' continued Jed with a humourless grin. 'I have but one more request. Actually it's more like a demand.'

Strang found himself looking down the barrels of two familiar pistols, both with hair triggers.

'I want my mare back.'

The hapless boyfriend's eyes widened in horror, his destiny to become a pile of ash stinking of brimstone loomed ever closer. 'No, not in a million years! Demonica will annihilate me!'

Keeping one pistol aimed directly at Strang's head, the highwayman attempted to unharness his grey mare Milady who promptly flattened her ears and snapped her teeth at him. Jed was taken aback, she had never, ever laid her ears back at him! Such loyalty!

'She's with us now,' sneered the only understandable Pooka, 'she's our girlfriend.'

Jed went around to unharness Strang's dour nag and got the same display of bad temper. 'And he's our boyfriend.'

Powerless in the face of such equine resistance, there was nothing he could do but escape on foot back towards the trees and the path beyond.

Nasty bastard Strang sighed at first with relief, Demonica would soon return to find her carriage team complete and fully harnessed and with no sign of a possible rival to usurp him. Then the relief turned to fear - what if the demonic female wanted to celebrate the fiery demise of another village? He was so exhausted, there was no way he could get anything useful up.

'No pleading with me to escape with you then?' A desperate Strang shouted after the rapidly retreating Moonraven.

'No way! Unfortunately for you I am an even nastier bastard!' was the fast fading reply as the highwayman made himself scarce.

With an explosion of light and swirling sulphurous mist, the heavy metal band Shrike Hell had their audience clenched tightly in the palm of their studded black leather gauntlets. It had been a riotous gig from the start, always a good sign to have a contingent of Vikings in the mosh pit. Fresh from a successful pillage, they were ready to party hard. The only downside was their horned helmets. With much grumbling and swearing involving various parts of Thor's private anatomy, they reluctantly handed their blood axes and swords at the door, but refused to remove their helmets. Provocative rumours rippled through the crowd, started by some drunken students from Knight School that the Vikings' impressive flowing locks of long blond hair were actually wigs and only stayed on because of the helmets. This was likely to cause a mighty ruckus later. But now the mood of the crowd was high spirited and enthusiastic.

Which made up for the last disastrous Shrike Hell gig when they had been mistakenly booked to perform for an order of silent nuns, the Sisters of the Perpetual Pained Expression. The holy sisters of the convent had actually quite enjoyed the loud, uproarious music in a silent sort of way until Zaff had performed his infamous party piece. That brought the house down, well, the convent's timber roof. The effect was the same.

'Its time, go for it!' screamed a maniacally grinning Lennie above the pyrotechnics and his crashing drums.

Lead guitarist Zaff strode forward, a magnificent sight in his tight black leather clothes, his wild, thick mane of raven black hair that fell to his waist. He was devilishly handsome and charismatic; his legendary guitar solo was always literally the climax of the gig. He threw back his hair, causing a hen party of wood nymphs to scream and faint. With a slight, sardonic and attractively cruel smile he began to play. As each flowing chord sensuously caressed the ears of the crowd, he lulled them into a comfort zone. Their eyes grew dreamy, seduced by the beauty of the music. Gradually picking up the pace, the rhythm became wilder, harsher, occasionally discordant and unpredictable but always mesmerising and exciting. Lennie joined in on the drums, pounding a heartbeat that grew more rapid as Zaff coaxed his black guitar into a more overtly sexual riff. Higher and higher and more intense, the music was orgiastic and wildly erotic. But he would not give them release, on and on, he stoked up the excitement to a fever pitch. Cleverly working the crowd, pushing them to the limit and beyond. They would do anything for him now...throw themselves off a cliff, cut their own throats, eat butterbeans; he could even demand that the Vikings take off their wigs and wear frilly dresses. They were his.

Lennie suddenly and dramatically stopped the incessant drumbeat. A single spotlight surrounded Zaff in a beam of yellow light. His dark eyes closed, his head back, he played a thrilling riff that hushed and stilled the crowd, even the raucous gang of flower fairies on a hen night and drunk on elderflower champagne stopped touching up the Vikings and listened. As the music built up to an orgasmic finale, Zaff threw down his guitar, set it alight with a flash of flame from his eyes and leapt from the stage. Hands shot up ready to body surf him across the crowd but instead he released his large black wings and ascended slowly above the auditorium to gasps of awe and screams of fright.

He was Zaphael, only son of the Prince of the Land of Darkness and Despair, a full blood demon. One who didn't get chucked out of the Infernal Realm like his old man but calmly strolled out for the sheer damned hell of it. Who now preferred to be called Zaff and play lead guitar in a heavy metal band. He was the devil with the best tunes.

Having reduced the crowd to panic and pandemonium, Zaff lightly descended and folding up his impressive bat-like wings, nodded his respect to those who hadn't bolted for the doors. No one forgot a ShrikeHell gig and no one forgot Zaff, though unfortunately not always remembering him for his virtuoso guitar performance. He didn't care; he was where he wanted to be, doing what he wanted to do. Few in this life could say the same.

The rest of Shrike Hell were human, well, the jury was still out on the bass player Rob, who boasted his father was part cave troll. Lennie heard his dad was really an accountant in charge of the banqueting bills up at the castle, that the cave troll bit was a desperate attempt to make himself more interesting to the voracious groupies. And to explain his squat stature and unfortunate lack of looks. A ploy which was always doomed to failure while they had Zaff in the line up. One thing not in dispute was that Rob smelled like a cave troll. But his habit of eating flies was another dead give-away that he was fantasising - cave trolls were allergic to them.

As the gig finished in a thundering, deafening encore of their latest hit; 'Run the Gauntlet of Doom,' burly roadies leapt to the stage to protect the gear from any pillaging, the inevitable downside of having a Viking raiding party at the gig. The sweat-soaked band grabbed towels and their instruments and protected by burly minders who actually were cave trolls, made a run for their sanctuary backstage, enduring the chaotic push and shove of their fans. Zaff was too cool for a towel, too terrifying to need minders, what fan would risk being reduced to a pile of ash stinking of brimstone? Auditorium cleaners across the land would testify that it was a quite a few.

He sank onto a squashy leather sofa, on a high from another successful gig, his mind full of his music, replaying the whole concert. He made mental notes how to improve his performance, sharpen up the cues from the rest of the band. They had only lost one band member to his unfortunate demon-ness recently. An ambitious prat called Deathrall Lorde... (Actually it was really Barry Spoons). It wasn't enough to be lead singer for Shrike

Hell. Being frontsman would have been glory enough for any other mere mortal, but he also coveted Zaff's role as lead guitarist. He shamelessly showed off at first during Zaff's electrifying solos, trying to draw attention from the handsome young demon's charismatic performance. That Zaff generously stayed in the background for most of the gig mattered not for Barry Spoons, sorry, Deathrall Lorde. One night, when drunk on powerful and semi-lethal bog chav moonshine, he attempted a playful, supposedly humorous pogo leap against Zaff just as he began his dramatic assent into the sky. One more pile of ash stinking of brimstone for the cleaners.

Since then, the band struggled on without a lead singer, taking turns on the vocals. It was safer that way, all the frontsmen they auditioned were egotistical wassocks and therefore doomed to a premature career change as a pile of smouldering cinders.

Helping himself to a leather flagon of African killer bee mead, Zaff closed his eyes. He didn't need to sleep but it helped him concentrate on composing new work. A tentative knock on the door told him it was one of the band, none wanted to end up like half the new roadies who hadn't learnt the folly of startling a demon. It was Lennie, draped by three buxom groupies, one brazen one still had her hand down the front of his jeans. Zaff yawned, he had no interest in human groupies and lived a celibate life since leaving Hell.

'Sorry to interrupt you Zaff, me old mate, but I think you might want to see this.'

'Er, I'll pass on that, man. There's nothing down there that will interest me,' replied Zaff with a grin.

'No! Not the contents of my jeans, though it is an awesome sight by any human standards. No, there's something outside you ought to see.'

They walked out of the theatre and onto a nearby hill to witness the night sky ablaze across the horizon. The stench of brimstone and bloodshed so strong it reached them in a foul-smelling miasma.

'F◆♏&;)(◆!' swore Zaff, who like all demons was capable of swearing in symbols – which is way cooler than speaking in tongues like the opposition. 'Looks like my old man's on the warpath again

Things were finally stirring in the Land of Darkness. Well, sort of. Prince Rafial strode purposefully through the endless gloomy, cobweb-laced corridors of his fortress. Flaming torches blazed from black metal sconces and as always they were already lit. No one ever knew who did it, but wherever the prince walked, there would be the torches flaring away atmospherically. Odd.

Following in his wake were a column of evil followers frantically scribbling notes, sidestepping the occasional new pile of ash stinking like brimstone. 'Take this down!' the demon commanded, 'I want a call up of all evil beings in my dominion. No excuses!'

He stopped abruptly which caused an underling following too close behind him to step on one of his trailing wings. Rafial raised a hand, the minion ducked and the one behind him copped it. As did another one about five back in the line who snurffled with glee at the other's misfortune with an unfortunate sound like 'cheeesushchrissshtt.'

'I want the Union of Scary Clowns involved this time, no nonsense about being too busy making strychnine-laced custard pies. And the skeleton army...I won't accept their whingeing about it being too cold this time of year to fight. They can wear grimly tattered cloaks made of their victim's skin like the zombies. Never have any trouble with them.'

Rafial walked on again. The evil minions were not used to seeing their master so enthusiastic and animated...it confused them, hence the many piles of ash. But the next time he halted again suddenly, they were ready. No one stepped on his wings or snurffled or sneezed or coughed. Then one farted loudly with a sound very like... a loud fart.

'How gross!' Was the last thing that particular lackey heard.

'Call up the werewolves, they can't all be recovering from their rabies and distemper shots. The wraiths, sprites, ghouls and spectres can get their wispy backsides back off that cheap package holiday to the Costa Lotte.'

The demon glanced down at the quivering note-takers, their quills shaking in terror. 'But leave the call up for the cave trolls, their aunties and the ogres until the very last. Greedy buggers devoured all the food in the fortress before munching away on my army last time. Not a single cursed black unicorn left!

'And,' he announced with a grim, dangerous frown, 'I want all the flying monsters stationed in the ruined haunted abbey in the dark woods. No dragons, Rocs, winged apes, or harpies anywhere near my fortress. It took two centuries to clean all the crap off my battlements after last time.'

When known as Valiant Castle, it used to be a shimmering spectacle of white marble. Tall towers capped with colourful pennants that proudly proclaimed the coats of arms of the royal family. Until a visit from Vinny Grimes, the slickest, most persuasive and successful salesman in the land. On a high from a successful cold-calling trip to the Bogs of Fuggis Mire, he had visited the castle. Now the entire edifice was stone clad. Dark enchantment murmured the citizens. *A sound and practical solution that will add value to my property,* thought the king. *One that will keep it safe from the ravages of time and weather and what that nice Mr Grimes called 'crepusculent marble blight'.*

'Let's rename it Petunia Castle!' the queen had announced on seeing the dramatic make-over. The change went unopposed, all would-be dissenters had lost the will to live as the first artificial slab was plonked onto the pristine ancient marble.

High in his beige stone-clad battlements, the king surveyed the baleful line of darkness along the horizon with a heavy heart. He had hoped never to take on the formidable Forces of Darkness and Despair in his lifetime, his father and grandfather and great grandfather managed to live trouble free reigns. Why him? It was so unfair. What had stirred up the usually indolent and easygoing demon this time? There had been no trouble between the kingdoms of Light and Darkness for centuries. His mind went straight to his son, Prince Pravis, all braying bravado and talk of noble quests and valorous acts. Had the knob-head attacked an important denizen of that hellish land?

Below him the sun still glistened on the shining armour of his knights, a sun that soon would be hidden by the ever-encroaching black clouds from hell. The king had summoned all the forces of good in the land, to his relief, the unicorns and kindly wizards had arrived promptly. As had a battalion of well-armed flower fairies. Never would lead-filled spider silk handbags be put to better use. Approaching from all directions, he could see a winding line of roving, taciturn and hooded lone heroes and young apprentices looking for their unknown destinies.

There had been some noticeable absences. His greatest allies, the elven warriors had not answered his call, some bizarre rumour about a poetry festival. The centaurs were in quarantine after a foot and mouth scare. Though he irritated the pants off him, the king wanted his son back at his side. At least the boy was brave and could fight.

In a cloud of expensive perfume, the queen wafted up to join him. 'Thadeus, is all this silly nonsense really worth it? Just two days ago, I ordered a total designer makeover for the throne room and I want to drain the moat and turn it into a sunken Japanese themed Zen garden. Now we have all these uncouth, dirty people turning up expecting to be fed and housed. Most inconvenient!'

Sighing, the king turned to look at his wife, her face red and shiny from a chemical peel of liquidised butterbeans and rancid toads. Her wrinkle-free expression permanently surprised, rigid from frequent injections of boggart phage. An unfortunate green tinge to her skin told she had been overusing the beauty treatment.

'Hemelda my precious, the forces of darkness are amassing, we will soon be under attack!'

'Pish!' The queen fluttered her extravagantly elongated false eyelashes of mascara'd dead spider's legs, 'speak to Rafial. Ask for a postponement of hostilities. Or better still; call it a draw and we can all get on with our lives.'

Shaking his head, the king replied sadly, 'it's gone too far, beloved. Someone has pissed the Prince of Darkness off badly. I am hoping it isn't our idiot son.'

'Nonsense!' shrieked Hemelda in the highest possible dudgeon and highest possible decibels, 'My darling golden boy would never do anything that stupid. Our giddy, silly daughters maybe. But not my lovely blue-eyed prince. My own wonderful knight in shining armour!'

'Talking of the girls,' replied the king, his ears still ringing from his wife's tirade, 'they are both looking rather plump around the midriff lately. We need to marry them off to suitable princes. But they will not be interested in taking lardy wives. I order they both go on strict diets from today.'

It was inevitable that Morven's little band would meet up with the disguised elf. Or was it a result of shamelessly engineered plot contrivance? Whatever.

'Oh look,' said the Goth lad, 'an elf travelling in disguise. Could my life be more clichéd?' He was feeling rancorous, elves were known for their epic poetry, his place as the Fellowship's bard was in danger of being usurped.

The travellers paused in the middle of the path amid much shuffling of feet and exchanges of awkward smiles or in Robard's case, awkward glowers.

'I am urgently seeking help,' begged Cylphie, in an unconvincing attempt at a deep mannish voice. 'The Forest of Mhmin is under great threat from the devilish fires. The folk who dwell within think magic will save them.'

'Great! So, nothing to worry about,' muttered Robard dourly. 'Got to roll – be seeing you. Not!'

Something deep within Wheatley stirred, was this the moment? The great revelation had finally arrived, that his hidden destiny was to rescue the imperilled inhabitants of the Forest of Mhmin? Then his stomach gave a low and thunderous rumble. Relieved, the apprentice realised the strange feeling was merely mundane hunger cramps.

Only Morven, still guilt ridden for breaking her sacred vows when she clobbered Prince Pravis's head with a dead rancid toad was not prepared to let the mystical inhabitants of the forest turn to smouldering embers or piles of ash stinking of brimstone. She had two able-bodied if rather pathetic human males, a fine young elf maiden disguised as a mysterious traveller, though she was weirdly garbed as a bog chav. Somewhere out there in the mire was her dashing highwayman, courageous, ruthless and a crack shot with those duelling pistols of his. So that would add the obligatory thief to their Fellowship. There could also be a brave and noble talking animal or friendly dragon but that was not mandatory. With the forest in such danger, there must be something they could do.

Despite an aching head and convenient complete amnesia to the events immediately leading up to being hit on the head with a solid lump of dragon poo, Prince Pravis awoke in a surprisingly good mood. The prospect of some serious smiting was a sure fire cure for problem ordure, which had magically dissolved on contact with the royal bonce. And without further misadventures, miraculously the prince and Squarf had finally made it out of the fiendish bog. Actually, it wasn't really that miraculous. With the forces of Evil and Darkness approaching, all the good beings of the land were being rallied. They simply followed the steady stream of water nymphs, unicorns and mages all the way back to the castle.

As the dull stone clad ramparts of Petunia Castle appeared on the horizon, the stream of land's defenders turned into a mighty river. Most had eyes gleaming with righteous fervour and burning religious zeal. Or else a maniacal gleam at the thought of having a bloody good demon arse-kicking punch-up ahead, as many notorious troublemakers and persistent brawlers marched under the flag of Goodness and Light. Many others walking with the crowd looked perplexed at all the talk of smiting and cleaving, they mistakenly thought they were on their way to a massive sale of sofas for their hovels. One that must end Monday!

Soon Pravis and his serf were swallowed up by the sheer size of the crowd. The prince tried to pull rank and commandeer a horse, preferably snow white as befitted a valiant, noble hero. 'Don't you know who I am?' spluttered the prince to a particularly uncooperative group of Benign Alchemists with their young apprentices. Most had packhorses laden with their potions and experimental tinctures. One horse was suitably snow white but that could have been with terror as the unfortunate beast was laden with explosive chemicals.

'No, sorry, should we?'

'I am Prince Pravis!'

'No, I'm Prince Pravis,' responded one wag behind him. This was instantly taken up in a ripple effect of merriment throughout the crowd of travellers. 'I'm Prince Pravis. No, I am Prince Pravis,' over and over again, including one toothless old crone who said 'I'm Prince Pravis and so is my mule.'

This was too much for the real Prince Pravis. He turned to his serf. 'Squarf - tell them who I am!'

Long-suffering Squarf thought it would be worth an arse kicking to continue the wind up. 'This *is* indeed Prince Pravis.'

The Prince looked around him in triumph - gesturing grandiosely towards his servant. 'See!'

'And so am I...' added Squarf, bracing himself for the inevitable.

Things were not looking too promising for Rafial's mighty army of darkness. The moon had done its best; it had never looked so brooding and foreboding, turning the deepest and most ominous shade of blood red. But so many visitors to the fortress had sparked off the defensive dramatic thunderstorms and soon it was surrounded by soaking wet creatures of evil and darkness. The stench was unbearable, especially that rising up from the werewolves' manky coats. And because the crowd consisted of creatures of evil and not fluffy bunnies or kittens, the bad weather had shortened already nasty tempers. It certainly triggered off a fearful row between the harpies and the flying monkeys. Soon the thundercloud filled, forever-night sky was strafed by screeching, scratching and spiteful wing tearing creatures.

Below them, the evil ones began to take sides and lay bets. Most money went on the harpies, who were formidable fanged and taloned flying female monsters. The wise money went on the monkeys. The harpies had spent a great deal of time carefully preparing to look good for the coming mighty conflagration and subsequent victory parade especially as most had a hopeless crush on Rafial.

All the monkeys had to do was perform their infamous party piece - throw their poo with great velocity and mind-numbing accuracy. Which they did. The harpies flew off to clean themselves up, muttering obscene threats of terrible vengeance - something involving using butterbeans in a most inventive and anatomically impossible way. But the damage to morale was done as the monkeys' obnoxious fallout from the battle had splatted down like malodorous rain on the already sodden crowds below sparking off a ferocious riot.

On his highest battlements, Rafial was furious, close to the edge of losing his famous tolerance, just one step from blasting the whole damn lot of them into piles of ash stinking of brimstone. It would totally depopulate his dominion but at least it would be a quieter and easier place to manage. Give him more time for his books and lists. He sent a few lightning strikes strafing the ground around the rioters and roared across the blighted valley, silencing and stilling the brawlers instantly.

'I will not have fighting! Not in my army!' These were to prove prophetic words.

The situation in the opposing camp was little better. The gathering army greeted each arriving faction with the usual vainglorious banter, though not always good-natured. It was never a good idea to have too many lone and mysterious hooded strangers in the same place. Being brooding and enigmatic was highly competitive. And there was a long-standing and irresolvable feud between the leprechauns and the brownies that had simmered for centuries and started, legend has it, over the ill-advised use of a tea cosy and a bottle of laxatives.

Emotions soared briefly as a bedraggled but still valiant Prince Pravis arrived, sword held aloft. Followed a few minutes later by his malodorous serf, bizarrely wielding a rancid dead toad, which he claimed was a lucky charm. But beyond the cheering and back slapping of the fully armed knights, not all was harmony and companionship.

In fact in the verdant fields beyond the recently drained moat, the atmosphere was rapidly deteriorating. The puffing out of chests and outrageous bragging was wearing thin as reality that they were all facing painful death in a real war began to filter through their minds. Queues began to form outside the Porta loos...a thicket of over-watered gorse bushes.

Nothing was helped by the conspicuously silent arrival of the Brotherhood of Noble Knights. A secret order of monastic hooligans always spoiling for a brawl. Mystical and world shattering conspiracy theories had always surrounded the order of BONK, all started by them to give them extra cachet. They were running out of ideas. The last one circulating that Elvis was living on the moon with Shergar and the last living descendents of Attila the Hun had fallen on deaf and disbelieving ears.

They wore dull brown monastic robes which were designed to fall open occasionally to reveal the flashy chain mail and tabards with their sacred secret symbol of an albatross made of day-glo yellow rhinestones that they wore beneath. One of the strict secret rules of their order meant they all had to be albinos. The ensuing shortfall in new members had been solved by purchasing one of Vinny Grimes's instant conversion kits.

The Brotherhood lurked conspicuously in the centre of the amassing army, the chink of many weapons showing they meant serious smiting business. Four of their order carried a large gilded chest aloft on long poles. The chest in the form of a... large box, hummed with ominous hidden powers.

It was to be used as a last resort if the battle seemed lost and all hope was gone. Then and only then must it be opened while the monks chanted secret and mysterious chants. Only then would its contents be unleashed on the enemy and as for what would happen then, may the gods have mercy on their souls.

Unknown to the monks, everyone knew it only contained a swarm of extremely irate bees.

Instantly lowering the tone, the Fauns and Satyrs arrived looking out for some action of another sort before marching off to war, the object of their lust being a party of attractive if rather formidable Amazons. But then the voles, being vile little stirrers whispered to the Amazons that all the Satyrs and Fauns had fleas and their breath smelt of old goat's wee. Which was true but it was still a grave insult.

Up in the battlements, the king was oblivious to all the seething undercurrents in his gathering army, too overjoyed to see his son home safely and ready to risk his life in battle.

A horse snorting in a nearby thicket gave Jed the first ray of hope in this new, long, dire day. He didn't care what state it was in or who it belonged to. All that mattered was there was an equine in the woods. And he could be a highwayman again and not a pathetic, footsore wreck on the run. Or in his case, undignified hobble. Knowing how nervous and easily startled horses were, Jed approached quietly but confidently. At first, he could see nothing but bog oak and stunted snivelling willows all with a bad case of the purple canker. But as his eyes became adjusted to the gloom, aggravated by the smoke-shrouded sky, he made out a black horse standing with its head down in a forlorn stance. Jed was delighted; a black horse was a dashing and dramatic addition to any highwayman's street cred.

But as he approached the sorry looking beast appeared more and more bedraggled. A broken black horn rose from its narrow forehead. A unicorn! A cursed black unicorn! *Oh damn!* thought Jed, backing slowly away, hoping the creature hadn't seen him.

'There's no need to run away,' it muttered feebly. 'I can't do anything with this useless horn.'

'But you could still bite and kick me and trample me!' answered the highwayman, still backing away.

'What's the point,' the unicorn sighed. 'I am useless, a pointless waste of skin.'

Jed stopped moving backwards but stayed wary. Lying and trickery were after all the tools of evil creatures the world over. Well, it worked well enough for him. 'So, what happened?'

Without raising its long head, its eyes hidden by a straggly and matted black mane, the unicorn began its sorry tale.

'I was a failure from the moment I was foaled. I came out a sparkling snowy white. Before anyone could see me, my dam covered me with dirt and fed me a diet of coal. It tasted vile but turned me a dingy dark grey which was just enough to pass for evil. It's not as if cursed unicorns are two for a penny these days. Especially now. I may be the only one left. Before the last Great War between the forces of good and evil, the cave trolls, their aunties and the ogres started eating all the cursed black unicorns. I fled.'

The sorry looking creature sighed, 'So as you can see, human, I am both a failure and an abject coward. A traitor to the memory of my kind.'

The highwayman took a chance and sat on a tree log, which not being enchanted did not object. 'What is your name?'

Again the dingy unicorn sighed, paused then whispered, 'Kudhles.'

'Cuddles?'

'NO! It's Kudhles. It means the Horned Mighty Wielder of Doom.'

'Then you really do have a problem, my friend!' replied Jed trying hard not to snigger. 'Listen, I have a better idea then languishing alone and miserable in this wood.'

Cuddles, er sorry...Kudhles groaned. (Actually Cuddles is easier to type and doesn't stress out the spell checker.)

'Oh! Let me guess.' The unicorn spoke, his voice laden with sarcasm. 'You want to con me into teaming up with you, pretend to be my friend because you really only need a lift out of the bog. Because highwaymen look ridiculous without a dashing steed. Am I right?'

'Yep.' Jed shrugged, 'No point in denying it.'

For the first time the unicorn looked slightly less depressed. 'Phew. You may be a notorious, murderous thief and a total scoundrel but you have given me the first honest answer in over five hundred years. You have yourself a deal. Hop on board!'

As Jed approached, the creature turned its head and gave a fiery glower that proved it truly was a purebred cursed unicorn and not the result of a night's amorous wandering over to the good side by his mother. 'But before you climb on my back, I have two provisos, highwayman. Break them and I will buck you off. Comprende?'

Jed paused and nodded assent.

'Firstly,' demanded Cuddles, 'you will remove those nasty sharp spurs. And thirdly you will never, ever call me Cuddles.'

'You have a deal Cu......oh Horned Mighty Wielder of Doom...' Jed carefully climbed onto the unicorn's scruffy, thin back, accepting he would inevitably get bucked off many times before reaching the world beyond this accursed bog.

Though after the prince's fiery outburst, the squabbling had died down and remained at the surly muttering and baleful glare stage, Rafial's army was still a disorderly, dysfunctional rabble. One likely to tear itself apart in a bloody clash of fang, talon, tentacle, knobbly bits and strychnine-laced custard pies long before it reached the Land of Light and Goodness. The prince needed urgent help in commanding the unruly gathering. Preferably someone from his own royal family. Promoting any of the evil minions to the status of commander was always doomed to failure. With the earth bound legions of darkness under their control, they inevitably developed megalomania and delusions of such grandeur that they always tried to usurp Rafial. More tiresome piles of ash stinking of brimstone. The demon's carbon footprint had long gone off the scale.

That left his family. With Demonica gone on her own hellish rampage, his thoughts turned to his full blood demon son Zaphael. Only problem was his dear boy was still down in the Netherworld, a place Rafial had not contacted since his embarrassing banishment. But with the Minotaur already threatening to head butt the leader of the Gargoyles over some slur over the size of its mother's backside and the zombies making everyone puke by popping out their decaying eyes and juggling with them, it was time to take serious action.

Alone, the prince donned his formal garb of fire salamander leather, tastefully trimmed with golden basilisk scales, and a flowing cloak with a high, pointy collar made of silver werewolf fur (the hardest pelt in the world to acquire as they usually turned back to human form when shot by silver bullets). Once suitably dressed to talk to the Boss down below, he strode deep, deep down into the fortress's deepest bowels to the Great Pit of Summoning. It was a formidable and suitably dramatic setting, one that was celebrated in the annals of High Gothic Demonic Architecture. In fact it had won many awards for its impressive atmosphere of Doom and Foreboding. And a gold medal for Baleful Oppressiveness. The sound effects were state of the art. In the background there was a booming suggestion of a vast heartbeat, highlighted by the occasional ghastly moan or heart-chilling scream from wretched damned souls. Theatrical but effective.

It had a high-vaulted ceiling shrouded in dark sulphurous clouds, walls ornate with gruesome blood-red stone carved with images of tormented souls, skeletons, gargoyles, dragon skulls and fearsome weaponry. And a giraffe in a tutu and a fat hamster riding a unicycle. No one knew why the evil minion stonemason carved them. But Rafial left them just in case the images had some vital shamanic or alchemical significance. 'Remove the carvings and the whole edifice will fall' or some other sort of secret, dramatic spell to that effect. He couldn't actually ask the mason responsible as the unfortunate minion was long turned into a pile of ash stinking of brimstone. It happened within seconds of Rafial discovering the giraffe.

Taking a deep breath to compose himself, the prince approached the edge of a mighty yawning abyss, the surrounding air burning hot from the roiling pit of molten lava so deep down it was impossible to measure. Though people chucked down it had plenty of time to guess before they hit the flames. Rafial raised his arms wide and began the solemn incantation of summoning, a long and elaborate ceremony. In a dramatic gesture, he threw some foul smelling incense into a skull-shaped golden salver on a high plinth in the form of a ferocious serpent; a substance believed to be butterbean based, hence the noxious fumes... In his deep, rich voice, the prince began an incantation, involving evoking all of the Boss's million names. To the prince's relief, a booming voice interrupted him by the fortieth name.

'That's enough Rafe. What beyond hell do you want?' The voice swiftly became less booming and more peevish. In fact, to be brutally honest, it was high pitched and shrill. Even a little girly in tone. Not what most people expected from His Satanic Majesty, though Rafial was used to it. 'I wish you hadn't taken that idiotic and stubborn stance over our eternal torment policy. I need you back down with me, I miss you.'

Rafial shrugged. He was in no hurry to return. Living with humans had its drawbacks but was infinitely preferable to his old job. No more eternity spent menacingly dangling food on long poles for this demon.

'Whatever you want, make it snappy, Rafe old boy. I have a large party of time-share salesmen on the way. Stupid bastards got food poisoning on the Costa Lotte. Only one survived. Some chap called Vinny Grimes.'

'I bring you good news, my Satanic Lord and Master,' announced Rafial, 'I am going on a war with the forces of Goodness and Light. But I need my son to help me. Could I respectfully implore you to send up Zaphael?'

The voice tried to return to its booming and malevolent mode but failed, coming out as an affronted squeak. 'Zaphael! Failure runs in your family...must be something wrong with your demonic bloodlines. Luckily that half-breed daughter of yours is showing great promise. So, you want Zaphael? Well I can inform you that the young fool calmly turned his back on all his infernal duties and strode out of Hell to become a lead guitarist in a human heavy rock band! He's already up there somewhere.'

The voice grew withering and contemptuous, 'I now have no one to supervise the pit for where damned souls go to spend all eternity up to their chins in human ordure. Mainly spammers, hackers and phishers. Most vexing. So you are welcome to him...' With that the boomingly squeaky voice faded away, leaving an astonished Rafial teetering on the brink of the abyss. The Master was the Prince of Lies, he couldn't help it. It was his job. He must be lying now, surely? How could a full-blood demon crown prince team up with a load of mangy humans, not to spread death and mayhem but play music? Though all that wide-legged posturing in studded spandex was pretty evil. Rafial now had another problem on his hands beyond the ill-disciplined rabble that needed to be shaped into an efficient fighting force. But how could he find and sort out his rebellious son and heir?

There was no sense of impending doom within the Forest of Mhmin. Sunlight still danced off the floating gossamer and mysterious but beautiful tiny silver bits. Though it had not rained, a spectacular rainbow arced over the top of the verdant treetops. Butterflies of every hue including some over-the-top glitzy ones fluttered through the carpets of fragrant flowers. The worst offenders being the garish day-glo orange and purple fritillaries; they had augmented their gaudy glamour with glittery legs having stomped about in cuckoo spit then danced in the tiny silver bits.

The poetry festival had recovered its composure after Cylphie's dramatic interruption and resulting riot. Apart from a few centaurs nursing sore heads and pulled tails and one unfortunate talking stoat hyperventilating, all was calm again. With the only sound being the tiny wheeze of the unfortunate stoat breathing into a brown paper bag, all were enraptured by an epic tale of subterranean derring-do performed by the miming moles. Or it could have been a tragic love story. Or a rip-roaring, knock about comedy, no one had ever worked out what the moles were trying to portray but it was a sincere attempt at High Art so everyone always applauded wildly and enthusiastically. Once again the moles were happy, so delighted by the rapturous reception their sagas received that they would be back again the next year with another baffling performance.

Excited squeaky voices and a sound of impatient shuffling heralded the arrival of the next performance. A determined group of male wood gnomes, piskies and other diminutive forest dwellers had forced their way to the front of the auditorium. Several tall, elegant elves stepped forward, one with a dazzling bejewelled harp, another with a sparkling quartz crystal mandolin. The third with a set of wooden spoons, he was down on his luck. The fourth elf was an exquisite raven-haired maiden, a feast for the eye with her flowing gossamer gown in shades of silver and jade. And she didn't wear Dr Martens. The group had set one of the divine Devin's interminable poems to music. They were joined by a troupe of water nymphs who had choreographed a dance to accompany it. As they floated on in a ripple of watery and diaphanous silk, the small beings at the front became more excited.

They had a book running over which of the nymphs, if any, wasn't wearing any knickers. When the high stepping and kicking of their river dance began in earnest, the wagering became frantic, threatening to disrupt the highbrow serenity of the elven music. But as the nymphs danced, a dark shadow passed over the sun, darkening the glade. Everyone shivered and looked up, except one of the bolder wood gnomes who took advantage of the distraction to look up a nymph's floaty dress. Everyone shivered at the sudden drop in temperature as the sun was obscured by a massive flyby of huge evil dragons heading for their rallying point in the Land of Darkness and Despair. Then they were gone and the sun returned.

'I've won!' bellowed the wood gnome, 'It *was* the wee lassie in the lilac gown

Jed and Cuddles were getting on very well together considering their short acquaintance. In exile for five hundred years Cuddles had been lonely for a long time and Jed enjoyed having a companion he could chat with unlike his surly former sidekick Oakham Strang and best of all the unicorn didn't smell as bad either. There was one odd annoyance, as they trotted along a track, Jed couldn't shake off a peculiar buzzing sound close by like an exceptionally angry wasp trapped in a bottle of Tizer. Jed looked around for any lurid orange fizz bottles with an irate stripped prisoner inside but there was nothing. As the buzzing intensified, Cuddles raised his head and shook his wonky horn in bewilderment.

'I can't believe it. I'm picking up a signal again – for the first time in centuries.'

'A signal?' asked Jed confused.

'A signal from the Satanic Messaging System – we call it SMS for short. Rafial of the Lands of Darkness and Despair uses it to communicate with his dark creatures. My horn acts as an antennae to pick the signals up. I've been offline for a long time. I thought it was broken.'

'What does it say? The signal.'

'It's a call-up signal to all dark creatures. Prince Rafial is mobilising an army against the Kingdom of Goodness and Light. It's all out war.'

'Are you going to answer the call?' Jed held his breath waiting for the answer. This could be the shortest partnership of his career.

'No. I'm the last of my kind and nobody in the Evil world even knows I exist any more. I told you I was a traitor. I'm too ashamed to go back. I'll stay with you for now, Moonraven, until I work out what to do next.'

'Your horn, does it have satnav?' queried Jed, now desperate to get to Morven before gremlins, cave trolls and their aunties overran the country.

'Satnav?'

'Yep ...you know, a device to find people...Searching And Tracking Nice Associates And Voles,' replied the highwayman.

'Ah, you mean Satanic Navigation, of course I have,' Cuddles answered, changing the angle of his horn by rubbing it on his knee. 'Now, who do you seek?'

In a blaze of fury that ignited several nearby and unsuspecting magic trees that ran away screeching towards the river as fast as their long trailing roots would allow, Demonica faced up to her most hated nemesis. Her half-brother Zaphael. She wouldn't lower herself to call him 'Zaff', that ridiculous coarse humanised name he insisted on using. She ground her fanged teeth in frustration. It was all so unfair. Her brother was the first born and a full demon. And as Rafial's only full demon son, he was next in line to the throne of the Land of Darkness etc etc. One she had no hope in gaining as a female and a mere half-human.

She'd been hearing about him since she was young enough to understand her father's nostalgic whining. Zaff this and Zaff that. She had grown up in the shadow of the perfect son, the perfect brother. The one who had stayed behind and prospered in Hell....ha! Sooo wrong there, Daddy Dearest. She loathed everything about him. Zaphael had three thousand titles! He had magnificent wings! And he had no interest in being a demon but only wanted to tour the world with his appalling heavy metal band. Demonica wanted to smash his handsome face in.

Zaff flew up into the sky and using his wings, beat out the flames on the unfortunate enchanted trees before returning to confront the insane half human harpy otherwise known as his sister.

'Uncool, sis. That screeching was hurting my brain. Had a heavy night.'

Demonica's upper lip curled in derision. 'What's the matter Zaphael, going soft? But what would I expect in a so-called demon who prefers to tunelessly thrash guitars and hang around with adoring groupies than to fulfilling his royal destiny.'

Dragging on a dubiously fat looking cigarette, Zaff shrugged. 'I won't touch human women. Too much risk of producing another half-breed spoiled brat like you.'

He waited till she stopped making the ground shake by stamping her feet in outrage before continuing. 'Anyway, you know it doesn't matter what I do, Monica. Our dear dad is immortal. There will never be a throne for me to inherit.'

She strode forward, one leather-spiked arm raised ready to strike him. 'My name is Demonica- Princess of...'

Fending her off easily with a swish of his wings and silencing her from tediously listing her paltry three hundred titles, he laughed in devilish delight, how he loved winding his sister up. 'I was there when your human mother named you. And during the Ceremony of Damning. You are officially entered in the register of Hell's Vast Dominions as Princess Monica.'

In the background, her sex slave / boyfriend, the nasty bastard Strang bit deeply into his arm to stifle a fit of the giggles. Also, hidden in the still unburnt enchanted trees, a well-hidden Cylphie marvelled at Zaff, at his dark beauty, her heart already falling in love or maybe more likely in lust with him.

'Prove to me you are worthy to call yourself the only son of Rafial! Go on 'Zaff'. Do something unutterably evil and demonic!'

'Some say my music is evil enough!' Zaff gave a wicked grin, 'The ladies representing Puritans Opposed to Rock Noise, a crusade to ban all heavy metal music certainly thought so!'

'What happened to them?' demanded Demonica, having never heard of PORN.

'Lennie had given me some pure Colombian and I sneezed. Hard'

He mimed the resulting conflagration of the Puritan ladies with a wicked grin.

'It's all so frivolous to you,' snarled Demonica, 'one feckless big game with no responsibilities. No demonic dignity. You have the power to turn the world into ashes and desolation. To rule your own kingdom of darkness and despair. Instead you have thrown it all away. Go on Zaphael, show me that you are still a royal demon worthy of the name!'

'Don't tempt me!' he laughed, knowing he could easily reduce her to a pile of ash stinking of brimstone and she could do nothing to harm him. Instead he did something nearly as vexing to the furious princess. He turned his back and walked away. Demonica began to shout a volley of horrific and insulting names from every language ever spoken. She sent a barrage of fireballs to explode harmlessly around him. Futile but dramatic. And not good news to a party of voles returning home from their attack on the St Epiligia Pedants. Without slackening his pace or turning around, Zaff raised one hand and gave her the finger.

'Now that's cool, that's what I call rock and roll,' whispered an adoring Cylphie, yet angry and disappointed with herself to have foolishly fallen in love with an evil demon.

The elf maiden hurried back to the rest of the newly formed Fellowship now boosted by the addition of a dashing Highwayman and a manky looking unicorn of undetermined colour. The rakish gentleman of the road was handsome, charming but one look at Morven's adoring eyes and the elf could see it was strictly hands off.

Cuddles had been right; the damaging attacks were all the work of Demonica and not the Prince of the Land of Darkness and his evil hordes. Yet. There was no doubt that Rafial was gathering a mighty army, the skies were filled with harpies and dragons heading north. The grass bristled and smouldered with slithering fire salamanders and three-headed serpents returning to their demonic birthplace. The war had not started but could break out at any time. Inevitably the mood back in the camp was despondent.

'What exactly are we supposed to do about it?' moaned Robard. 'We are hardly the stuff of heroes!'

'But we are,' replied an equally miserable Wheatley, 'everything that was pre-destined is in place now. We have the requisite members of a Fellowship; we are the ones that must end this conflict.'

'How?' sniped the Goth lad. 'Chuck custard pies at them, bombard them with bagels? Pelt them with pastries?'

'Yes! If I have to!' Wheatley responded heroically, though alarmed at the thought of such flagrant misuse of quality baked goods. 'We were all brought together for a reason.'

'Or a convenient plot contrivance,' Robard muttered dourly.

Alarmed at the failing morale, Morven held up her hand. 'I am not going to stand by and watch the Forest of Mhmin burn to the ground. We may not be a team of fearless warriors, sorry, apart from you Cylphie of course, but we must find another way. Use our brains.'

'That counts you out Moonraven,' muttered Robard, 'your brains are all in your trousers!'

'That's it!!!' a delighted Morven cried out, 'We will set a honey trap to win over Zaff to our side. The only being strong enough to stand up to Demonica and win!'

'Ridiculous!' grumbled a still highly affronted highwayman. 'Zaphael is a full-blood demon...he won't help us.'

'He put out the burning enchanted tree...' Wheatley pointed out.

'And called Demonica rude names...' added Cylphie.

'And plays in a human heavy metal band...' continued Robard.

'Exactly!' Jed finished throwing up his hands in triumph. 'He plays diabolical music...that's all the proof I need that he's on the other side through and through!'

The argument became heated and rapidly deteriorated into a full blown domestic between Morven and Jed who was convinced she was going to put herself up to entice the young demon.

'Oh! A bloody typical man. Jed Moonraven - you can tumble into bed with any doxie that catches your eye but if I even suggest chatting up a demon in order to save our world, you become all jealous and domineering!'

The highwayman threw up his hands in exasperation. 'Jealous? I'm not jealous. I just want to stop you turning into a pile of ash stinking of brimstone!'

'This isn't getting us anywhere....' interrupted Wheatley.

'Butt out baker!' said Morven and Jed in unison.

'Actually, I was never a baker, I am only an apprentice, out to seek my hidden destiny.'

'The only hidden destiny you have is that fast deteriorating stale Chelsea bun you have stashed in your red spotted hankie,' retorted Jed unkindly.

Wheatley's face reddened with fury, 'My lucky bun! How did you know about that? Have you been rifling through my things?'

'Of course!' smirked Jed. 'Highwayman!'

The apprentice ran to his hankie and desperately searched for the ancient rock hard bun, but in vain. 'You've scoffed it! Prince Pravis was right! He should have run you through with his sword, you vile scoundrel!'

'I'm a highwayman, not a greedy, garbage-guzzling boggart. I never touched the disgusting thing.'

The argument was interrupted by the sound of equine coughing. Then copious retching. Yes, yes, it is a well-known fact that horses can't be sick but this was a unicorn. 'Yeeeuurchh...' spluttered Cuddles, 'I shouldn't have eaten that!'

'MY LUCKY BUN!! How could you?' Wheatley exploded into fury; this was too much for a simple apprentice lad to take in.

'Er...evil cursed unicorn?' replied the evil cursed unicorn.

'I cannot believe you people!' Cylphie picked up her bow and began to walk away. 'We have formed a brave and noble Fellowship to fight the Forces of Darkness and this is how we prepare? Ridiculous petty squabbles? Over a stale old bun?' She was appalled. Had she made a mistake by teaming up with these fools? The raging hell fires were nearing her enchanted home... and they fight over buns?

'It *was* my lucky bun,' Wheatley snivelled feeling both bereft and foolish.

'It tasted disgusting,' muttered Cuddles, threatening to ignite the row again.

Cylphie sighed; she had indeed made a terrible mistake teaming up with these idiots. She needed tough, valiant and focused warriors if her home was to be saved. She began to walk away, expecting them to stop her but they were too engrossed in the Battle of the Bun to notice.

At last the Army of Darkness and Despair had got its act together and began to move slowly away from the fortress to the steady rhythm of pounding kettle drums played by a percussion club consisting only of the cave trolls' maiden aunties. It was their hobby. More interesting then dead flower dis-arranging.

Rafial picked out a fabulously evil looking dragon to ride, a masterpiece of shiny black scales, elaborate baroque spines and horns, massive leathery wings and a very long barbed tail. A very, very long tail.

The column of evil beings made an impressively horrendous sight as they passed through the baleful Valley of Bones, despite the odd trip over ribcages and the zombies' distracting urge to play football with the skulls. The entire army was soaking wet from passing through the obligatory thunderstorm and a blood red moon shone with ominous splendour off the sodden armour and weaponry. And the shiny bald heads of the ogres. Well, most of the ogres. There was one who sported a very obvious ginger wig that was always slipping to one side, but he was far too brutal and huge for anyone to point it out. Or dare to snigger.

An impressive flypast in formation by the legion of Malign Butterflies with their guest performers the Malevolent Moths flitted over the heads of the horde, their black wings suitably ragged, their tiny feet clad in impressive hobnailed bovver boots, their minute teeth sharpened to painful pinpricks of poisonous menace. Everyone cheered or roared or snurffled at the precision flying except the gnats and mozzies who could only fly in disorganised clouds. They just seethed and buzzed, eaten up with jealousy and muttering that the fluttering show-offs were too short-lived to even reach the battlefield. Indeed there had been a morale-boosting display organised by the Macabre Mayflies. But they had all died after the first rehearsal.

Equally discontent were the were-wasps. They had boycotted the entire war because once they flew into the Land of Goodness and Light they would become ordinary wasps again, only fit for annoying people at picnics and vulnerable to swatting. The only worry for the werewolves was turning into naked, grubby humans with dental hygiene problems...they always carried spare underpants, socks and toothbrushes on campaigns. Just in case.

Sweeping high over his mighty army on the back of the impressive dragon, Rafial was still uneasy. He hated the idea that his son Zaphael had sauntered up from Hell, was now consorting with humans and was nowhere to be seen. He was nervous about keeping this rabble of monsters together as a cohesive force. Was he losing his touch? Were the long centuries contentedly pootling about the fortress now taking a toll, compromising his ability to command? He was about to be thrown his first serious challenge of the campaign. The leading battalion comprising of the Union of Scary Clowns and the least decayed zombies entered one of the land's blighted forests. At first all was as it should be. Then a horrified blood-curdling scream carried on the sulphurous air. Pandemonium began to spread like a Mexican wave through the ranks of the damned.

Furious at another crisis so soon into the campaign, Rafial urged the great dragon to swoop down to the ranks to see what in damnation was going on.

As the dragon alighted at the forest edge, a panic-stricken clown, greasepaint running down his contorted face, ran passed the prince, screaming 'He's in there! Aaaaarrghhh.'

Rafial turned him into a pile of ash stinking of brimstone for the temerity of not bowing in his presence, which was a bad move as he needed to know more. He did not have long to wait.

Yet another clown followed by a fairly fresh-looking zombie, probably only in its grave for a month, burst out of the woods. 'He's in there! And hungry!' Or something close to that, zombies were not known for being terribly coherent, what with their decaying tongues and rotting windpipes.

This time Rafial did not blast them into piles of ash stinking of brimstone but made them halt and explain themselves. Their fear of what lay in the wood equalled their fear of their demonic dark lord, the clown had wet himself, his multicoloured curly wig was full of twigs and dead leaves from his panic-stricken bolt from the blighted forest. The zombie had lost an arm and seemed in no mood to go back and retrieve it. The demon prince grabbed the clown by the throat - he didn't dare do that to the zombie as their heads fell off so easily. 'Who or what is in the woods?' The clown turned pale which was some feat considering the thick white grease-paint makeup his face was plastered in. His whole body shook which set off his large black and white whirling bowtie. A rubber chicken fell out of his over-sized baggy patchwork jacket. And a trumpet. And a pistol that had a flag shoot out of the muzzle with the word BANG! on it. 'Enough!' roared Rafial, determined to get the truth before the string of sausages fell out. And the damned annoying string of endless coloured hankies.

The quaking clown began to stammer and stutter, displeasing Rafial would have serious and permanent consequences.

'It's HIM! Back from exile in the Forest that Looks Enchanted but is really rather Mundane.... Nutsferatu!!!!'

The sound of that name being spoken out loud began a ripple of panic through the army.

'Rubbish!' howled Rafial with the full power of his commanding presence. 'I banished that little bastard from this land two hundred years ago!'

Few could forget Rafial's fearsome ire at being pelted by conkers by the much detested forest dweller. So disrespectful! But he was far too quick for Rafial, dodging with contempt the prince's flaming bolts of demonic power that would have reduced Nutsferatu to a small pile of ash stinking of brimstone. The demon's pursuit of his nemesis was costly in terms of destroyed blighted enchanted trees. And the evil creatures that dwelt there. With one too many singed werewolf, there was no choice but to ban the virulent little gobshite far, far away from the Land of Darkness and Despair forever. But Nutsferatu was back. It seemed forever did not last as long as it used to.

Zaphael, still amused by his encounter with his half-sister Monica, crouched up high on the last remaining tall tower of a ruined abbey on the edge of the bog lands. It once belonged to the holy monks of the order of St Minusculus.

All the holy men who served there had to be less than five foot high in honour of the tiny saint, which led to considerable recruitment problems. And finding suppliers of suitably small habits. Though the order's strict dietary requirements for a butterbean only diet did not help matters. When numbers were at an all time low, a decision by the Holy Abbot to raise the height limit for inclusion to the monastery led to conflict and a mass walk out. Well, a stroll out by the last two tiny monks. They looked extremely miffed though.

Flexing his massive wings, Zaff pondered his next move. He had no desire to join up with his father and the army of darkness. But there would be no gigs with a massive and punishing war on. Was it too late to try to stop it? The band had bookings all across the land and a new album to promote. And he knew his father Rafial had always been half-hearted about waging war, preferring to stay in his fortress reading and making lists. He was still wondering what to do when a pretty female voice wafted on the smoky air up to his roosting place. Groupies! They were the most determined creatures that ever existed, even more persistent than time share salesmen for hovels on the Costa Lotte.

'Sorry darlin'.' The gig's knackered me. No action tonight.'

Eyes widening, the elf maiden put her hands on her slender hips and shouted back up at the demon. 'Can you come down? I need to speak to you.'

'If you want an autograph, you can climb up here and join me.'

Perhaps forgetting she was dealing with the demon crown prince, sole heir to the Kingdom of Darkness and Despair, Cylphie seethed, the arrogance of the creature! But with the mission at stake, she gritted her teeth and began to quickly climb the unstable and precarious brickwork. When face to face with the demon she pulled off her bog chav baseball hat and let the luscious waterfall of silver blonde hair tumble down her slender back. Zaff was delighted. A beautiful elf maiden! As she wasn't human, she was therefore automatically on his 'able to fuck' list and she was stunningly beautiful. All thoughts of finding his father faded, his mind was totally captivated by the enchanting elf warrior.

Risking a small fire, though what was a few flickering flames compared to the approaching conflagration, Morven cooked some flat bread. Simple traveller's fare spiced up with her unique topping of tinned anchovies and dried apricots sprinkled with ginger. Robard turned a shade paler and pulled a face as she handed him a slice.

'Go on, eat. Looks like you could do with a hearty meal or three. It won't harm!'

Wheatley took his with a weak smile of gratitude and a sad sigh. By now the bakery would be down to the difficult to shift items, the ones he excelled in selling. The last forlorn flaky pastry topped with grated coconut, lurid orange fondant fancies, bundles of deeply dull, dry cheese straws. He bit into the bizarrely flavoured bread, tears of homesickness and bun withdrawal rolling down his cheeks. Morven felt guilty about her past impatience with Wheatley and was moved to comfort the unfortunate lost and ageing boy apprentice when she heard the sound of Jed's pistols being primed. They had visitors.

Through the gnarled spinney came Cylphie accompanied by a magnificent looking young demon, his dark wings folded back, his walk an indolent, arrogant swagger.

'Unbelievable!' gasped Morven; the young elf had actually succeeded in winning the support of the crown prince of The Land of Darkness and Despair.

'Way too cool!' muttered a deeply impressed Robard. Finally there was someone he could connect with. This was a dude who would appreciate the dark beauty of his tortured soul.

Oh shit! thought Cuddles trying to find somewhere to hide, he was a runaway from the Land of Darkness and Despair, a traitor to the cause of evil and doom.

'No way!' grumbled Jed. He fully expected to spend eternity in the company of demons like this but not before he danced a final jig at the end of a hemp rope.

'Gllllooorrfllle snurffleeghhh,' choked Wheatley on his flat bread in abject terror.

Behind his dark shades, Zaff carefully took in the group, looking at him in the usual and predictable mixture of terror, awe and lust. With an added emotion this time - expectation. Apart from the hot elf, there was a pale-faced black clad teenager who would no doubt want to sell his soul and be his slave, a highwayman who by rights was on the side of evil already, a terror struck middle-aged man, a stunningly beautiful redheaded witch. One of the good ones. Zaff grinned to himself... for now! And a faded, grubby and sorry excuse for a cursed black unicorn futilely hiding behind a blighted bog oak bush.

Turning to his new companion, the delightful elf maiden, Zaff shook his head in disbelief. 'So, let me get this straight, this ill-matched rabble is actually going up against my sis?'

With his wings folded tight, Zaff lent indolently against a tree, and began to smoke a spliff.

'We are not a rabble!' retorted an outraged Wheatley. 'We are a Fellowship.'

'The winged dude was right the first time,' answered the Goth boy as he bravely strolled over to Zaff to cadge a few puffs.

Passing Robard the whole spliff, the demon addressed the group. 'Hey, guys. Do what the f♦ⓂⓅ&; you like. It's a free country - at the moment.' He winked at Morven, 'Shame to fry such a fine-looking chick though.'

'I am not some chick! I am Morven, the Unwise Woman of Fuggis Mire!'

She made a show of being affronted but this ultimate bad boy's attention made her blush, to the fury of Jed. In the league of desirable but totally unsuitable men, Jed was a lightweight compared to the demon. And the bastard knew it.

'Babe, you could be the Queen of f♦ⓂⓅ&;ing Sheba. If you piss off Monica, you will still end up as toast.'

Queen Hemelda had decided the only answer to all the dissent and chaos amongst the Forces of Goodness and Light was good design and careful accessorizing. She had spent the night nose deep in the Book, her ultimate design bible. So many wondrous ideas and unexpected ways to use voile and sequins.

She called up every seamstress and tailor in the land and after hours of intense toil, had kitted out all the army in matching tabards of gold lamé with a tasteful petunia motif worked in cerise and aqua sequins. The knights received a total make-over. Pink plastic flamingos purloined from a nearby garden centre replaced their tournament-worn crests of battered boars and damaged dragons. Their helms were also trimmed with four foot long red ostrich feathers. No armour had ever shone so brightly, the sun light dazzled, bounced off the mirror-like gleam, blinding several serfs and setting fire to twenty campaign tents. Morale slumped to an all time low.

The overwhelming urge to tear off their tabards and stamp on them spread like a Mexican wave through the ranks except among the friendly giants who thought the colour brought out the blue in their eyes.

Prince Pravis stepped on a prone Squarf's back and mounted his noble steed. His father the king approached and beckoned him to lean forward so he could whisper in his ear. 'Once you get out of eyeshot of the palace, they can take those awful tabards off. It's up to you my boy to bolster the morale and get this army ready to take on the Forces of Darkness and Despair. The survival of our world depends on you.'

'Have no fear father,' proclaimed the prince in a booming, heroic voice. He wanted to stand up in the stirrups and address the elite corps of noble knights around him. Give a stirring speech that would put fire in their blood and a sharper edge to their swords of righteousness. But it was difficult for any of the knights, himself included to stay secure in the saddle with the armour and chain mail so shiny. One by one, as their impatient steeds became restless to leave the courtyard, the knights began to slip and slide about in their saddles.

The weight of the plastic flamingos and ostrich plumes unbalanced their helms, tipping them down over their eyes. Their horses sensing their lack of balance and co-ordination took advantage and began to play about. Soon the courtyard in front of the palace was full of un-seated knights and horses squealing, shying and bucking about in a giddy melee. The surface of the courtyard didn't help. The ancient cobblestones had been dug out by the Queen's orders and replaced by a pink and gold brick driveway in a clever parquet effect. The knights would soon have a perfect view of the castle's latest improvements when they tumbled off their rebellious steeds.

Pravis tried to restore order by roaring out an order in a suitably heroic voice which only wound up the unruly horses even more. Squarf could see what would happen next. One over-excited beast would see the open gate and bolt for the grassy meadows beyond the castle, starting a stampede. He could have easily stopped it by running over and hauling down the portcullis. Leaving it open was far more fun.

A scrawny chestnut mare succeeded in shying so abruptly that her rider flew through the air in an impressive arc before landing in a crumpled heap of dazzling shiny metal, ostrich plumes, flamingos and very long pointy shoes. Unencumbered, she gave a huge buck, squealed then galloped out of the castle, followed by all the other horses, some with knights on board, still clinging on for dear life. Squarf risked a good kicking by laughing uproariously. The likelihood of punishment confirmed when he convulsed into further loud hysterics at the sight of Prince Pravis's snow white steed joining the other bolters. Across the whole courtyard, sniggering serfs and pages did their best to stifle back their giggles before attempting to rescue their fallen masters.

'Squarf! Run after them! Get those crazy horses back,' commanded the mortified and bruised prince, struggling to his feet, the flamingo on his helm now askew at a drunken angle.

'If you don't mind my Liege, I'd rather just take the kicking. There's no way I'm going after those eejits!'

Pravis did not argue with his rebellious serf. He took off his helm and threw it across the courtyard in an explosion of vexation. The ignominy of the last few minutes was unbearable. All his life he had trained for this moment. His shining, golden moment of nobility and glory. All the tough years at Knight School had prepared him only for victory. The training, the bruising tournaments, the bizarre and humiliating punishments for failure. He shuddered at the memory of being immersed up to the neck in a barrel of butterbeans for not bowing to a smelly old badger, the school's official mascot. He had borne his chastisement with stoic resignation and not a word of complaint. As a royal prince he could have substituted Squarf, let his serf stand in and take his punishment. But he did not. It seemed worth it at the time. But not now.

Up in the battlements, the king was also about to explode with embarrassment and fury. His great army of Goodness and Light was a humiliating fiasco. Rafial easily could take this land without igniting another hovel. In fact the king was sorely tempted to hand the castle keys over to the demon without a fight and let the country go hang itself. Rafial was even welcome to his wife. He could then fulfil his dream of retiring to a new-built castellated villa on the Costa Lotte. One he had recently invested in. 'Safeguard your future in shining white brick in a serene land of sun, sea and golden sands,' Vinny Grimes had whispered of such tantalising images in his ear and they made a deal straight away.

Crash, clank! The sound of another of his elite corps of knights hitting the deck was his reality now. The king covered his eyes with his hands. An invasion of the Forces of Darkness and Despair would come as an act of mercy.

Queen Hemelda was also about to explode with embarrassment and fury. The bolting horses had smashed their way through her delicate and delightful new Zen-inspired garden, scattering the artfully raked gravel and knocking down an expensive but fragile Japanese-style bridge. Such unspeakable vandals! Shattering her dream of having a full colour spread in **Sycophant!** A glossy magazine which delighted in rubbing peasants' noses in how rich and extravagant their rulers were.

The night passed uneventfully and Morven handed out the last of their meagre and eccentric rations such as fly cemetery biscuits with real flies in them for breakfast. She spotted the elf maiden walking away from the camp to sit on a bog oak log and drop her head into her hands. Clearly time for girl-talk. The Unwise Woman sat down next to her after checking for woodlice and bum-boring beetles.

'Do you want to talk?' she queried, her voice warm and compassionate.

Cylphie sighed, knowing she was being idiotic. Jed and Zaff were still away, using the cover of nightfall to check out the lie of the land. It was only a brief recognisance mission but it meant Zaff was out of sight and with no guarantee of him returning,

'I must admit I was surprised to see you so smitten with lust over that handsome devil, ' Morven ventured, ' I thought you elves were on a higher realm of existence, wandering through moon-lit glades or wafting about on clouds and rainbows being all creative and ethereal.'

'We are. But we also like to bonk.'

'Right,' Morven replied, non-plussed. 'But you can't expect a passionate romance from a creature like Zaff. For one thing he is probably a wildly promiscuous demon, will do anything with a pulse that isn't human. And he is in a heavy metal band. Which is pretty much the same thing.'

Cylphie sighed, a crystal tear ran down one porcelain-pale cheek. 'Its not just lust. I've fallen in love with Zaff.'

Highly unlikely, thought the Unwise Woman, Cylphie had known him for little more then a few hours.

'Sorry to sound so blunt, my dear,' Morven soothed, handing her the last clean hankie. 'I know all about bad boys, as you know I'm in love with one myself. They will not change, the love of a good woman - or good elf maiden, will not tame them. I accept Jed for what he is; I have to turn a blind eye to all his womanising and debauchery. He can't help it. It is his birthright. He was born on the morn of Tumesantide.'

So was Cylphie's aunt Gerifalee, an elven woman so prim and proper she would have sewn her legs together shut permanently if physically possible. So repressed, all mention of 'that awfulness' was banned from her home. She didn't get a lot of visitors. Tactfully Cylphie kept that story to herself.

'But he always comes back to you,' the tearful Cylphie responded, desperate for some tiny ray of hope that she stood a chance of some sort of relationship with Zaff.

'One day he won't.' It was Morven's time to become tearful, knowing the fate of all highwaymen. Since meeting and falling in love with Jed, she spent her life in the shadow of the gallows.

Cylphie's hand shot to her mouth, mortified at what she had said. 'Oh! I am so very sorry. That was so callous and stupid of me. Can you ever forgive me?'

The Unwise Woman gave a sad smile and put her arm around the young elf. 'The only one I cannot forgive is that bloody Cupid! I wish I wasn't sworn to harm none. I would turn that little creep and his damned bow and arrows into a rancid toad!'

'Or an incontinent boggart's bottom!' added Cylphie with a giggle.

'Too good for him. What about a fat boar's bollocky backside!'

'Zombie armpit sweat?'

'Sea hag toe clippings!'

'Flying monkey poo!'

'No, I have got the ultimate punishment,' laughed Morven, 'a big festering bucket of cold butterbeans abandoned at the back of a nasty old greedy goblin's store for a month!'

'Make it six months and it's settled!'

The two women fell about laughing. But as the already smoke-hazy sun was darkened briefly as Zaff returned in a flurry of his magnificent wings, Cylphie's mood returned to sadness.

'I don't suppose you can mix me up a potion to make him love me. Or one to help me forget my love for him.'

Morven took both her hands and gave them a gentle squeeze.

'Hon, I cannot. I must do no harm and altering another's emotions is to do harm. The sensible advice would be to forget him, before your heart gets broken anymore. Find a loving, loyal elf boy to love. A handsome warrior to match your skill with a bow.'

'Actually, I am complete rubbish with a bow,' Cylphie confessed, 'but I am an elf, upholding convention and all that.'

Morven was saddened at the crushing blow her words had to the elf maiden's still flickering flame of hope. But what the hell, the world was about to end! 'I am the Unwise Woman,' she added, 'my advice is go for it, rock his Underworld more than anyone ever could.'

Cylphie, who had never known another's intimate touch, blushed prettily. Unwisely, Morven gave the elf maiden a glimmer of hope,

'Mind you, demons were angels once, before the Fall. Angels are meant to be full of love, perhaps enough celestial blood remains for Zaff to learn to love you.'

Cylphie's fey features lit up, eyes shining with renewed hope, and the two young women embraced, already friends.

Their sad mood changed as an excited Wheatley rushed up, for the first time his face wreathed with smiles and excitement. Hope rose in their hearts. The war was over? Rafial and Demonica had gone home? Robard had cheered up?

'I found it...the unicorn had only taken a bite, it's a bit battered and smells of vomit a bit, but I have it back!'

Morven and Cylphie glanced at each other, non-plussed.

'My bun! I have found my lucky bun! It had rolled under a juniper bush!'

'Right!' snarled Rafial. 'I have had just as much as I can take from that little tosser!'

He ordered his army to halt and flew his dragon as low as he dared over the tangled branches of the malign wood. Somewhere in the gloom lurked his archenemy, a fiend so mean tempered it would prevent the forces of darkness and evil from safe passage through the forest. How dare it! He was prince of this desolate land of sorrow and despair. With no creature man, werewolf, zombie or ghoul enough to take Nutsferatu on, Rafial decided to sort the wretched thing out himself.

As he focused hard on the trees, scanning for any sign of the menace, the great dragon's wings drummed the air in a foreboding rhythm; hopefully the sound alone would make Nutsferatu see sense and surrender. But the dragon's long tail, its very, very long tail whipped too frantically, getting caught around a tree. The startled dragon pulled up so short that Rafial was pitched from the saddle to plummet down to the earth for a second time since the Fall. It was only when close to reaching an embarrassing and painful landing that he remembered he had his own wings. With feet to spare, he recovered and landed in a clearing.

The incongruous sound of slow handclapping announced he was not alone. A conker landing on his head announced he was in the company of Nutsferatu.

'Come down and face me, you little bastard!' Rafial demanded. Two more perfectly pitched conkers hit him square on the forehead. The outrageous lack of respect was intolerable. And painful.

'Not bloody likely!' piped a squeaky little voice with a pronounced Transylvanian accent. 'You vill zap me. I do not vant to end up a small pile of ash stinking of brimstone!'

'It is all you deserve! How dare you come back to this land. I banished you.'

'Zat's gratitude for you! Typical demon, all arrogance and mindless zapping.'

There was a flash of red through the treetops, a gleam of tiny glowing eyes, the flash of moonlight on sharp fangs. 'I came all ziz vay to join ze Forces of Darkness and zis is the only zanks I get!'

Rafial's glowing fire eyes glanced around the forest floor, at the large and fresh piles of bones at the base of the trees. 'I won't have any army left for you to join at the rate you are getting through my citizens!'

'Do not vorry my Prince. I am qvite sated now. I vill save my appetite for ze enemy. Zo, I vill join your army?'

'I would be a fool not to utilise such a vicious and successful evil killer. Of course you are welcome to join my mighty army of Darkness and Despair.'

A delighted Nutsferatu skipped merrily down the tree trunk and onto the forest floor where he was instantly zapped into a pile of ash stinking of brimstone.

Rafial stormed over to the pile and gave it a hearty kick. 'When I said you are banished, you damn well stay banished! Go on, you little shit. Regenerate from that!'

Retrieving his dragon, the demon prince freed its very long tail from the branches with his sword and flew high above the forest, giving a victory roll that inspired a rousing cheer of relief and celebration amongst his cowering troops at the woodland's edge.

'No bloody vampire squirrel messes with this demon. Nasty little gobshite!'

'So what exactly *are* we going to do?' demanded the Goth boy, emboldened by finishing Zaff's spliff. A question that was on everyone's mind but none had dared utter it aloud.

'Let's face it,' Robard continued, 'a few miles away from us, there is a vast army of bloodthirsty cave trolls, zombies, werewolves etcetera led by an evil demonic prince...er, no offence Zaff....'

'None taken, man...its cool,' shrugged Zaff, unconcerned.

'And we are a so-called Fellowship comprising of an Unwise Woman, a thief mounted on a mangy talking unicorn, an ageing apprentice obsessed with cakes, a love-struck elf and a demon. And me. A youthful pacifist poet with a deeply troubled soul who...'

He was silenced mid sentence by a glare from the highwayman. But he was right, what exactly were they supposed to do?

'Don't look at me for an answer,' Zaff replied, 'this is your gig.'

Ignoring an appalled Cylphie, the demon flew up into the nearest high tree and watched out for signs of the approaching Army of Darkness and Despair.

'What a pillock,' muttered Jed trying not to show his seething jealousy. Until the demon's arrival, he was the dashing, handsome bad boy, the focus of all the attention. Now all eyes were on the darkly glamorous Zaff.

Morven ignored him; her greater concern was the Goth boy's pertinent question. What exactly *could* they do against the vast and deadly army of Darkness and Despair? The honest answer was probably nothing. But the Forest of Mhmin was under the most immediate threat. And with Zaff on board, surely they could stop Demonica?

The Unwise Woman risked Jed's displeasure and strolled over to the tree and called up to the demon. 'We are not complete fools, Zaff. We can't do anything to stop your father and his rampaging army on our own. But we could stop your sister burning up the Forest of Mhmin.'

Zaff shrugged unconcerned. A few barbequed piskies and charred wood nymphs...what was that to him? Morven saw his lack of interest and controlling her temper as best she could, fully aware of how dangerous a being he was, called up to him again.

'The forest is the home of that beautiful elf who fancies you, Zaff. You wouldn't want to wreck your chances with her. If you do nothing and her home and family get destroyed, you stand no chance.'

The demon smiled broadly, a wicked gleam in his fiery eyes. 'Ok babe, you've convinced me. And it's always fun to wind up my sis.'

With a smoke-darkened sky and the crackling of burning bog grass, it was getting harder for the ethereal inhabitants of the Forest of Mhmin to ignore the approaching danger. The wisest joined the elven Elders to retreat to the ethereal, crystalline Temple of Serenity and Contemplation where moonbeams magically sparkled amongst the fragile glassy columns, even by daylight. Within minutes heated and rowdy arguments broke out, factions and alliances were hastily formed, some insisting their woodland home was safe, that magic would protect them, as it always had. Others that something should be done. What exactly was to be done was another question that divided them up into even more factions and alliances. The treetops and glades surrounding the Temple echoed with heated debates and with every minute wasted in chatter, the fires of doom broached ever nearer. At least some of the enchanted trees were decisive, dragging out their long roots from the ground, tucking their companion logs under their branches and escaping. Very, very slowly.

Demonica hauled her mixed team of Pookas and horses to a screeching halt. Actually it wasn't the team that screeched, it was the nasty bastard Strang who got his leather, studded codpiece trapped in a wheel. Ignoring him, she climbed to the top of her coach, teetering a little on her spiky high heels and surveyed her next helpless, innocent target with an evil and maniacal laugh of triumph. In her mind, she could hear the screams of petite flower fairies with their delicate, flimsy wings on fire. The futile pleading for mercy from the lofty and superior elves ringing in her ears. The forest floor littered with the charred corpses of talking fluffy bunnies. This was wickedness on a scale her useless demon of a father could never envisage, a deed so heinous it would surely reach Him Downstairs who would reward her with the keys to Rafial's kingdom. He could hardly give them to that appallingly disinterested Zaphael!

The sound of slow handclapping however was not in her reverie, that was all too real. Demonica spun around to be confronted with an odd group of beings, a Fellowship no less. She climbed down from the coach to approach them warily glancing anxiously along the line, wondering who had the great power that could overwhelm her. There was always one, even if they didn't know it until their ever-loyal best friend/doomed lover or lovable though sometimes irritating talking animal pet was threatened/killed by the baddie. In this case, her. A Japanese fellowship might include a so-called lovable but always intensely irritating small animal or robot. And all would have big, round eyes. This was definitely a local Fellowship, all had filth and mire up to their knees from the bog. And normal sized eyes.

Any great power was well hidden, Demonica carefully surveyed the group, a comely redheaded witch - she looked kindly. A white witch and therefore forbidden to do harm, so she was out of the frame. With his hands on his hips and his hat at a rakish angle, the blue-eyed highwayman was handsome if a tad wiry in build for her tastes, but it was rarely the thief who had the powers. Thieves stole amulets and potions for the true hero to use and often died heroically protecting him. Or her. That left a female elf warrior with a bow and arrow and wearing male garb as a disguise - a distinct possibility. The wretched looking Goth boy was another strong contender.

But what in Hades was the last member of the group? Not a mage, not a lone, mysterious and taciturn roving hero. And far too old to be an apprentice. But he was holding tightly onto something in his pocket, something of great value to him. Demonica glared at him in great trepidation. He must be the one! The hidden thing had to be some primeval sacred stone or an ancient amulet to ward off the powers of evil, perhaps a magic knife that could burn through immortal demon flesh. As she was only half demon, it would do even more damage to her!

It would be useful to finish off Zaphael though, leave her the only heir to the Land of Darkness and Despair. But how to separate the magical treasure from that so mundane looking human?

The tense, silent standoff was interrupted by the worst sound in the world, the rhythmic downbeat from her half-brother's wings. What was blasted Zaphael doing here?

'Hi, sis...how's it hanging?'

'Leave this place now! I have business with that forest.'

'Listen to old bossy britches! What's the matter Monica? Got your leather studded knickers in a twist?'

Fire streamed from her angry eyes, from her fingertips, futilely sending flame bolts to attack Zaff. All bounced harmlessly off him. It was no use, she had to have the Fellowship's secret weapon! Only that would destroy her infuriating brother.

'I am not here to get into a family tiff. One you couldn't win in a million years. I want you to leave the Forest of Mhmin alone. There's plenty of other things you can burn to cinders. Staines for a start.'

Demonica stopped the bombardment of fire and glared at the full-blood demon with a look of sheer hatred.

'Or you could join our dear old dad. He's about to march into this land with a vast conquering army.'

'Don't be ridiculous,' spat Demonica, 'he never leaves the fortress. Too busy with his lists. You are trying to wind me up.'

Zaff lit up a cigarette and shrugged, unconcerned. 'Whatever.'

Keeping a wary eye on the human with the magic knife/amulet/stone, Demonica climbed back on top of her coach and looked to the horizon. There was no doubt a large number of evil dragons, harpies, winged monkeys and thick clouds of gnats and mozzies had gathered in a swirling cloud of black evilness. Noooooo! This was her idea! Her invasion! It was to be her ruling in triumph over a cowering, conquered land of terrified slaves.

'I can see you are as happy about it as me,' added Zaff. 'I have important gigs all over this land, can't play to a crowd of charred corpses. Though they may be livelier then some of the gigs I've played in the past!'

She wasn't listening; she leapt down into the driver's seat and tearing the reins from the nasty bastard Strang, whispered in his ear. Then whipping the Pookas and horses into a flat out gallop, drove the coach straight through the startled Fellowship, scattering them out of the way of the demonic coach. Amazingly, it galloped away from the Forest of Mhmin. Robard began to cheer, a bizarre expression contorting his pale face...a smile?

Jubilation turned to shock as Jed spun around. 'Where's the apprentice?'

'Oh no! It looks like that horned bitch has kidnapped him,' answered a distressed Morven, 'but why?'

All eyes turned to Zaff.

'What's the matter? Why are you looking at me like that? I didn't take him!'

Morven stood, hands on hips. 'But you can get him back. Jed and the manky unicorn could never catch up with those Pookas.'

'I bloody well could!' interrupted an affronted highwayman, all dented alpha male pride.

'Oh no I couldn't,' muttered a truthful Cuddles.

Zaff shook his head. 'Not my problem, I saved your damn fairy forest. That's my part in your little adventure over.'

He stretched out his wings, ready to fly away to re-join his band. In a rash, impulsive move, Morven ran over to the demon and whispered in his ear. No one knew what she was saying, but Jed in particular, did not like the wide, wicked smile spreading across the demon's handsome face.

'Throw in the dashing highwayman and we have a deal, witch.'

Zaff flew high into the sky, laughing, not maniacally but in the deep, melodic voice of the fallen warrior angels he was descended from. Within seconds he was lost from sight.

'What hellish pact have you contracted with that monster?' Jed demanded, grabbing the Unwise Woman's arm.

She daren't tell him, how could she? It was a typically outrageous demand from the demon. Agreeing to a give away her soul in return for Zaff rescuing Wheatley? Morven reached up and kissed her highwayman on the lips.

'You have nothing to worry about, my love. I had my fingers crossed on both hands!'

Rafial's conquest of the Undead, one squirrel scourge that was Nutsferatu, had a rallying effect on his army. All squabbles were forgotten and a new sense of purpose and discipline spread through the ranks. As one, the great army of Darkness and Despair moved steadily through the blighted forest, no longer worried about a tiny blur of red fur and black cape leaping from the twisted and gnarled branches. Lost time was rapidly made up, even allowing for the inevitable delays caused by zombies retrieving their body parts. The renewed fervour spread to Rafial who had been on the verge of calling for a postponement of hostilities. He had reluctantly done that once before, a millennia ago, when all his evil minions had gone down with the elbow rot phage. A vexing complaint not suffered by the ghostly vapours, spectres and phantoms but they alone an army of darkness did not make. Far too diaphanous.

Soon they reached the border between the two opposing lands where the ever-night of Rafial's domain became the bright, blessed world beyond. As one, the now tightly disciplined army paused to don the regulation sunglasses. An evil minion followed by lesser lackeys marched beside the ranks of the damned carrying the cardboard boxes full of sunglasses to distribute to the night-bred troops. But the evil minion's grim, grey, gnarled face blanched to a horrified chalk-white when he opened the first box. Then the second. And the third...in fact whimpering in disbelief and terror, he tore open every box, throwing them onto the floor in despair.

Due to an appalling clerical error on his part, Rafial's administrative evil minion - now soon to be a very ex-evil minion had ordered the wrong glasses from the supplier – Ghoul About Town. Instead of suitably fearsome, intensely dark shades with cool black rims, the evil minion had taken delivery of musical day-glo Barbie-pink ones complete with plastic gems around the edge of the frames. The only thing preventing another riot was the proximity of the sun, that hated, accursed bright orb that so hurt their eyes used to ever-night. Doing their best to ignore the jingly-jangly rendition of 'You are My Sunshine' that emanated from the hideous pink specs, the hellish creatures of the night stoically donned their glasses. There were surprisingly few grumbles. In fact the banshees were openly delighted; most of them harboured a secret fantasy of wearing pink for once in their afterlives. So apart from the inevitable casualty among the ranks caused by maniacal sniggering - the gargoyles being the worst offenders, the army of Darkness and Despair was ready to invade.

Unaware of the latest fiasco to befall his army, flying high above the border, Rafial searched in vain for the opposing army. Where were they? Would they really be that stupid as to let his invading force simply stroll into their territory unhindered? Or was it a cunning trap? He flew ever wider and found evidence of Demonica's handiwork. The line of scorched villages, the charred crops and trees. 'Good girl,' he thought. At least one of his family had been productive and suitably demonic. Rafial's eyes flared with angry flames.

Somewhere down below him was his useless son Zaphael. It would not be a happy family reunion.

The army of Goodness and Light were also ready to march to battle. Still seething and grumbling about the tabards, they lined up in an almost orderly way, all were eager to get going, to do some serious demon bashing. The problem was trying to get the noble knights sorted out. Prince Pravis was supposed to be at the head of the army with his elite guard of mounted knights. Most of their horses had been rounded up and caught but any attempt to remount was met with disaster. Most of the by now very spooked animals refused to go near the ultra-shiny armour again. And any that did lost their rider again within seconds.

'I refuse to be super-glued into the saddle!' stormed an outraged Pravis to a suggestion from his serf Squarf.

'Rafial and his evil hordes will be soon knocking at the castle gate,' Squarf pointed out, 'my Liege you have to think of something - double quick!'

'This is the Army of Goodness and Light...We have wizards, wise women and seers at our disposal - call for the wisest of them all.'

Squarf shook his head, 'with respect, they are all mostly arrogant old gits. And highly competitive. Asking for the wisest will create a massive feud that will drag on till Doomsday.'

Sighing, Pravis agreed. 'Ok - just pick one out at random.' For some unknown reason his hand went up to the big painful bump on his head, he called after Squarf, 'But not that comely red-headed witch from the bogs.'

Squarf strolled down the ranks of wizards, mages and wise women; many were showing off creating dramatic flashes of lightning or conjuring colourful clouds of swirling smoke. The surrounding army were getting pissed off with this. Many now had headaches and fits of coughing from the flashy displays of magic. But no one dared complain for fear of being turned into a rancid toad or a bucket of butterbeans. Unless this army could get moving swiftly, this could end in another time-wasting squabble, the thought of Rafial's well-disciplined evil horde so close quickened the serf's step, searching the ranks for a likely wise being.

He walked briskly passing the flamboyant ranks of wizards with their show-off blue velvet robes covered with arcane silver symbols and moons, long white beards and tall, pointy hats. The highest percentage of downright frauds were here or the 'All Show and No Glow brigade' as their more cynical or jealous peers would say. Squarf also gave a wide berth to the hooded, dark robed mysterious ones whose faces couldn't be seen. They may have been the most brilliant magicians but they gave him the willies.

He also averted his eyes and quickened his step as he approached a battalion of stage magicians wearing spangled tuxedoes and top hats. There was always a risk of being splatted on by their doves or bitten by their rabbits. The wide, cheesy and dazzlingly white grins from the magicians and their sequin-clad assistants, usually ageing lasses with ostrich plumes on their heads made Squarf feel nauseous. He hoped they would have the same effect on the enemy.

The serf felt a tug at his cloak and whirled around to see no one there. Squarf shuddered, in the presence of so much magic he was feeling spooked enough.

'Sor! Ye'll be needing a wee bit of help Oi imagine. So ye will.'

A leprechaun! Oh bugger, not now! thought Squarf pretending not to hear and walked off too fast for short legs to follow. Leprechauns were the least trustworthy of all ancient spirits; they loved to take the piss out of humans. There had been enough of that all ready. 'This was going well,' he fumed to himself. There must be someone or something with the answer to the slippery knight problem. He wished Morven was here, there was something about her gentle manner that he trusted - a peaceful lass apart from clonking that prat Pravis. And though her potions were weird, they did no harm which reminded him that as Morven called herself the Unwise Woman, Squarf decided the best solution was to find a proper Wise Woman this time....

Within an hour, all the Knights were securely reunited with their wayward mounts. Their armour was still shiny but their bottoms were not, thanks to the rough but effective administrations of Olde Mistress Knotteweede. It was amazing what you could do with a large piece of wire wool.

Now well beyond the bog and the Forest of Mhmin, Demonica decided it was far enough from Zaphael to rein in the Pookas and horses who were all by now frankly completely knackered. It was time to find another form of transport, preferably flying. She spotted a dark, deeply tangled wood with a small path just wide enough for the coach and pulled the team to a shuddering halt. Actually it was only the evil minion/ nasty bastard Strang who shuddered, the woodland was shady and cool and he was only wearing a leather studded codpiece.

'Sweetheart!' Demonica demanded, 'Scan the skies. Look out for evil dragons!'

'Er, how do I know they are evil?'

'If they don't laugh at your leather studded codpiece, they are evil!'

To be on the safe side, she gave Strang a magic whistle fashioned from the thigh bone of a cursed overzealous traffic warden who once ticketed St Goodilia the Benevolent on a mercy mission among the bog chavs, the whistle was guaranteed to call down evil dragons. And clouds of gnats.

Demonica returned to her quivering, weeping prisoner. Hardly the stuff of heroes but maybe he didn't know his hidden destiny yet. At least that gave her an edge. She did her best to make her voice soothing and conciliatory. It came out as plain creepy which made Wheatley wet himself in terror. Demonica did her best to ignore the dampness spreading across her plush velvet carriage seats but she would make him pay for the desecration once she had his secret weapon under her control.

'You know I could turn you into a pile of ash stinking of brimstone with one flash of my eyes?'

Wheatley nodded, lost in his abject misery.

'But I don't want to do that. It would be a shocking waste of such a fine fellow.'

Her red taloned fingers stroked his knee; Wheatley thought he would die of fright.

'I have a proposition, one of mutual advantage.'

The apprentice's eyes widened. What on earth could a terrible she-demon want from him? He didn't want to be her sex slave and wear only a leather codpiece! His knees trembled uncontrollably, his mind sought comfort by listing all the cakes and buns in the bakery, including cinnamon Danish whirls on Wednesdays. So frightened that he didn't realise he was listing them out loud in a continuous incomprehensible litany.

A spell, an incantation! Demonica did her best to hide her fear. Heroes with hidden destinies and unknown powers were the most deadly of foes to demon kind. She backed off and attempted to smile.

'You have something in your pocket I need. In return I will not only let you go free but I promise not to harm your friends, your brave little Fellowship.'

The apprentice unsuccessfully tried to gulp back his fear rising like a choking gobstopper in his throat. 'Lady, you are very er...beautiful. But I have sworn to celibacy until my wedding night.'

Demonica laughed, a cold, hard sound like a crack breaking in a glacier. 'What a ridiculous thought! I wouldn't want anything of yours to touch anything of mine. You repulse me! What I want is the object you are holding so tightly in your pocket.'

Wheatley tightened his grip on his lucky bun. 'No way, lady. No one touches this but me!'

'Is it worth your life? Or that of the pretty witch? Or the black-clad, sad boy?'

The apprentice had to agree it was not. The lucky bun gave him such comfort, a last reminder of the perfect, warm, cosy and safe life he had abandoned to go on this insane quest. But it was still only a hard, stale Chelsea bun. The thought of anything bad happening to Morven was unbearable. Unthinkable! If he was being honest, he was rather less concerned about Robard. Warily he climbed out of the coach and reaching into his deep pocket, retrieved the bun, safely concealed in a green velvet pouch, a gift from Morven. He held it high in the air and whirled the bag around by its drawstrings, before hurling it deep into the forest. 'If you want it, you must find it first!'

Demonica screeched with fury and screaming for her boyfriend to help her, ran into the woods. Wheatley didn't hesitate, with a fleetness of foot he had no idea he possessed, he ran as far away from the monstrous female and her monstrously attired human cohort as he could.

Strang was delighted that his dragon-watching task was over. He had never been so humiliated in his life. Well, apart from earlier that day when his old partner in crime Jed Moonraven had laughed at him for being dressed as a sex slave. Strang had used the magic whistle to call three passing dragons down and they all had laughed uproariously at his codpiece. So much for Demonica's theory! Because, two were definitely evil dragons, their scales were either black or deep purple, they had bloody bits of flower fairy stuck in their teeth. And both sported badges saying 'Eveel Rools, OK?' Dragons were not known for their spelling.

To add to Strang's mortification, his exposed bottom was red raw from some particularly malicious clouds of gnats also summoned by the whistle. This was the worst lifestyle choice he had ever made. Worse than giving up a steady job with a good pension as a draper's assistant to become a notorious highwayman. And an evil bastard.

To her relief, Demonica saw the rich green of the velvet pouch hanging on the darker leaves of a holly tree. 'It's all right, boyfriend - go back to the dragon spotting. Find one - now! I want to be on my way.'

She pulled the pouch off the snagging, prickly branches and was heartened by its solidity and weight. She was right; it was an ancient sacred rune stone, forged from the elements when the newborn earth was still being formed. Created by the formless and all-powerful Ancient Ones as an enduring symbol of their dominion and a mighty weapon to all that wielded it. Before she could open the pouch and claim her treasure, the downdraught from familiar mighty wings nearly knocked her to her feet. Zaphael! What wonderful timing! She could rid her life of this accursed nuisance once and for all.

'We meet again, sis. Not by my choice. But I will get some seriously hot action if I do the Fellowship a small favour. I just want the baker dude.'

Demonica's face broke into a broad smile, already tasting the sweetness of her victory against her half-brother. 'It's all just a game to you, Zaphael. Play your vile loud music. Get laid. Score some dope.'

'Sounds good to me, Mons,' replied Zaff with a mischievous grin.

'That you are of high born demonic royalty, that you are the Crown Prince of the Land of Darkness and Despair - none of that matters to you?'

Zaff's wings shimmered with his complete disinterest. 'Nope. Not a damned thing. I couldn't give a flying f◆♏&; for any of it.'

Reaching into the velvet pouch, Demonica grabbed the hard object and thrust it towards the winged demon. 'Then die Zaphael! You are too worthless a demon to live!'

At first nothing happened. Then Zaff dropped like a stone off the tree he was perching on, to collapse shuddering on the ground. Demonica roared with delight.

She had done it! She ran over to the still twitching body, to watch and gloat over the last agonising moments of Zaff's miserable life. For good measure, she took aim with one of her high spiky heeled boots, ready to kick him in the groin.

Demonica screamed as his hand shot out, grabbed her boot and toppled her over.

The merriment in his attractive face had turned to flame-eyed, white-faced fury - briefly. Then he began to laugh. And laugh. And laugh some more. 'A bun? You actually tried to kill me with a stale old bun? Oh, Monica, you crease me up!'

Horrified, she glanced down at the sacred rune stone. It was indeed a stale old bun. Probably Chelsea or possibly even a Bath bun.

'What are you going to do? Turn me into a pile of ash stinking of brimstone?'

Zaff's hand went up to his chin, as he made a mocking show of contemplating her fate. 'Nah! What's the fun in that? I can't wait to see what you come at me with next. A festering old ham sandwich? A tin of tomato soup? Aaaarghh noooo, she's armed with a carrot and is not frightened to use it!'

'Cocky git!' seethed Demonica, more determined than ever to kill Zaff one day. But not with any confectionery or baked goods. Or any form of raw vegetable.

'A cocky git that can fly out of here,' laughed Zaff as he grabbed Wheatley's lucky bun from her grasp and rose high above the trees. 'You, sister dearest, face a long, long walk. Your evil minion has freed the Pookas and buggered off with the two horses.'

Her hand went to her neck, 'Hell's Cavity-filled Teeth!' Strang had taken her dragon-summoning whistle too!

Zaff could hear her screams of fury and humiliation rising up from the woodland to spread across the land, her cries accompanied by furious bolts of flame. Nothing hit any targets though. The wood was comprised of enchanted trees that worked out regularly. They were able to scarper out the way.

'Just not your day, sis,' quipped the demon as he scanned the ground for signs of the fleeing Wheatley.

An overcast afternoon stretched onto to a gloomy early evening. Jed walked away from the much diminished Fellowship and watched the sky. Though cloudy, at least the acrid smoke had cleared leaving an optimistic hope that the demon had sorted out his rampaging sister and perhaps the Forest of Mhmin was safe. That just left Zaff's father's mighty army. So that was all right then. A rare visitor, the shadow of doom spread fear across his soul, Jed reached into his jacket pocket and pulled out a slim hipflask with some raw, potent moonshine brewed by the more intelligent of the bog chavs. Most blew themselves up making the liquid dynamite brew but that was never enough to stop more trying to make the moonshine. Jed was glad of their suicidal stubbornness or stupidity as the burning liquid scorched the back of his throat.

Why was he here? He was not a hero. He was a notorious thief and scoundrel, a role he never regretted. Jed had no intention of being involved in a pitched battle with monsters, the politics of the land held no interest. He followed his own path in life and would thrive whatever the outcome of the conflict. But he was concerned about Morven. She was so caught up in this idiotic Fellowship notion. Being a kind and compassionate Unwise Woman dishing up her odd but harmless potions to all who sought her out was one thing, taking on the forces of evil head on was ridiculous. And fatal. And what about that mysterious pact she'd made with that damned demon? All very worrying because for all his womanising and debauchery, Jed loved her.

'Spare me a swig?'

Jed turned to see Cuddles stroll towards him. He poured some brandy into the palm of his hand and waited till the cursed unicorn lapped it up. 'It is hopeless isn't it?' The highwayman sighed. 'None of us will survive a battle with Rafial's ravening horde.'

'Of course not!' agreed Cuddles. 'That's why I am leaving. This unicorn maybe cursed but not insane. I've got room for one on my back.'

It was tempting, so very tempting. But what about his beloved? Two big beating wings agitated the evening air. Zaff had returned with an unharmed Wheatley tucked safely under his arm. What was the point of Jed hanging around, how could he compete with that? A heroic, powerful and immortal demon? Morven would be safer under Zaff's protection than his. Jed leapt onto the unicorn's back, who turned around to address him. 'Same rules as before...no spurs and don't call me Cuddles.'

Jed rode away without risking a backward glance; any sign of Morven and his resolution would shatter to pieces. He pulled his tricorne hat low over his eyes and pulled the collar of his caped great coat high. Within a few hundred yards of their departure, a puzzled Cuddles halted. 'What is that strange sound, highwayman?'

'Ignore it, my friend. It's just the sound of my conscience knocking, trying to escape. You see I've locked the self-righteous bastard away in a chest.'

'Don't tell me. She's dumped you for a younger, fitter model?'

Ex boyfriend, ex sex slave but still nasty bastard Strang turned abruptly on his heel to discover the highwayman approaching, riding of all things a manky, cursed unicorn. Or a good unicorn with personal hygiene issues.

'Sod off Moonraven!' snarled Strang, still embarrassingly scantily dressed in his leather straps and studded codpiece. With all his weight loss due to Demonica's voracious and frequent demands, the fetish gear hung loosely on him, exposing hairy, dangly objects that are best left un-described. The reader may be having lunch.

'Though I don't suppose your mistress gives out redundancy deals, so I have to deduce you have narrowly escaped.'

Nasty bastard Strang roughly yanked the horses away from the stream where they had been drinking. He had made no plans, just to get as far away from Demonica as possible. For a fleeting second, he wondered about asking Jed whether they could team up again but the thought of the humiliating mileage the highwayman would get out of his situation was unbearable. He had little dignity left and what tattered scraps he did have, Strang wanted to keep.

'Think what you want Moonraven. She is still on the warpath and after you. A small matter of a big bag of pilfered rubies not to mention vandalisation of her father's best coach.'

'What can I say?' smirked the highwayman. 'I am already a wanted man for thieving from kings, why not demonic princesses?'

Cuddles, enraged by the rough treatment of the tired, still thirsty horses, gently dumped Jed to the ground and head down charged towards the nearly clad man. Strang screamed and scrambled up the nearest, thankfully not enchanted tree.

'Call your tatty unicorn off!' he bellowed down from the branches.

'Sorry, old friend,' replied Jed with an extravagant gesture of helplessness, 'The Horned Mighty Wielder of Doom has a mind of his own. I do not control him.'

The cursed unicorn patrolled around the tree, snorting and pawing the ground in a truly impressive and menacing manner. A forgotten sense of pride flooded through him, he was an evil unicorn again and he loved it! He did not want to merely frighten the human but run him through with his horn over and over in a gory extravaganza of destruction and carnage. A pang of homesickness added to the surge of emotion coursing through the black blood in his veins. Cuddles waited until Jed had rounded up the two horses, calmed them, allowed them to drink their fill and then climb into Milady's saddle.

'I will keep this naked poltroon at bay while you take off with the horses, then I am off to join Prince Rafial's army of Darkness and Despair.'

Jed nodded, it was the right thing for the unicorn to do, Cuddles had found himself again. And so had he. 'Thank you my friend, I owe much to you.'

'And I to you. We will meet again if fate allows.'

'I look forward to that,' laughed Jed, 'it will be good to see a friendly face in Hell.'

'And what about me? Your old friend and partner in crime?' shouted nasty bastard Strang from his precarious perch high in the tree, 'Are you really going to ride off with both horses and leave me to the mercy of this crazed creature? And with no money or clothes?'

The irony was not lost on Jed but he merely tipped his tricorne hat in Strang's direction. 'I told you before, my friend. I am a much nastier bastard than you will ever be!'

Riding to the summit of a conveniently well placed small hill and halting his horse, Prince Pravis surveyed the lush valley below. The enemy's lines were at last in sight, a seething malodorous mass of misshapen dark forms resplendent with spikes and fangs. A roiling cloud of winged nightmares circled high above the army of Darkness and Despair. The stillness and discipline of the evil foe's ranks was disconcerting as was how far the enemy had advanced into their territory. Worrying close to the Forest of Mhmin, though Prince Pravis was still in a snit with the elven warriors for putting a poetry festival over preparations for warfare. Getting a bit of a battering from Rafial's rampaging zombies and trolls might shake the elves down from their lofty ivory towers...if they had any.

Squarf kicked his fat and lazy war mule to canter up the hill to join his master's surveillance.

'My Lord, it will soon be time to parley.'

The prince's face turned puce with horror, 'Parley? Parley with a damned demon?'

'It is customary,' returned the serf, 'often the matter can be settled over a nice cup of nettle tea. Or mead. And whatever Prince Rafial drinks, virgin's blood or liquid sulphur. I'm not that knowledgeable about the drinking habits of the hell spawned. Anyway, there may well be no need for bloodshed.'

'Of course there is need. The purity of the Land of Goodness and Light has been violated by these depraved creatures spewed forth from the deepest pit of Hades. I mean to put every one of them to the sword!'

Squarf expected that answer, the prince was raised to be valiant and heroic, not sensible. 'But surely preventing the needless deaths of so many of your subjects would be seen as an act of supreme valour. They will worship you for it!'

The serf thought Pravis would explode, so pumped up with patriotic fervour and desire to win his spurs in a big, bloody battle. 'An outrageous suggestion! Would you rather cower under a demonic yoke...live under the tyrannical shadow of Rafial's dark wings?'

Yeah, why not! If it meant not wearing sequinned tabards depicting petunias, thought Squarf to himself in a fit of treacherous pique. The blue clashed badly with his ruddy complexion. And the damned sequins kept falling off; he had found many of them in surprisingly intimate locations.

'Anyway, My Lord Prince. A parley is a convention of all war in this land. Talk first, exchange archly witty pleasantries that are supposed to hide a chilling threat but never do, then bandy about some insults and curses, throw down a gauntlet, storm off back to your army. Only then is it time to get down to the actual fighting. It has to be done that way. It is expected.'

Pravis sighed heavily. His manservant was right of course. There were rules of etiquette and conventions to be upheld, anything less would be an act of lawlessness and he would be no better than that debauched scoundrel Moonraven.

Summoning his mounted elite of noble knights, now all safely secure in their saddles, the prince prepared to ride down to confront Rafial for the first time.

'Don't forget a phial of Holy Water secreted about your person,' called out Squarf, 'just in case you insult the Prince of Darkness and Despair a tad too much.'

Pravis nodded and patted his tabard to show it was already on his person. The thought of being turned into a pile of ash stinking of brimstone did not appeal.

Over in the opposing camp, Prince Rafial was equally ill at ease. 'How many times do I have to go through with this charade?' He moaned to his evil minion personal assistant. A highly prestigious though short-term position. 'Millennia have passed yet I still have to pretend to be challenged by some jumped-up little prick of a human prince. It is all so tedious.'

The minion wisely kept his counsel; he had stepped over what remained of his predecessor on his way to the prince's side, an evil minion who had unwisely pointed out that conventions must be upheld.

'Find me a suitably impressive equine to ride down to the parley tent. My enemy will be mounted on a prancing snow white stallion. I need something to top that.'

Quaking with terror, the evil minion bowed and scraped his way out of the demon's presence. What in The Deepest cesspit of Hades could he find? All the cursed unicorns had been eaten by the cave trolls, their aunties and the ogres. Princess Demonica had stolen all the Pookas. There wasn't even an evil Pantomime Horse left since malevolent clothes moths attacked the last one.

Head in hand, he walked past the lines of creatures searching for something remotely rideable that wasn't a dragon. It was considered bad form to use a winged conveyance for a parley, they always blew away the special tents and banners that appeared as if by magic exactly halfway between the two opposing armies. Then just when he thought he was doomed to become a pile of ash stinking of brimstone, the evil minion was given a miracle. He nearly said 'Thank God for that!' Which would have been wildly inappropriate and earned him a duffing up from the nearest evil creature. There was his salvation! A cursed unicorn standing in the ranks next to the wraiths. Manky, with its coat colour a bit close to a dirty dark grey than jet black but a cursed unicorn all the same. It needed a good makeover and perhaps some magic to transform it, but Rafial had his ride!

None too gently, Zaff dropped the unharmed apprentice in front of Morven. To his relief, Wheatley's embarrassment was spared, for the flight across the plains had dried out his damp britches. The demon himself alighted beside her, a wicked gleam in his dark eyes. He was not in the slightest interest in collecting souls for the big boss downstairs but did enjoy a bit of stirring humans up, they fell for it every time. Zaff lost count how many idiots 'sold' their souls to him to be rich and famous and were now selling used tissues to other beggars. Or cold-calling telephone salesmen unaware they had no souls to trade. Zaff glanced around eager to see the elf maiden again, he had realised as he flew back to the Fellowship that he couldn't stop thinking about her. It must be some sort of enchantment but one he liked.

'He's gone,' snapped Morven, she had no time for the demon's antics now. 'Jed and the unicorn have disappeared!'

'Good trick, could come in useful.'

Morven's green eyes flashed with grief-fuelled fury. 'This is serious. He has abandoned the Fellowship! Oh screw it, who cares about that, he's abandoned me!'

The Unwise Woman's strength and courage failed her, she began to weep. Wheatley attempted to put his arms around her but she brushed him aside, instead dropping her head on Zaff's well-muscled chest.

Before the startled demon could react, a gang of armed men surrounded the greatly reduced Fellowship. Or the closest equivalent. The elf warrior attempted to raise her bow but was knocked to the ground by what appeared to be a big, burly, hairy man in a dress.

'Muriel!' gasped Morven, 'what the hell are you doing? And leave the elf alone! She is on our side!'

Morven glanced around, most of the troops with their weirdly tacky pale blue and cerise sequinned tabards were from the mummer troop. Their leader, Salatious Prink stepped forward and gave a low mocking bow.

'Why, my Lady of the Swamps, we meet again. And I see you have our defecting songbird with you.'

He stepped over to Robard and gave him a painful clip around the ear. 'I love this boy, treated him like my own son. Without our best troubadour, we bombed at the castle. Voted the worst performance of St Epiligia Revels ever. The shame! The ignominy! Our punishment was to join the army.'

Prink glared balefully at the Goth lad. 'You brought us to this misfortune. But now I have captured a scouting party for the enemy, maybe Prince Pravis will let us go as a reward.'

'What rubbish! We are a noble Fellowship, trying to stop this war,' responded an outraged Wheatley.

The leader of the mummers walked up and down the captured Fellowship, his face contorted with scorn. 'Fellowship? What kind of fool do you think I am? You have a witch, a bloody great bat-winged demon, you have a black clad emu and a supernatural archer dressed like a bog chav. I'm not sure what the tall man is supposed to be. A shape shifter? A very fresh zombie? It makes no odds. You are the enemy.'

The Unwise Woman tried to stay calm, she was avowed to cause no harm but if she did nothing, Zaff would blast these buffoons into several piles of ash stinking of brimstone. At the moment, their posturing merely amused him. One step too far and it would be zap, sizzle, plumpf!

'We are indeed a mis-matched band, but we have already beaten Princess Demonica and saved the Forest of Mhmin from being turned to charcoal. And that demon has just saved the life of an innocent human.'

'A human with a killer bun in his pocket!' laughed Zaff. 'Watch out! He's lethal!'

'Shut it man,' bleated Robard, 'you are not helping!'

'I am immortal, these clowns can't hurt me,' shrugged an unconcerned Zaff.

'But they can hurt me,' Cylphie murmured, gazing directly into the demon's face, her lustrous eyes brimming with crystal tears. 'You wouldn't want to lose the chance to... you know what with me...'

Zaff would not let Cylphie be harmed and pulled the elf close to his side, wrapping his wings around her before glaring at the newcomers with his angry eyes flaring dangerously.

That was not helping either. Morven didn't want the demon to blast away at these fools, their only crime was to be stupid. Well, not quite their only crime. Muriel's dress clashed horribly with his sallow complexion.

Tall, hooded and ominous Necromancers bearing long poles from which flew black and gothically tattered banners emblazoned by grinning fanged skulls, walked in front of their dark prince's procession. They in turn were flanked by jet-skinned, cold-eyed Drow mercenaries from the UnderRealm. A doom-laden dirge accompanied the party, played by eternally damned musicians, mostly members from split up boy bands and purveyors of novelty Christmas number ones.

Rafial rode down to the Tent of Neutrality on a high-stepping jet black unicorn. Fire flashed from its eyes, its long, twisted horn glittered like black diamonds. Huge ravens and sharp fanged vampire bats circled in formation above them, ten sleek werewolves padded at his side. Rafial knew how to make an entrance. He had plenty of practice.

It was Prince Pravis' first time and it showed. Oh, he had the fluttering banners borne aloft by his mounted elite, their armour still glinting in the gathering gloom. But the petunia emblem rather watered down the effect. As did all the slipping and sliding. Hours in the saddle had undone the good work of Olde Mistress Knotteweede and her wire wool; the knights' bottoms were getting shiny again. Tightly holding the reins of their highly excitable warhorses and bearing long, heavy poles was taking a toll. Muttered oaths and curses combined with lopsided and red-faced knights did not make a good impression. Prince

Rafial was able to cock his leg over the withers of the unicorn, sit back, fold his arms and wait for a disaster. The demon did not have long to wait. As Pravis pulled his stallion to a halt, the demon drawled, 'shall we get this farce over and done with?' Gracefully alighting from the unicorn without waiting for an answer.

Pravis nodded a terse agreement and attempted to dismount, but his backside was so slippery that he slipped off sideways to land in a crumpled, tinny heap on the ground. Mocking sniggers from the werewolves were bad enough, hidden giggles from the normally grim and austere Necromancers were humiliating but a burst of nervous guffaws from his own knights was beyond bearing.

'How very unfortunate, need a hand getting up, old chap?' said an amused Rafial in his deep, melodious voice.

The prince growled in fury and embarrassment, brushing away the proffered demonic hand. He would get to his feet alone, even if it took till Doomsday. Why had he insisted on the correct procedure and left Squarf behind. Noble knights only? They were next to useless.

While all the talk was going on between the leaders, some used the opportunity to switch sides. In truth, it was mainly across to the Army of Darkness and Despair, clearly the winners in terms of menace, numbers and discipline. The surviving time-share salesmen lead by Vinny Grimes were first to bolt. Followed by many wizards. One of the tuxedoed stage magicians tried to defect but one glance at his cheesy grin and he was chucked straight back where he was beaten up by his elderly glamorous assistant and three rabbits for being abandoned.

The only defector to the Army of Goodness and Light was a couple of ghostly vapours. But they made little difference, wafting about and moaning mournfully didn't count for much in a pitched battle.

'We meet at last Prince Nobbit...' Rafial lounged indolently in a highly ornate gothic throne, a leg resting over the arm. He picked at one fang with a long, stiletto sharp dagger. How the throne and the large oak table before it got there was another unsolvable mystery. Prince Pravis ignored his own official royal chair and chose to stand. For three reasons. He did not want to go through the humiliation of trying to get up in the slippery armour; one embarrassing scramble about on the ground, finally hauling himself up with a stirrup iron was bad enough. Secondly, the chair had received a make- over from his mother's interior designers. All royal chairs were once gold with a tasteful and understated oak leaf and ivy gilded carving. Not any more. This one had been rubbed down with wire-wool then painted with a bright day-glo lilac crackle glaze, stencils added of pale blue petunias which were picked out with gold and had emerald green sequined leaves. Lovely.

The third reason was he wanted to look proud and heroic. Virtuous and valiant. Morally superior as the champion of Goodness and Light, towering over this louche and loathsome demon. In his golden armour, his long blond hair and perfectly chiselled features, he knew he looked the part. Once the battle commenced, Prince Pravis would prove he had the courage and fighting skills that would make him a legend.

'I am Crown Prince Pravis, heir and champion to the land of Goodness and Light. *King* Nobbit the Tireless was my great, great, great, great grandfather.'

'Whatever,' yawned an indifferent demon. All this endless line of human rulers were prats.

'I believe it is customary to have an ironically worded toast at this stage in the proceedings,' seethed Pravis, desperate to smite the demon with his specially blessed broadsword. It had been anointed by a relic of St Pugnacious, the saint of righteous battle against the forces of demonic evil. Though St Pugnacious was often wrongly evoked for any major barney. Theologists decided that was why so many armies lost despite being far superior in manpower and weaponry...it had pissed the notoriously short-tempered saint off.

Shuddering at the dragon and skeleton themed goblet, the cup made from the top of an upturned human skull, Pravis handed the demon fresh virgin's blood, while he raised a plain golden chalice of blessed altar wine, to ram home his righteousness. Prince Rafial took a swig then leapt to his feet, spluttering and gagging.

'Fool! Are you trying to poison me? An Immortal! I can turn you into a pile of ash stinking of brimstone in a second!'

Genuinely astonished and understandably alarmed, Pravis stuttered an apology.

'Absolutely not, Prince Rafial! I would never stoop to such low, underhand tactics to beat my foe. I am a noble champion, I look forward to meeting you in pitched one to one combat on the battle field.'

Pravis retrieved the goblet and gingerly sniffed at the dregs of its contents. The unmistakable smell of fresh tomato juice. It seemed the only experts that could be found on matters demonic were a sect of Vegetarian Satanists.

'Enough of this nonsense!' stormed Rafial. 'Concede now. I outnumber your forces in every measure. Save the lives of your people and surrender.'

'Never!' Pravis growled. 'We have good on our side. Light will always overcome Darkness!'

'What - like this?' Rafial leant over and snuffed out a candle with his fingers.

'To battle!' declared Prince Pravis.

'To an utter rout,' replied Prince Rafial.

Before both rulers could storm out of the Tent of Neutrality, a shiny knight, his flamingo crowned helmet under his arm, sidled up to Pravis and whispered in his ear. The prince's face broke into a wide smile of delight and triumph.

'I believe it is my turn to demand that you concede, demon. Which you will as soon as you see what awaits you outside this tent.'

He hauled back the flap to reveal a sorry looking group of prisoners, mostly human and astonishingly, a heavily chained winged demon.

Rafial gasped at the sight of his son Zaphael in chains. Why was he held captive? He could break free at any time if he wanted to. The prince looked him directly in the eye and saw the glint of mischief and a familiar wicked grin. Zaphael was playing a game with his captors. Relieved that all was well, Rafial had time to reflect. He had forgotten how handsome his son was and also realised that his boy's obsession with messing around with humans and playing in a rock band meant he was no threat to his reign over the Land of Darkness and Despair. Both human and demon societies had many tales of ambitious sons murderously overthrowing their fathers to gain power. Rafial did not have to worry about his son. Just his daughter!

'So - what are you showing me that will make me concede?'

Pravis's eyes bulged with disbelief. 'Durr - I have your only son and heir in chains? And many of your loyal evil minions, caught as spies in my land.'

'They mean nothing to me, do with them what you will.' Replied Rafial with a convincing show of complete indifference. Indeed, the bedraggled group with Zaphael were all indeed complete strangers.

Zaff smiled. Morven kept quiet. The others began to shout in outrage.

'I am not with the evil army, I am a misunderstood dark poet!'

'I am a noble elven warrior from the Forest of Mhmin!'

'I am the wielder of the lucky bun that defeated Princess Demonica!'

'Take them away, lock them up securely. I do not have time for nonsense from a load of head cases,' muttered a deflated Prince Pravis.

'To battle!' He declared again.

The Tent of Neutrality was silent. A bemused Rafial had already gone back to his army.

Insulted, thrown roughly into a holding tent, the bruised and battered and singularly unsuccessful Fellowship struggled to come to terms with the injustice. Their courageous crusade against the forces of evil had been tossed back in their faces. Even the Prince of the Damned didn't want them. Not even his own son.

Cylphie made sure she was first to comfort the young demon, despite being tightly bound, wriggled across the floor. 'I'm so sorry Zaff...your own father...that must have been so hurtful.'

Zaff smiled and attempted an indifferent shrug despite the tight and heavy chains, 'No worries, babe. It's cool.'

'None of this is cool!' Wheatley exploded. 'This whole week has been utter pants!'

He had been cast out of his home and comfortable safe life, got stuck in a boggart-infested mire, had his lucky bun eaten and regurgitated by a manky unicorn. He had been threatened by a female demon, taken on a terrifying flight in the arms of another hell-born thing of the night, accused of spying and treachery by the Prince of the Land of Goodness and Light. And now he was bound hand foot and chucked onto a filthy floor. Could it get any worse? He glanced longingly at the new love of his life, one he would happily give up his life long interest in quality baked goods for. Her withering look at his pathetic outburst cut through him like a knife.

As did the real knife cutting through the canvas beside him and a familiar face peered in.

'Jed!'

The apprentice's heart slunk to a new low as the highwayman tore open a flap of canvas and stepped in, rushing to cut Morven free. 'Quickly my lovely...we've only got seconds to get away.'

The Unwise Woman allowed her bonds to be cut but wouldn't leave. 'Not without the others! This is a Fellowship'

'This is a farce!' Jed hissed, he didn't give a stuff about the others - especially that accursed demon. 'I can only rescue you - I have only one spare horse and little time.'

Ignoring him, Morven grabbed the knife and cut the others free. 'There's nothing I can do about those chains, Zaff.'

'Sorry old chap,' shrugged an unconcerned Jed, 'Now let's go...now!'

'I said it was cool,' replied Zaff, 'they can't harm me, I'm immortal.'

'I'll stay with him!' Announced Cylphie predictably.

Jed grabbed Morven's arm and hauled her out of the tent. 'The supernaturals can sort themselves out, we are mere humans - lets go!'

'We all go or none at all!' proclaimed Morven proving once and for all she was indeed the Unwise Woman.

'You do realise what will happen to me if I get caught.'

Morven's eyes widened with horror at her foolish posturing, she tried to apologise but it was too late. Armed guards surrounded the tent. The men pushed Jed and Morven back into the tent and began to argue who was going to claim the huge bounty on the highwayman's head. Especially the one who owed Vinny Grimes for an insurance premium on his stone clad hovel in the Costa Lotte.

Doing her best to get close to her beloved scoundrel, Morven's eyes streamed with tears. 'I should never have doubted you, my love. You risked your life to rescue me and I have ruined it! They will hang you and it was all my fault!'

'This is getting way too heavy!' moaned Robard.

'Sigh,' sighed Wheatley, knowing Morven would never weep like that over him.

Cylphie looked at Zaff not just with longing but with expectancy.

'Damn,' the demon muttered, 'this is no longer any fun.'

He stood up, snapping the chains, shaking them off as if they were made of flimsy paper, stretched out his magnificent wings which ripped the tent to shreds. 'Now which of you gentlemen wants to be the first to be turned into a pile of ash stinking of brimstone?'

The guards fled shrieking leaving the startled Fellowship alone and free.

'Let's scarper!' Shouted Jed.

Zaff carried Cylphie and flew up into the darkening sky while Robard with his precious book and Wheatley and his lucky bun jumped up onto the bay gelding. All instinctively headed in the same direction, the only place they all had shared. Morven's hovel in the bog.

Jed reached down, ready to haul Morven onto the grey mare's bony back. But she stepped back and shook her head. 'Ride like the wind my love, you must escape but I will stay here. If there is a battle to come, I must treat the wounded, comfort the dying. It is my duty as a healer.'

The highwayman's dark blue eyes flashed with surprise and concern. 'Are you crazy?'

'No.' Morven gave a brittle laugh, not really masking her own fear. She whacked Milady's bony rump sending the mare bolting away in a startled gallop and cried out after the fast disappearing Jed... 'Just Unwise!'

The setting sun cast a ruddy glow over the battlefield, dramatically glinting fire off the knights' shiny armour and highlighting the glistening, dripping fangs of the werewolves. Both armies faced each other, close enough to smell each other's breath. A fact not relished by either side. Especially as the wood nymphs had been eating wild garlic sandwiches and the zombies had pickled troll eyes for lunch, though in truth every part of them stank to high heaven.

With the sun disappearing over the horizon, the Army of Darkness and Despair were able to discard their garish pink sunglasses which landed on the ground in a discordant cacophony of un-synchronised verses of 'You are my Sunshine.' Their enemies flinched at the bizarre and incongruous sound. A good start and a sign the pink glasses weren't such a disastrous idea after all.

Steely glares from the Lone, Wandering and Mysterious heroes locked onto to malevolent glowers from the gargoyles. Obscene gesturing from the Flower Fairies was met with a rude response involving bananas from the Union of Scary Clowns. Taunts of 'Pravis is a Pillock' rose from the evil ranks and also from the army of Goodness and Light. Actually, it was all from the army of Goodness and Light. No one taunted Rafial, not with his readiness to add to the carbon footprint.

All was ready for the catastrophic battle to commence...

Only nothing happened. The half-hearted taunting gradually lost impetus, stopped and a tense silence spread across the still pristine battlefield. Then a pink and silver maned unicorn let out such a loud and spectacular fart it caused a ripple of nervous laughter to spread through Pravis' army. At such a hair trigger tense moment, such a thing could normally spark off a sudden charge but nothing moved, even the evil butterflies stopped their threatening fluttering. There wasn't even a pre-emptive strychnine laced custard pie being lobbed, the Union of Scary Clowns were always the first to let rip.

In truth, the Army of Goodness and Light were too scared of their grim, hell-spawned foe that they refused to move. And the Army of Darkness and Despair would not move because of the orders from their demonic prince earlier. His exact words, 'I will not have fighting! Not in my army!' still rang in their ears or nearest equivalent.

Overhead the two opposing battalions of flying creatures amassed, ready for battle. But the long delay created problems for those circling in readiness above their armies, some had to go to the loo with unfortunate knock-on effects for those beneath them. Others were getting tired being airborne for so long.

On Rafial's side, the air was agitated by the mighty wing beats of huge evil dragons, of many harpies, flying apes and gargoyles. And lesser though no less determined wing beats from the vampire bats, menacing moths and evil butterflies. On the side of good, there were kindly dragons, flying horses, battalions of fairies. The downdraught from all these circling, flapping wings grew and grew till it became of hurricane proportions, as the bored winged ones tried to out do each other by showing off their flying manoeuvres.

Beneath them the trees in the Forest of Mhmin bent and swayed alarmingly, the enchanted trees hanging onto the normal ones for support. There was nothing anyone on the ground could do to stop the powerful wind but hang on tightly to their headgear. Mostly in vain as a wave of flying flamingo topped helmets, wizards' pointy hats, scary clown wigs and zombie ears tumbled across the battlefield.

The sky darkened as a huge, spectacular and glittery cloud comprising all the floating gossamer and mysterious silver bits from the forest - and the abandoned pink sunglasses - was wafted up by the wind. Carried on the stirred up air towards the armies, it circled around, mesmerising the onlookers beneath it. Then it plummeted down, enveloping both armies in a sparkling, pink and gossamer laden cloud. At first nothing happened. The

Army of Goodness and Light became even more like
ballroom dancers with glitter added to their sequins. The
Army of Darkness and Despair tried to brush the ghastly
glitter off. Except the banshees who thought it added to
their allure and some wraiths and ghostly vapours who felt
a tad more substantial.

It began with one loud, snot-laden sneeze. Then
another and another. Soon explosive sneezing crippled
both sides, their eyes streaming uncontrollably.

'Retreat!' howled a near-blinded Pravis.

'Retreat!' commanded a furious Rafial from his high
vantage point in the sky as his once disciplined force
descended into a helpless, sneezing rabble. Creatures on
both sides were falling into each other blindly, picking
fights with whoever wiped their noses on them.

In complete disarray the armies bolted for their home
bases without raising a finger or hoof or tentacle in anger.

In the tumultuous scramble to escape the glittering wind,
there had been the inevitable casualties. Broken
fingernails among the flower fairies, a tragedy to their
vanity, already bruised knights taking yet more tumbles
from their bolting horses, near trampled magician's
rabbits needing comfort and carrots. A traumatised
unicorn with its magnificent tail bitten right off, though
this was a case of suspected friendly fire. Morven and the
others of her wise womankind moved amongst them,
dispensing care and unguents.

Having run out of her famously useless woodlouse, fig
roll, lemon curd and shaving foam bruise salve, Morven
decided it was time to slip away unnoticed and rejoin her

highwayman back home at the hovel. Her plans were interrupted by the unwelcome arrival of Prince Pravis and Squarf.

'I told you she was a good 'un!' announced the serf with a broad smile on his squashed-up features. 'Look how she is helping our side's casualties.'

Pravis was glad to concede he was wrong about the more than comely flame-haired witch. If only she had been of royal blood, then he could forsake his chivalrous vow of chastity and insist she married him. He bowed his head to thank her for her work among the wounded. 'Good Mistress Morven. You have travelled a long way to administer healing and kindness to my army, you have my gratitude.'

Bowing low in feigned respect, Morven smiled prettily. 'It is my calling as a woman of the Craft, my sacred vow is to do no harm, help birth babies and heal the sick.'

'Then you also must have ancient and arcane knowledge. What exactly is this extraordinary stuff?' demanded Pravis as he tried in vain to brush off the glitter from his armour, hoping it wouldn't start off another fit off coughing.

'You really don't want to know,' sighed Morven, averting her eyes. She had enough of war and only wanted to enjoy the peace by celebrating with at least a whole week in bed with her highwayman.

'I am the prince of a victorious army, I demand you tell me, witch!'

Still a pompous prat then, she thought, 'Its magic dust from the Forest of Mhmin, that's all you need to know.'

'Then we must gather it all up in stout barrels and keep it safe within the castle vaults. That vile demon may chance his arm with another dastardly attack and this time we will be ready to repel him!'

Morven walked away, a warm throaty laugh escaping as the Army of Goodness and Light spent the rest of the night gathering up armfuls of a millennia's worth of dried fairy snot. The filthy little madams never did use hankies.

Aftermath

Footsore, exhausted from seething and hating, Demonica finally found some transport, an enchanted Larch that had skipped some of its workout sessions to have long lie-ins. With the threat of being turned into a large pile of ash stinking of brimstone, it reluctantly permitted the demonic female to sit high up in its branches as it slowly lurched towards the Land of Darkness and Despair. The tree's frustratingly slow pace at least gave her time to think. Maybe her father would now see her potential for creating mayhem and allow her to rule their desolate ever-night land. Let him enjoy his books and list making. For by now surely even Rafial would realise that his son Zaff was a pointless waste of skin?

Whatever the outcome, Demonica used the tedious slow journey to plot and plan her many revenges. Starting with those two wretched humans, her first ex boyfriend, Strang and the bun toting Wheatley would be toast for betraying and humiliating her. As would that highwayman scum for stealing her rubies and vandalising her coach. Ok, technically still her father's coach. And she would have to search the remote and mystic places of the world to find a way of killing Zaff, preferably as slowly and painfully as she could. The thought of this revived her spirits. The battle with her hated half-brother was not over - it had not yet begun!

Apart from making pithy comments pointing out the obvious to the idiots that comprised the Fellowship, what purpose did Robard play in this saga? That's what the gloomy black clad boy pondered as he flicked through his precious grimoire of maudlin poetry. He hoped he was more than a plot contrivance, maybe his own hidden destiny lay in future adventures?

In the meantime though he would not show it, he enjoyed helping the Unwise Woman set up a New Age hovel on the edge of the Forest of Mhmin, so much more pleasant a location then that filthy mire. The forest itself had a great mystical atmosphere, especially at night when the sparkling, ethereal mists intertwined through the trees. He would wander in there and write his own wonderfully dark and angst-ridden poetry.

Poetry that the elves and other magical forest dwellers actually seemed to appreciate. They had even given him the slot in their next poetry festival normally taken up by the miming moles who had finally discovered the annual appreciation for their great works of art was merely patronisation and that no one understood what they were portraying. Angry and humiliated, they had burrowed off muttering colourful and anatomically graphic mole-ish curses, including one that included a sock, some pickled butterbeans and a soupspoon.

From her vantage point on a newly built roof garden on a Petunia Castle battlement, Queen Hemelda was able to catch the first sighting of their returning army. Her green tinged perma-tanned face broke into a pained, thin smile, her taut features restricted by recent phage injections, but inside she was beaming. At the sight of her son at the head of the troops, she jumped up and down in delight causing the newly laid and varnished decking to creak in protest. Her glorious golden boy was home!

Hemelda was also delighted that all the army still sported their petunia-emblazoned tabards, strangely even more sparkly. A victory for co-ordination as well as over the forces of evil. Later she was to shudder in horror that many of the ill-bred ingrates had used their tabards as hankies and worse, but for now she was overjoyed.

Prince Pravis glanced up at his wildly waving mother and saluted her heroically as he returned with Squarf at the head of his triumphal army, his troops now burdened down with barrels of the miraculous magic dust. Except for the defecting ghostly vapours who wafted about getting in the way and moaning.

Tonight the halls would resound with celebration and feasting. Troubadours would sing out extravagant odes and paeans of praise to his courage and resolve. He would go down in legend as the saviour of the Land of Goodness and Light. The only downside was he had no gory trophies to make the ladies of the court swoon in feigned shock and to impress his father. Rafial's head on a plate would have been the most desirable. Failing that, a zombie's still moving arm or the wings of a flying monkey. He would also have loved to have seen Moonraven's corpse swinging from a gibbet. All in good time.

The only one not to enjoy the fun was his loyal serf Squarf. The prince had him detained in the castle's dungeons for the duration of the feast. It seemed a curmudgeonly act but a necessary one. The serf would inevitably get very drunk during the celebrations, and all sorts of bizarre versions of the prince's quest and subsequent battle against the forces of evil would emerge. Rubbishy tales of the prince being taunted by a boggart and felled by dragon's poo. Or falling off his horse at the feet of the demon prince. Who would believe such tosh? But it was best to be on the safe side and avoid a PR disaster.

Returning to his little town in triumph, Wheatley was haled a true hero and borne through the streets on the shoulders of the cheering townsfolk. A precarious journey as one after another tripped over their modish long pointy shoes, nearly pitching their new champion onto the dung covered cobbles. Wheatley was beyond caring, his heart and soul soared with his achievement. He had finally found his hidden destiny. He had singlehandedly taken on the appalling Demonica and faced her down, armed only with a stale lucky bun. The demon Zaff's considerable contribution was mysteriously lost in translation.

Wheatley was given a bakery of his own by the grateful citizens and he took on many young apprentices to cover the shortfall if one of them decided to go on a quest of his own. In fact he bought an insurance policy from Vinny Grimes in case they all should leave at the same time on the next Feast of St Epiligia.

Surrounded by the warm, yeasty smell of fresh baked bread and cakes, Wheatley was at last content. But not happy, only having Morven at his side would make him happy. But her compassionate and foolish heart was still lost to that rakish ne'er do well Jed Moonraven. His unrequited passion for the lovely redheaded witch was not hopeless. He was a patient man. One day soon she would lose her highwayman to the noose and he, Wheatley would be waiting to comfort her. Show her the love of a decent, faithful man. Until then, he ended every evening and started every day touching the lucky bun in a glass cabinet in its place of honour above his bed. Sighing and wishing to be with the lovely Morven.

In the course of time, Jed's fickle but swift mare grew considerably larger behind the girth area. After one particularly risky raid on a coach bearing Queen Hemelda's portly sister - Princess Delicatia, which yielded the highwayman a fortune's worth of fine gems, he narrowly escaped being caught. Milady's exceptional turn of foot had failed her. For the first time she sweated up and blew hard mid gallop. A worried highwayman took her straight to Morven for some healing herbs, to be greeted with peals of warm laughter. Jed's mare was pregnant! A few days later, she presented him with a pitch black colt foal with huge sulphurous eyes and a magnificent black-diamond horn, its first act after standing up on wobbly legs was to glare at Jed and swear at him in fluent Irish. As stated earlier, Milady was a fickle mare.

Salacious Prink and Muriel escaped their unwilling posting into the Army of Goodness and Light and bolted to the Costa Lotte where Vinny Grimes found them work at a beach side cabaret. However the sight of Muriel in a low-cut and very tight pink and orange flamenco dress caused a riot among the outraged locals and they were forced to disguise themselves and run a Punch and Judy show on the beach to earn enough groats to return home. They are believed to be planning a comeback tour.

Zaff had rejoined his band, for now with the war that never was over, Shrike Hell's full tour was restored. Refreshed from his adventure, the young demon was ready to rock hard all night with the band which was still without a lead singer. The queue of would-be vocalists had not surprisingly dried up once news spread of the unfortunate fiery fate of Deathrall Lorde.

The last anyone in the Fellowship had seen of Zaff was when the demon immerged from the forest, buttoning up his leather jeans and wreathed in weary but triumphal smiles after a tumultuous night of marathon love making with Cylphie. He had immediately flown away with his beautiful elven lover in his arms in a tight embrace to seek out Shrike Hell and resume his place as the band's infamous lead guitarist. Keeping half an eye open for Demonica of course, she might lob a lethal can of mushy peas or a dangerous baguette at him at any time.

Life in the Forest of Mhmin returned to normal, indeed with the temporary lack of sparkly bits floating amidst the wafting gossamer and subsequent marked decline in hay fever, all was going very well. The resident elves of course were shocked and saddened that their fair maiden hero wandering the world beyond in disguise had not returned but had shacked up with a demon. It was the first big scandal to affect the noble and lofty elves. Well, since the best forgotten incident when the Elvin Lady, Erinora had a short-lived affair with a centaur. They parted due to an obvious physical incompatibility.

That one of their kind actually preferred a life of mindless hedonism and debauchery with a foul demon created a ripple of refined shock and elegant distaste. Meetings resumed in the Crystal Temple to discuss whether to rescue their errant elf Cylphie from entrapment caused by obvious dark enchantment. But at least the old belief that magic protected the forest had been strengthened. And beyond the almost heated debates within the Crystal Temple, all was calm and serene again.

Serene was not a word applicable to the St Epiligia Pedants, still nursing their bruises - mainly on their backsides after the shameful rout at the Boggarts' picket line. But being hard-line Pedants, they could not let the matter drop. Indeed, they had never been so determined, so galvanised and so angry. Until they were vindicated, they would protest to their graves. And beyond if need be! They had time to plot and plan their next move. Earnest letter writing to the newspapers was not working, handing out leaflets and conducting door-to-door surveys was hazardous to life and limbs.

The Pedants retired to a distant cave and in the dust, gloom and inevitable piles of bat poo, made their plans for a spectacular protest, something so outrageous they would be listened to at last.

Or die trying as martyrs to their righteous cause of truth and wisdom.

And deep in their riverside burrows, the voles quietly resumed a normal rodenty existence. Scurrying about, living out their unremarkable small lives. Ignoring the supercilious but actually downright jealous sneering of stoats and the surly mutters of the miming moles determined to hold a grudge against the whole world. A life concerned only with finding grubs and worms to eat and raising bijou little volettes.

Until twelve moons had waxed and waned in the night sky and the dawn of the next Feast of St Epiligia.

Part Two
The Pagan Feast of Wolfsbane

Excitement and expectation hung as tangible as an over-inflated badger bladder ready to pop outside the Ye Olde Moote Hall, the heart of Burpinton-Not-On-Sea's town centre. The crowds had started queuing at dawn, bringing thick but smelly sheepskins to sit on and flagons of ale and mead to while away the long wait. The very long wait. The notorious death thrash band Shrike Hell were not due to perform until midnight but none of their fans wanted to be stuck at the back even though the mosh pit was so dangerous. Not just from the odd fatal stabbing from pogoing Vikings who still refused to remove their horned helmets. That was bad enough, but the band's lead guitarist could get carried away sometimes at the height of his spectacular performances. The risk of being turned into a pile of ash stinking of brimstone was very high, mainly because the band's axeman was a full blood winged demon. A royal crown prince of Hell no less, who had turned his back on all that infernal torturing of the damned to become part of Shrike Hell. So, not that much a change of direction.

Backstage, as the roadies grumpily bustled about doing all the vital and important work of setting up the stage, the band themselves were in disarray. Five minutes after midnight was the official starting point for the Pagan Feast of Wolfsbane, one of the most important nights in the calendar. It began a week of ancient and esoteric celebrations of the start of winter, including the hazardous but enthusiastically enjoyed pumpkin hurling, earwax flanging and bounce the weasel's wig. But there was no sign of their lead guitarist, the charismatic and handsome demon Zaff.

The band's leader, Lennie called an impromptu meeting. All had toured as Shrike Hell for many years, except their increasingly nervous new lead singer. The band had a bad reputation for getting through so many over the years and Vic Blood-Rage knew it. As the band also knew his real name, Desmond Ainsley Pheeps.

'Right, fess up. Does anyone know where the winged wonder is? Anyone holding back on me will get a right old bollicking.'

After a few minutes boot staring and shuffling about on be-jeaned bottoms, the drummer Tofus Grossle-Snerd, which was his real name, slowly raised a hand. 'I think I know, Len. I saw him earlier over in the park having a major domestic with his old lady.'

'Great! That's all we bloody need,' muttered Lennie, nostalgic for the good old days when Zaff was fancy free and celibate, refusing to bonk any humans for fear of siring a monstrous half-breed like his sister Demonica. Now he had an elven lover, his behaviour had become erratic and unpredictable. And more dangerous. Cylphie, the elf ex-maiden was stunning and feisty, anyone that annoyed her or came on to her risked Zaff's wrath and the ever likely fate of becoming a pile of ash stinking of brimstone. It was bad for the band's PR and diminished the fan base.

A furious Cylphie was perched high up at the very top of a particularly tall tree, where her demon lover has placed her. Making it impossible for her to storm off in a hissy fit. He flew around her, trying to get her to see sense.

'Sweetness, it was nothing! There is no one in my life except for you.'

'A groupie? You screwed a groupie! I am so angry I could explode!'

Zaff hovered in front of her, worried sick, not knowing much about elven metabolism beyond enjoying her elegant and beautiful body and voracious libido that almost matched his own. 'Errrr...Is that likely to happen?'

'Maybe - so you'd better keep out of the way!' Cylphie yelled, too angry to look at him, knowing one glimpse of his dark beauty and she might weaken her resolve and the bastard would get away with it again. She loved him so much, that was the problem. Too much to share him with his hordes of crazed fans. As for the demon, was he capable of loving anyone? The jury was still out on that. He could certainly shag for Hell though. No! She forced aside all thoughts of that, her treacherous body would force her to cave in, knowing making up for their rows was so amazing, so mind bendingly, earth shatteringly good.

She was being a complete little fool of course. Morven, the Unwise Woman of Fuggis Mire had warned her that being in love with the ultimate bad boy was madness, heartbreak waiting to happen. Morven herself had years of experience, being the lover of notorious highwayman Jed Moonraven, a commitment-phobic womaniser. But Jed adored his flame- haired witch. Worshiped the ground she walked on. Cylphie did not have the comfort of knowing whether Zaff loved her or was even capable of love. He was an evil demon, one who had strolled up from Hell after all.

'I didn't do it!' pleaded Zaff in all honesty. 'It is just that muckraking tabloid printing lies to sell papers!'

Outraged, Cylphie held up the offending newspaper, The Daily Excess, read out the lurid headline;

"My wild night of love with Hell Boy, Zaff. An ex Miss Basingstoke tells all."

'Pixiepants,' the demon pleaded, 'as if I would! Ever! I would never touch any human especially one more plastic than flesh...and have you seen her lips? I'd rather kiss a sea bass.'

'Then why don't you?' Cylphie seethed, her anger kept the tears away...just.

The angry confrontation had not gone unnoticed. The lacewing curtains on a stone-clad hovel close to the park had not stopped twitching since the start of the argument. Even a pig herder has standards.

Forclosia huffed and puffed to no avail. Her husband had made himself comfortable on a straw pallet on the floor, tucking into a bowl of cold gruel and would not be moved. Not without socks. She grabbed a broom and stormed off towards the tree. No yobs were going threaten lasses in her village!

With a groan of alarm, Cylphie saw a behemoth of a broom wielding peasant housewife bearing down on the tree, her round sweaty face red with fury. She meant business, her trailing skirts hitched up to expose maggot-white knees, sturdy limbs powering her along like a dray horse's legs. And nearly as hairy.

Oh dear! This was not good. An innocent bystander thinking she was a fragile maiden needed rescuing. A well-wishing busybody about to be a considerably large pile of ash stinking of brimstone. The elf maiden had to move fast. 'Zaff! I am really sorry to be so possessive and jealous, please forgive me.' The demon flew in closer. Cylphie held out her arms to him, 'Take me away from here, I want you...now!'

A wide grin spread across his darkly handsome features, he swept her up in his arms but before flying high into the air, kissed her in a long languorous, passionate embrace. One interrupted by a well-aimed broom connecting to his posterior. Bruised and startled, Zaff reacted instinctively and yet another pile of ash stinking of brimstone marked his passage through the Land of Goodness and Light. As they flew away to a nearby cave for an afternoon of tumultuous lovemaking Cylphie sighed sadly. She had done her best.

A chill autumn breeze ruffled through King Pravis's flowing blond locks as he surveyed his new Kingdom of Goodness and Light. Symbolic, he decided, of the wind of change that he had started. He stood high on the battlements of a real castle again, a mighty fortress against the ever present forces of evil that lurked at his country's border. His father had abdicated, using the embarrassment and debacle of the war that never was as a convenient excuse to scarper down to his bolthole in the Costa Lotte. After refusing to tone down her shrill protests, his mother Queen Hemelda was confined by armed guards to her quarters. Pravis's first act as king was to undo all the interior and exterior design changes, sending the queen's team of makeover experts fleeing the land under threat of the sword.

No more stone cladding, no more roof gardens, the moat fully restored with deep and ominously murky water again. The tearooms were once again dank and gloomy dungeons, shelves formerly laden with homemade jam and tins of ginger biscuits now replaced by racks and thumbscrews. Castle Valiant shone out again, a gleaming white marble beacon to all that was noble and righteous.

Pravis returned to his throne room, a marvel of bristling weaponry proudly displayed on the walls that were now plain rough stone, all trace of the hideous watered silk and gold chintz wallpaper expunged. He saw his new second in command leaning over a table, sorting out a project dear to the man's heart, a new paper, The Burning Times. Ex-highwayman, ex evil minion and ex sex slave but still nasty bastard Strang was now the official Worthy Witch Hunter, a post created for him by the king. Still reeling from the threat of the demon Prince Rafial and his army of Darkness and Despair and the ruinous rampages from his awful, destructive daughter Princess Demonica, Pravis wanted a tough new regime. Centuries of tolerance would soon end with one royal decree to be posted in Strang's newspaper. The Land of Goodness and Light was to be a magic free zone, a pagan free zone. A Feast of Wolfsbane-free zone. As this would be as popular with the general populace as a dose of bubonic plague, Pravis's troops were ready to suppress the enraged masses once Strang's specially trained agents began their work in earnest. For weeks they had covertly infiltrated the populace, making notes and sending information back to their new boss.

'I've made a list,' growled Strang, 'noting all the names of those most wanted.'

He handed it to the king. Not surprisingly Morven the Unwise Woman of Fuggis Mire was on it, the king had insisted she headed the list. Pravis was still reeling at her insolence, letting a whole army march back in triumph covered with dried flower fairy snot! He also insisted her lover, the notorious highwayman Jed Moonraven was next. That particular scoundrel had got away with his criminal exploits for far too long.

The king was puzzled by one entry. The less obvious inclusion of a heavy metal rock band called Shrike Hell.

'You see, your Majesty, they don't just play the devil's music,' explained Strang patiently, 'they have an actual evil winged demon for a lead guitarist.'

Again, the king was perturbed. Part of being a valorous leader was to be just. 'We cannot condemn people for having dubious taste in music. Otherwise we would have to list barber shop quartets or Balkan Eurovision entries.'

The new witch hunter snapped his fingers and a small, meek looking but clearly angry peasant stepped out from behind a pillar. The throne room now stunk of pig poo and old turnips. And possibly butterbeans. He bowed and scraped, tugged his forelock and cringed in suitably grovelling peasant mode, stinking so much so that the new king began to gag. Most unseemly in a monarch. 'Enough! Desist my good if somewhat pongy serf and tell me your story. But stay where you are.'

In halting words, Gorblime Prud related the sorry tale of how his beloved wife was reduced to a pile of ash by a winged demon after she heroically stepped in to save a damsel in distress. 'I've checked with my insurance but Vinny Grimes insists I am not covered for Acts of Devil. It's not fair! I feel conned! And we are no longer safe in our own land with a monstrous thing flying around zapping honest poor folk at will!'

'A sorry tale indeed,' murmured Pravis, fishing out a gold coin and handing it to the startled and grateful Prud. 'And what of the fair maiden?'

'That was the strange thing, Your Majesty. Just before my beloved Forclosia got toasted, the damsel was actually snogging the demon! Really full on. I thought they would start to make out in front of my eyes,' his voice trailing away as he recalled his disappointment.

Strang pushed the little man out of the way and flourished his list. 'You see, my Liege! A good woman reduced to cinders, a fair and chaste maiden corrupted to open debauchery by dark enchantment.' He lowered his voice to sound more ominous, 'The Land of Goodness and Light is being tainted by evil. We must purge it.'

He pounded a nearby desk with his fist. 'With blood and fire!'

The witch hunter had stuck a deep chord with Pravis. He had a vision of the Land of Goodness and Light as shining as the refurbished castle's white marble walls. A land of virtue, nobility and chastity. Where honest men could walk unafraid and women pass safely without being debauched by demons. Where his noble knights could ride abroad on noble quests safe in the knowledge they were leaving behind a peaceful, blessed realm.

'Do what you have to, Worthy Witch Hunter Strang. I leave this matter in your more than capable hands.'

The king marched out, overdue some smiting practise. Strang strolled over to the peasant and snatched away his gold coin. 'Down payment my good man. For your uniform. You are now a member of the witch hunter's hit squad.

'It's not fair! I'm bored...and I'm hungry!'

Actually the exact words were punctuated by foul language so coarse it would make a demon blush. Or one of the nuns of the not at all silent order of St Tourretia. Words that certainly did not belong to a delicate looking and gangly unicorn colt foal. The highwayman Jed Moonraven pulled down the brim of his tricorne hat and urged its mother, his mare Milady to a faster speed. Wind driven rain drenched them in horizontal stinging lashes. With no sign of any coaches full of rich pickings and highborn ladies to flirt with and this accursed colt's constant verbal abuse and whining, he was rapidly losing the will to live. Too far to reach the welcoming arms of his lady, Jed decided to risk seeking shelter at a nearby small town. A clean (ish) bed, a couple of hot, willing strumpets to warm it and a tankard or three of ale would soon drive away thoughts of this wretched and unrewarding journey.

There was danger there of course, the reward on his head was now so high, it was only a matter of time before he made that last walk up certain wooden steps. But life was for living and for living his way. He pondered the possible alternative, the thought of retiring, spend a life of tedious good behaviour dusting Morven's potion shelves and feeding the guard goats and security toads. He shuddered and this time not from the chill, rain laden wind. No way!

His love for the Unwise Woman had not lessened but his horror at the thought of domesticity had grown. The couple were worlds apart and always would be. There was a curious comfort to be had that he would not make old bones, that there would never be a doddery old Jed Moonraven wrapped in a blanket, sitting by the hearth, regaling anyone who passed with endless, tedious stories of his past misadventures. Not like his own father, Jake who retired early at forty and became the town bore, a bitter, miserable git of one at that. No doubt still was somewhere out there, Jed had no intention of having a family reunion.

As they clattered over the slick cobbles stones, the light from the tavern revived his flagging spirits, not long now and he could put this dreary night behind him. Even the troublesome colt cheered up and trotted up by its mother with ears pricked, rain dripping off its black spiral horn. Poor Milady at least did not have to feed the colt herself anymore now it was weaned; nursing a horned foal was a painful trial for even the most patient of equine mothers. In truth, Jed did not know what to do with the creature. It hampered his progress across the country, its foul mouth was a liability when lying in wait for a passing coach. And how anonymous could Jed be with a Pooka/Cursed Unicorn/ordinary horse crossbreed at his side. It wasn't exactly an everyday sight.

Ahead, the dark street briefly lit up as the tavern doors opened, a pair of ghostly vapours wafted in, soon to be ejected from the bar, accompanied by angry shouting. 'Oi, you two. Get out! I told you once before, I won't have any moaning and wafting about in my tavern. Puts off me regulars. You don't even buy any ale. From now on, you are barred!'

Jed waited till the landlord returned inside and rode over to the ghostly vapours. 'Tough break guys.' The ghostly vapours wafted mournfully. But then, they always did.

'I tell you what,' continued the highwayman. 'I only want to go in for a drink, a shag and a couple of hour's kip, I'll pay for two nights. If you can keep watch, howl, moan, shake your chains or whatever it is you vapours do if the militia approach, you can have my room free for the rest of the time.'

Wafting in what Jed hoped and assumed was assent, he left the ghostly vapours on guard and walked around the back of the tavern to stable his mare and colt. He handed the stable lad a generous payment and insisted that Milady remained saddled, remarking that he was only popping in to the tavern for a quick drink. No doubt the accursed colt would contradict him just to wind Jed up. But this was deadly serious. Being able to make a quick escape meant the difference between wearing a collar of fine lace or of hemp rope.

His rampaging half human daughter did not return to the Land of Darkness and Despair. Neither did his thankfully useless full blood demon son. But it meant a furious Prince Rafial had to bear the humiliation of returning to his fortress alone at the head of an evil army covered in sparkling glitter. With some, mostly the banshees, insisting on wearing pink sunglasses that played 'You are my Sunshine'. Would the damn batteries ever run out? It was beyond bearing. Even the thunderstorms that sparked off whenever anything approached his grim fortress could not wash the vile glittery stuff off giving the inhabitants of this baleful land an unfortunate frivolous and festive appearance.

And just when the demon prince thought nothing else could go wrong, to really ruin his night, there was an inspection waiting. A deputation from the Boss Downstairs to see how Hell's conquering domain on earth was progressing.

'Bollocks!' he swore as he entered his throne room. Four sour faced demons waited, with clipboards and stopwatches. To be accurate, only three had stopwatches. One, a bit shamefaced had a baby blue and lilac Swatch. *He must have lost his own timepiece on the way up from the inferno*, thought Rafial, uncharacteristically charitably.

'Your timing is impeccable, gentlemen. I have just walked in the door after waging war on the forces of goodness and light. You can report straight back to the Boss that I am satisfactorily continuing his work up here.'

Rafial gestured imperiously in dismissal. 'Now, if you will excuse me, I have much to catch up on, work piles up when a prince of darkness is at war. Enjoy your journey back down under. To Hell that is. Not Australia.'

'Not so fast, my Lord Prince,' sneered a skeleton-thin demon. 'We have only just arrived. The inspection has not begun.'

The fat one with the Swatch began to wander about the throne room, touching stone gargoyles, checking for any serious lapses in gothic atmosphere such as lack of dust and cobwebs. Then he began to snoop about, looking in old chests for cursed treasure and skeletons. And all the time making copious notes on his Star Wars clipboard. Even the Boss was having trouble recruiting suitable staff.

Rafial snapped his fingers and summoned a quivering evil minion who nearly died of fright on the spot at the sight of four more hellish demons. He had sold his soul to work for just one demon! A contract signed in blood. His saintly grey-haired old mother had warned him not to work for the hell-spawned. But would he listen? Oh no....

'Take these fine demonic gentlemen to my office. I have made detailed lists of all my troop numbers, my armaments, invoices for the pits of sulphur, flow charts for the torture chambers. Quality control reports for the cess pits.' Rafial turned to the demons with a humourless smile. 'You will see that everything is in order.'

The demons seemed satisfied with that and followed the slimy lackey, now near catatonic with terror. 'Good!' Smirked Rafial. 'Those lists will keep the nosey beggars occupied for at least a century!'

His latest apprentice was a boy genius, a master baker already at the tender age of thirteen. Shame he would lose him come the next feast of St Epiligia, the official start of the questing season. The lad had a look of hidden destiny in his eyes. That or an unfortunate squint. But that was nearly a year away, Wheatley the Heroic sauntered down the filth-strewn cobbled street of his home town and breathed in the sweet, yeasty aroma of perfect freshly baked goods rising triumphantly above the squalor as he approached his bakery. The finest in the town. By now, the crowds would be queuing patiently outside, eager for the rapidly diminishing supplies of custard doughnuts, bread pudding and scones. What he wasn't expecting was a riot.

An angry mob of his regular customers were yelling colourful oaths and graphic abuse at a group of grey clad men, one armed with an official looking proclamation and protected by heavily armed militia. *Phew,* thought Wheatley, at least they weren't angry at him or his cakes and buns. Running out of jammy doughnuts too early was practically a hanging offence in this town. The baker pushed forward through the crowd and demanded to know what was going on.

'They are trying to ban the Pagan Feast of Wolfsbane! Bastards!' yelled a normally meek and mousy peasant housewife. 'They are closing you down! Wheatley the Heroic closed down because he sells bat cup cakes, meringue wraiths and gingerbread werewolves to kids.'

Astonished, Wheatley glared at the little man with the vellum scroll. 'Novelty items? Since when has it been a crime to bake light-hearted cakes for a national festival?'

'Since today,' sneered the man with the unfortunate pinched and puckered face resembling a cat's behind. 'The Pagan Feast of Wolfsbane is forever banned. Celebrating it in any way is now a crime. As are harbouring the following criminals for their transgressions against the righteous and honest populace of the glorious Land of Goodness and Light.'

He began to read from a long list, many were the usual suspects, boggart serial killers, bog chav thugs, notorious thieves and scoundrels headed by that infamous highwayman Moonraven. Then the list became more and more disturbing. Some were pointless as enemies, totally ineffective beings such as the defecting ghostly vapours or three evil butterflies that had broken free of their chrysalis on the wrong side of the border.

Or harmless eccentrics like the Hedgerow King of Tring, a wandering vagrant dressed as ... a hedgerow complete with sparrow's nests. His only crime was to shed leaves in autumn. And snagging ladies clothes on his brambles, though they didn't complain about his blackberries. Or the Dancing Druid of Durham who apart from being exhausting to watch and always off the beat was inoffensive and well, just a bit silly. But Wheatley's heart turned to ice as his beloved Morven The Unwise Woman was listed as the country's most wanted offender against righteousness. Lovely, compassionate Morven who always obeyed the rule to do no harm? It was monstrous!

Wheatley turned on his heels and ran, recklessly abandoning his bakery as the well-guarded men in grey began to gleefully tear down the town's Wolfsbane decorations. Children wept as their carefully crafted chains of cheerful paper bats, grinning comedy skulls and jolly werewolves were reduced to torn and trampled shreds. It would soon get nasty, as their mothers armed with rolling pins waded in, ready to do their best to reduce the officious vandals to torn and trampled shreds. The baker saw none of this; his only thought was to get to his beloved Morven and save her from this madness.

With a wide, lazy grin, one arm possessively around Cylphie's neck, the other hand holding a suspiciously fat cigarette, Zaff nonchalantly strolled backstage to rejoin the band. It was less then two minutes before the Shrike Hell was due on stage. And the band had already deliberately kept their fans waiting two hours. It was expected.

Enraged, the new lead singer was about to give their demon lead guitarist a well-deserved mouthful but thought better of it when Lennie kicked him hard in the shins, a sharp reminder that the evening could start off with a new pile of ash stinking of brimstone! It would have been the all-time record for shortest time with the band. And it was too important a gig to go on without a vocalist.

In the hall, the crowd were already stamping and slow handclapping in good-natured impatience. There was the usual enthusiastic crowd of Vikings including an off duty minor demi-God from Valhalla slumming it, a family outing of cave trolls without their aunties, a hen party of water nymphs, a stag party of stags, human moshers and heavy metal fans sporting the band's latest tour t-shirts. A raucous gang of drunken flower fairies were still outside, barred for carrying offensive weapons. Another gang barred from entry for their own safety were Zaff's fanatic and spite-filled groupies, all wearing tee shirts emblazoned with vivid and inflammatory slogans such as 'Flit off elf bitch!', 'I saw him first!' and 'Elves Fail!'

Less likely gig goers were a large group of silent, grim faced men sporting buttoned down grey shirts and crisply pressed dark grey trousers. They spread to opposite ends of the auditorium and stood, their backs to the wall, arms folded, impassive and strangely silent.

One way or another they looked like trouble.

As were a rowdy gang of latecomers, barbarians from Thrangthroor, By the Acid Lake of Skraagkar on the Outer Reaches of Doomguarde. All attention went from the grey-garbed strangers to the powerful, near naked broad chested barbarians, their well-oiled pecs bulging manfully, their square jawed chins jutting heroically, their loincloths disappointingly pitifully filled. They stormed in with a flower fairy on each arm, the little madams triumphantly giving the finger to the overwhelmed and defeated doortrolls.

A nervous flicker in his eyes, Lennie glanced across at an equally anxious Gordon and an unconcerned Zaff, 'Rough crowd tonight, lads...We'd better be on guard for mayhem breaking out. We can't afford to replace all the instruments again!'

The demon threw back his mane of waist length black hair, his dark eyes flashed with flames, a manically mischievous grin lighting up his darkly handsome features. 'f◆♏&; it. Let's give them Hell!'

Months of embarrassing journeying across the many provinces of Goodness and Light had taken its toll on the demon Princess Demonica. Transport had been a major vexation. Her mission of conquest and mayhem had started so well, transported by a magnificently decorated gothic coach pulled by a spirited team of purebred Irish Pookas. But its loss meant grabbing whatever she could, a slow but lofty enchanted Larch tree, a fat dray horse, a few hours triumphant soaring on a hang glider, she'd worn out several peasant donkeys and mules and now humiliatingly continued on foot. It was autumn now, the nights were drawing in, her revealing scraps of studded leather clothing did nothing to protect her against the cold rain and frosty nights. How had a high born princess of Hell come to this? One word...Zaphael!

Demonica blamed every misfortune not on her raging arrogance and ambition, her refusal to act on forethought but on impulse, her short temper. No. All the calamities that had befallen her were brought about by her half-brother. A situation that was about to end for good. The princess had finally reached her destination, the distant shores of the Sapphire Sea, home of a Selkie.

Few had travelled this far and those that did wished they hadn't. For never had something been so wrongly named, probably by the Vinny Grimes owned PR company, Phibs R Us. Those expecting to see a magnificent silver shoreline complete with deep blue waves were met instead by a wide vista of sludge and silt, interspersed with razor-sharp pebbles. No white foam-capped waves crashed dramatically against the beach, only the feeble lapping of oily brown water stinking of rotting fish and rancid old seaweed. Not surprisingly it had never become a popular resort crowded with drunken bog chavs sunbathing themselves to the colour of boiled lobsters. The Sapphire Sea's loss was the Costa Lotte's gain. That was exactly how the Selkie wanted it. Solitude and serenity broken only by the plaintive cry and occasional squabble of the sea birds.

Solitude and serenity now shattered as a footsore and tetchy Demonica stomped up to her cave and entered unannounced and uninvited. The Selkie had done her best to adorn her magical grotto in the customary mystical décor of the sea witches. It was just there was so little raw material lying around the beaches of the Sapphire Sea. No unusual and exotic shells, though she had made creative use of limpets, no fronds of graceful sea grasses, but plenty of dried brown bladderwrack. Her grotto was not graced by a still lagoon of clear water nor were the walls of her cave glistening with natural crystals. But it was amazing what could be done with recycled plastic ring-pulls, old bottles and cans found washed up on the beach.

At least the Selkie herself was striking, her shimmering floor length hair a magical shade of silver-green that needed no ornament, her pale, ethereal face lit by huge iridescent eyes of ever changing shades of green, purple, azure and turquoise - all the colours that should have been reflected in the Sapphire Sea but weren't.

'At last!' panted Demonica, plonking herself down on a lump of wet stone within the Selkie's grotto. 'You have no idea how difficult it has been to reach you.'

The princess expected an instant show of deference, bowing, grovelling and refreshments. But all the Selkie could see was a dishevelled, deranged female, smelling of donkeys and clad only in scraps of torn and filthy black leather, her unkempt hair matted and full of larch leaves and twigs.

'I'm sorry,' murmured the Selkie, her voice as gentle as the waves of another sea caressing a different shore, 'am I supposed to know who you are?'

Somehow Demonica summoned up the strength to stand tall on her worn stiletto-heeled boots, and flash fire from her eyes. 'Bow to me witch or suffer the dire consequences of my fiery wrath! I am a royal princess of Hell, only daughter of Prince Rafial, all-powerful ruler of the Land of Darkness and Despair!'

Demonica had forgotten the awesome power of the sea; the Selkie's mood could change in an instant from gentle and nurturing to a raging, destructive tempest. As it did now. The sky darkened to pitch black storm clouds ominously rumbling across the heavens, a vicious wind agitated the turgid waters to something resembling crashing surf, the Selkie's gentle sea-green-blue eyes were now the turbulent black waters of a maelstrom.

'I am Kirsty! Queen of these Seas, I bow to no one, especially the half-breed whelp of a demon!'

Ooops! thought the demon princess. She had made more than a slight miscalculation. Demonica did something bizarrely out of character. She apologised. Profusely. The storm abated, calm restored, the two unearthly women agreed to a truce, settled over a full, unopened bottle of rum, no doubt washed overboard from some passing pirate ship. Somewhere out there in the endless, world encompassing ocean was a well pissed off, thirsty pirate.

'You have travelled far and in some great discomfort. Why have you sought my counsel?' Asked Kirsty, stone cold sober, Selkies could drink like a fish.

Demonica, more than worse for wear from the rum, slurred her words as she proclaimed, 'Revenge! I seek a painful, tortured and prolonged death for my half-brother!'

Recklessly, she grabbed the rum bottle off the Selkie and finished it off. 'A toast to Zaphael, the cause of all my misfortune! I want a spell, a potion, an amulet...anything that will permanently rid me of that arrogant, mocking bastard!'

Then she passed out.

Leaving the princess to sleep off the effects of exhaustion, rum and pent up frustration fuelled by hatred and failure, the Selkie walked to her scrying pool deep with her grotto. It should have been crystal clear water seeping from the mountain above into the cave but she had to make do with a stagnant puddle of seawater. Was this Zaphael as good looking as his father? Kirsty had known Prince Rafial, known him very well indeed. The still waters cleared and showed her the winged magnificence that was Zaff, resplendently flying above his frightened but adoring fans at a rock concert. He was wild, arrogant and utterly gorgeous. Kirsty would make Demonica an amulet all right! Potent with a powerful spell but one with unforeseen consequences for the jealous and spiteful bitch! One who incidentally wasn't the demon Prince Rafial's only daughter!

Blissfully but perilously unaware of the chill wind of change swiftly sweeping across the Land of Goodness and Light, Morven the Unwise Woman put on a woollen shawl and stepped out to feed her guard goats and security toads. Her assistant the Goth boy Robard was still in bed, near comatose with sleep in the way of all teenagers but she didn't mind. When he was awake, he was a dutiful if rather melancholy helper around her new hovel and 'Spangles Newe Ayge Shoppe' on the edge of the Forest of Mhmin. Morven did not miss the stinking bog with its rampaging boggarts and the graffiti spraying bog chavs. Once, when her goats and toads had let her down badly, she awoke to find 'Morvin is a wich!' sprayed on her hovel. Hardly an insult, apart from the atrocious spelling, it was the truth.

Nor did she miss the steady stream of enlightenment-seeking knights on quests, her encounter with Prince Pravis, now the king, had been the last straw. No more tin-clad, sword-wielding pompous pillocks for her! Instead, she had a new clientele, gentle, spiritual humans and forest Folk seeking New Age remedies and spells. Robard had a talent for design and creativity and the hovel sparkled with delicate hanging crystals that sent tiny rainbows dancing on the white lime-washed wattle and daub walls. It was fragrant with incense, lush essential oils and rare spices. The cool morning air tinkled with the mixed jangling song of many wind chimes and light dazzled from spinning glass things that caught the early morning sun. The new look suited Morven, she felt truly herself here in a flower-strewn meadow on the edge of an enchanted forest. Her first real home. Only the absence of her highwayman cast a shadow on her new life.

One she would have to learn to accept or cut him out of her life altogether, what any wise woman would have done years ago. There was no spell or potion that could turn the love she had for the wayward Jed into more convenient indifference. Unable to change Jed's nature, she was stuck with him and all his careless, hurtful bad behaviour. He had always been that way and staying with him was her choice, one she would have to live with as cheerfully as possible, relishing the brief good times and ignoring the long absences. What she couldn't blank out was the dread of knowing one day, destiny in the form of a man on a faster horse would catch up with her highwayman lover. At least she had been proved wrong about the unlikely pairing of Cylphie and her demon. For all his rock god, bad boy reputation, Zaff was devoted to the elf girl, how she envied their happiness while wishing them well.

The sound of something stirring in the spare bedroom snapped Morven out of her gloomy reverie. It was either the teenager finally getting up or the smelly socks and underpants left under his bed transformed into sentient life forms and off out to discover the world on their own.

Rubbing his kohl-lined eyes, Robard finally staggered out of bed and sought out his employer and friend. 'I have a great idea for a line of novelty gifts for the Pagan Feast of Wolfsbane. Little models of spooky accursed scarecrows dangling on a string. The kids will love them. I need to go to the river to find some dried reeds. '

'Love that idea!' Morven laughed. 'They will sell like hotcakes in the town at the Wolfsbane Fayre on Smattersday!' She put her arm around the lad's shoulders, 'But first, breakfast! There is hardly anything of you.'

With a sinking heart, Robard nodded assent to keep her happy. Making Morven happy felt so right. But in truth staying deathly pale and painfully thin was more important to him then one of her well-meaning but weird concoctions. She served up prawn cocktail crisps, prunes and marmite on toast yesterday. Morven was sworn to do no harm but there were times when it became a close run thing.

After snatching a quick breakfast, this morning Morven had served up a hot and creamy oat and Stilton cheese porridge sprinkled with capers and raisins, the lad hurried off to the reed bed to stock up on scarecrow making materials. He also needed time alone to work up the courage to ask Morven something very important, momentous. He had changed his mind about being a tortured poet, though he would still write torturous poetry if the mood took him. Nor was he content to be a shop assistant to the Unwise Woman's shop, agreeable though it was. Robard wanted more. Much more. He wanted to be Morven's apprentice

Watching from the side of the stage, Cylphie could not take her eyes off her bad boy lover as he transfixed the crowd with his virtuoso guitar performance. Even the air guitar playing barbarians barging through the Vikings and taking over the mosh pit, stopped their muscle-bound gyrations to watch, open mouthed.

Cylphie was transformed by her time with the band. The elf ex-warrior maiden had cast aside the swirly, flowery silken garb of her kind and now wore typical rock chick clothing. Her slender elven figure now clad in a ripped scrap of what was once a black tour tee shirt, a tattoo saying 'I love Zaff' on her exposed midriff, the tightest, skimpiest pair of denim shorts, long stripy socks and her beloved Doc Martens boots. The combination of elven ethereal feyness with tough, kick-ass attitude was devastating and she knew it. She drove Zaff wild with lust and had him wrapped around her little finger. If only he was able to love her in return, that would make her life perfect.

She had forgiven him the so-called dalliance with the very ex Miss Basingstoke, in fact, there was nothing to forgive. Of course it was all just money grubbing lies from some botoxed bimbo. A human bimbo. All the band confirmed Zaff never had any interest in humans beyond target practice.

Her attention was reluctantly drawn away from her demon to some furtive movement in the crowds. For the first time she noticed the grey clad men around the edge of the crowd, not leaping up and down and singing along with the band. Not even looking in the band's direction. And nobody could take their eyes of Zaff when he was in full flow. Trouble. Some instinct warning her of impending danger kicked in and she was sharply alert. One of the men caught her eye more than the others, he was nervous, agitated, glancing every few seconds up to the ceiling. Her sharp elven vision followed his gaze, a huge metal net was strung across the high vaulted wooden beams, right above where Zaff would fly at the height of his spectacular solo. A trap!

What on earth could she do? Anyone interrupting Zaff when he was lost in his music risked being turned into a pile of ash stinking of brimstone. She had to cause a panic, a diversion that would snap Zaff out of his trance-like state long enough to alert him to the snare. But what?

She ran on stage and wrestling the mike of the lead singer, screamed at the top of her voice, 'Run away! They are coming! They are hideous! Horrible! It's the Fungus Badgers!'

The effect was instant. A water nymph screamed and triggered a wave of terror and panic whipped up by Cylphie. 'Save yourselves!' and 'Run for your lives!'

In a riot of screaming, flailing arms, trampling hooves and gouging horned helmets, the crowd raced as one for the exit, sweeping all before them including the men in grey who could do nothing to stop the stampede. One managed to release part of the net before being swept away by the living tsunami of panic. One corner of the metal net dropped drunkenly, entangling a party of pogoing satyrs high on magic mushrooms too stoned to notice the stampede for the exit but the net missed Zaff.

'What the f◆ⴏ&?' He growled, eyes on flame, 'I didn't get to finish my set!'

Cylphie ran to his side, 'That net was meant for you!'

The band fled from the chaos, abandoning their equipment. Zaff, gently but firmly holding his beloved flew above the others as they ran out of a secret back entrance only normally used as an emergency escape route by truly terrible comedians and mime artistes. And once by a magician in a tuxedo whose doves had all perished in the laps of an audience of pre-schoolers on a birthday party treat. He had not realised how fast outraged mothers could run.

Zaff could see movement in the main square outside the theatre and flew over a huge battalion of Pravis' militia. All armed to the teeth and grim faced, they made a belated and clumsy attempt to surround the theatre. What the bloody hell was going on? He had toured the land for years with Shrike Hell without attracting the interest of the militia. Even when he 'accidentally' torched the strident but unarmed PORN protesters.

Exhausted from their headlong flight, the band reached the shelter of a stand of birch trees, fortunately normal ones because enchanted ones, if sufficiently bored, might have given their position away just for the perverse thrill of it. The demon gently let Cylphie down onto the ground beside the band and prepared to fly back and barbeque the town. A distraught Cylphie tenderly laid her hand on his face and with her lustrous eyes glistening with tears pleaded with him to spare the town.

'I know you have no concept of innocence, my beloved. But there are people down there who had nothing to do with the trap. Kindly old ladies who knit crinoline lady loo roll covers for charity, families with little kids. Babies. And fluffy kittens. Lots of little fluffy kittens playing with balls of wool.'

'Its true, man,' added Lennie. 'Who will book us in the future if you trash the town? Way, way too uncool.'

A furious Zaff conceded with ill grace. He really wanted to burn something alive for pissing him off and ruining his performance.

'And what the soddin' hell is a Fungus Badger?' He grumbled, kicking a rock fifty feet into an enchanted privet bush that dared not yelp for fear of becoming charcoal.

Cylphie shrugged. 'Haven't the foggiest! I just made it up.'

'Stand and deliver!' the lass had gleefully demanded and Jed Moonraven had duly delivered, several times before collapsing into a far deeper sleep then he intended but his post bonkathon rest was short-lived.

One moment in a deep, satisfied slumber entangled in the limbs of the well-proportioned busty serving wench, the next sharply alert, Jed heard the fearful warning wail of the ghostly vapours. Pausing only to leave a gold coin on the wench's ample cleavage, Jed hauled on his britches and boots, grabbed his sword, pistols and coat and made rapidly for the door. He had kept his hat and shirt on throughout the bedroom fun.

The militia were outside, doing their best to manhandle the ghostly vapours with little success being that they were so flimsy and insubstantial. This caused so much hilarity that the whole neighbourhood awoke and were out on the street, transfixed by the farcical spectacle, giving Jed time to bolt to the stables.

Luckily, the stable lad had been true to his word, apart from a warm rug thoughtfully thrown over her back, his mare Milady was saddled and ready to flee. Not so the colt who lay snoring, flat out in the deep clean straw. The highwayman leapt into the saddle and shouted at the infuriating colt. 'Oi! You...up now...We have to fly like the wind to escape!'

Yawning, the colt sneered, 'Whatever!' and dropped its head back onto the straw.

Whickering her anxiety, its mother urged it to rise, 'It's not fair!' it whinged petulantly. 'I didn't ask to be born!'

Jed pulled out one of his pistols and aimed it at the truculent colt, 'Two choices, you flee with us now or I leave you here with a lead hole in your head.'

'Not without alerting the troops! One pistol shot is all it takes!' It threatened. 'Be nice to me or I'll hasten your journey to the gallows!'

Luckily for Jed, his mare Milady had enough of her offspring's bad manners; she reached down and bit it hard on the bottom causing it to leap to its feet with a yelp. She continued to bite and harass it until they were out on the open road and galloping towards freedom.

Subsequently, Jed never knew the militia were not after him, in fact did not know he was in the tavern. They were delivering proclamations on the new laws and posting wanted posters, with Morven at the head of the list. Arresting or at least attempting to arrest the ghostly vapours was no more than a badly judged coincidence.

Dropping his velvet breeches to warm his broad behind against a wide hearth blazing with oak logs, the official witch hunter smugly reviewed how good his life had become. Outside a peevish autumn wind stirred the fallen leaves, a feeble portent of the winter season just weeks away. He had no worries about the cold weather to come; he was warm, safe and a man of great importance in Castle Valiant. No more riding through thick mud crouched low in the saddle against wind lashed, flint hard rain. No more picking his way through hard frozen rock-hard ruts in the road, riding with hands too iced up to hold his horse's reins.

All that exhausting, perilous life as a so-called Gentleman of the Road was over. He never dwelt on his brief but lurid time as the boyfriend of a princess of Hell and it would not appear in his forthcoming autobiography; 'My Rise to Greatness' currently being penned by Vinny Grimes. Now he had a huge section of the castle to call his offices with a luxury penthouse apartment at the top of a battlement. Many obsequious staff at his beck and call and an army of ruthless and fanatic grey-clad agents scouring the land for his enemies.

He helped himself to a generous measure of rare vintage wine in a pure gold goblet and raised it in a silent toast to his benefactor the pompous pillock he had to call King - for now. How easy Pravis had been to manipulate. There was no doubting the man's chivalry and valour on the tourney field or on perilous though pointless quests. He was probably equally valorous on the battlefield but that was yet to be tested. But Pravis had a weakness, an Achilles heel. One that he exploited shamelessly to gain power. The king was terrified of his mother.

It had been so easy to harry and banish the Queen Mother's protective coterie of interior designers, landscape gardeners and makeover experts. Once alone, he threatened to withhold her beauty treatments unless she voluntarily accepted house arrest within the castle walls. Queen Hemelda reluctantly accepted, the nightmare of losing her precious injections of boggart phage abated but he would have just as happily thrown her over his shoulder and chucked her in the dungeons. He had the taste for power now and it was so sweet, intoxicating!

Soon the witch hunter formally known as nasty bastard Oakham Strang would have his revenge on the world. But most of all on his former partner in crime Jed Moonraven, the highwayman's mocking laughter burnt forever into his soul. It was a shame about the comely witch Morven, The Unwise Woman of Fuggis Mire. She had done him no harm save for making a vile-smelling and ultimately useless unguent to cure a boil on his bottom that had stunk of rotten cabbage for weeks. Probably because the main ingredient had been rotten cabbage. Her demise was sad but inevitable, the waste of a comely if eccentric woman. No matter. The lovers would perish together. How romantic...

'My Lord!' an evil minion asked cautiously. A rare long-term member of the prince's staff, he had avoided being turned into a pile of ash stinking of brimstone by being very circumspect. Never coughing or sneezing with sounds that were blasphemy to the demon's sharp hearing.... sounds like chhhheeesuss or ghooooddd. Never taking bad news to Rafial also helped so today he had taken a great risk. For the news he brought was just plain weird.

Rafial looked up from writing down his latest list, reasons why he was happy not to be human, mostly concerning unfortunate body functions but addiction to Big Brother was there too, as was ... Impatient to get on with his work, he listened to his snivelling underling, finger poised to zap.

'We have had a party of humans arrive at the borders, saying they were fleeing the Land of Goodness and Light and are seeking asylum here.'

Startled, the demon put down his list and fixed the creature with a piercing stare that had it quake and go weak at the knees, had its long run of good fortune finally run its course?

'Here? They actually seek sanctuary in the dread domain of the doomed and damned?'

'Seems so, my Lord and they are most adamant they want to speak to you.'

Curious at who would be daft enough to willingly enter these ever-night, cursed and frankly downright hazardous lands, Rafial ordered them to be brought immediately to his presence.

Minutes later, a group of humans were ushered in. But far from being terrified and overawed by the exiled prince from the fiery pits of Hell, they boldly strolled up to his throne and after extravagant, theatrical bows, introduced themselves as a collective of cutting edge interior designers and makeover experts. They were dressed in plain, dark clothing...all could have been mistaken for associates of Puritans Opposed to Rock Noise, but no hard core PORN member would wear their hair half shaved or dyed pink, have piercings and sport such a large amount of abstract bling.

One stepped forward and brushed aside a long lock of floppy blond hair from his forehead. 'You must have heard of us, Prince Rafial. Our work is renowned. We've done a complete makeover for The Most Revered and Imperial Pangolin of Sharpei, reworked the sacrificial chamber of Ultimate Doom for the Barbarian Queen of Hhruthruduul. Delightful woman but a bit short in the sense of humour department. And of course our award winning work for Queen Hemelda of the Land of Goodness and Light.'

Another chipped in, wailing, 'All undone, all torn down and trashed by that utter philistine brute of a son.'

Rafial's passing interest in the newcomers to his land had already finished, he was deciding their fate when a lean, bald designer began to stroll around the throne room, inspecting the décor. 'Who did this for you? A disgrace! So last millennia! All this heavy, doom and gloom-laden Gothic Uber-kitsch! Laid on with a heavy-handed trowel by a moron with no taste. Bring it all back to bare walls, lose the flaming torches and rag roll with a bright, breezy pale cerise - open it up for a full on neo-classical pastiche!'

Another took up the commentary, 'You are so right Tarquin, let us dump all these dated, depressing stone skeletons and gargoyle statues, keep a few carved stone bats for irony. And what about a feature wall completely covered with a huge blown up picture - again something witty and ironic?'

'A picture of the prince as a baby - on a white fur rug?'

'An abstract mural of interlocking reversed crosses? Overlain with stencilled 666's.'

'Angels! With wonderful spreading glowing white wings and golden halos, so deliciously out of place. They will look fabulous! Divine!'

'A giraffe in a tutu?'

Interrupting the growing excitement and creative rapture, Rafial coughed. 'Gentlemen and er...lady? You do realise you are in the throne room of a royal prince of the Infernal Dominions of Hell?'

'Absolutely!' sang out Loobis Croom, a renowned designer who had made a name for himself with outrageous design statements involving frog-skin and gold paint. 'But that doesn't mean you have to live in a miserable, dated, cobweb-dusted museum. One straight from the wet dreams of a spotty heavy metal-loving teenager.'

Croom strode about the room, pointing out the appalling décor with a sneer. 'You are a great and mighty prince, you deserve so much better. Be bold; tell the world you are not a meek follower of out-moded clichés... that you have your own signature design statement!'

One of Croom's cronies insinuated himself beside the great man, 'The Charloos Emperor Mingo of Vargon Prime hated his lakeside Summer Palace makeover at first, but Master Croom is a genius!'

Rafial was outraged. First he had the insidious and impertinent demon inspectors measuring the depth of his dust and cobwebs, now these human poltroons insulting his suitably demonic décor.

'Yes,' burbled on Croom's crony, oblivious to the flickering angry flames in Prince Rafial's eyes. 'The Emperor was shocked at first at losing centuries accumulation of gaudy pure gold walls encrusted with gems, so vulgar, utterly ghastly! But now he adores the minimalistic taupe hessian wallpaper coupled with a playful bamboo monkey motive.'

At this point Rafael raised his hand, ready to reduce them all to designer piles of ash stinking of organic, hand blended brimstone. But it was far too quick and merciful a fate. Ordering up some evil minions, he instructed to take the designers away.

'I have an area of my fortress in dire need of urgent re-decorating. It has had the same colour scheme for at least ten millennia. Time for a complete makeover.'

The designers bowed low, 'My Lord,' announced one smugly, 'I can assure you, you will not be disappointed.'

'And you have my assurance that I will be completely satisfied,' agreed the prince, smiling as the designers were led off to be immersed up to their necks in the infernal cesspits.

Deep within Prince Rafial's dungeons, a ferocious argument could be heard echoing through the labyrinth of gloom and doom-laden chambers. Voices raised not in wailing or gnashing of teeth but in shrill and heated debate. In the vast chamber of cesspits where offenders served out their term up to their necks in ordure, were a team of cutting-edge designers and avant-garde make-over experts.

'It is chocolat with an overtone of burnt umber!'

'Never in a million years, are you colour blind! Bistre and Taupe with witty streaks of ochre.'

'You two are so, so passé! Definitely bole and liver with mahogany highlights as a playful retro pastiche.'

Taking a deep breath, one announced as he frantically trod water...er...cess - 'I can top all that retro garbage after all it was I who wrote the best selling book Interior Design for Idiots. It is multiple shades of autumn, ecru, zinnwaldite and bronze. And a bit of russet thrown in as homage to the Pre-Rafialite movement. So there!' And in his own homage, he blew a playful, witty, retro, pastiche of a raspberry.

The cheek of the scantily clad demon bitch! Queen Kirsty the Selkie fought hard to keep her tempestuous temper in check, but there were signs of a storm brewing. Dark clouds gathered along the horizon and the sea became brown and choppy with foam cresting the agitated waves. The cause?

No sooner had Demonica awoken from her rum induced stupor, sprawled on the floor of the grotty grotto but she was demanding transport and the whereabouts of Zaphael.

'I know you have one of those scrying pools back in your grotto. I saw you use it!' she had insisted.

Using every ounce of her self-control, Kirsty tilted her head with a suitably fey and mysterious expression. 'I can indeed find your brother. I have the power to seek out your heart's desire. In your case fratricide.'

'Half brother!' screeched Demonica.

'Whatever. Semi-fratricide then.' Sighed the Selkie, 'But how exactly am I to provide you with transport? I can only command the creatures of the sea. I could try to find you a large, cooperative and ultimately suicidal halibut to attempt a journey across land, I suppose. Or a shoal of easily fooled mackerel.'

'Don't be ridiculous!' Demonica snapped.

'Alright. I suppose I could arrange an army of self-sacrificing lobsters to carry you across the land. I don't know how far you would get before they all conk out though.'

Demonica chose not to rise to the Selkie's sarcasm. The demon had run out of options.

'But there is a river opening up into the sea nearby,' she declared. 'Have you anything strong enough to swim upstream and tolerate fresh water?'

Stifling the urge to giggle, Kirsty nodded. 'Actually, I have just the creature!'

The Selkie, still biting her finger to stop herself laughing, rummaged through the jumble of esoteric items in her grotty grotto and produced an impressive large conch shell and a velvet pouch containing an amulet. She held the talisman in both hands and infused it with a powerful spell. Then carrying the shell, walked to the now calming shoreline and blew hard into the conch. A loud, discordant wailing sound resonated across the sea. Then silence.

'Now what?' moaned Demonica, the conch noise still ringing irksomely in her head, already painfully pounding with her monstrous hangover. Kirsty did not answer, but stood on the shore line, the sea breeze feathering through the fronds of her long hair.

The sea before them began to roil and bubble, something large, monstrous and strange was approaching the shore, a dark shape ploughing though the waves at great speed. Demonica felt a quiver of fear run down her spine, then became angry with herself. She was Prince Rafial's daughter for hell's sake! There was nothing on this land she couldn't blast and turn into a pile of ash stinking of brimstone...apart from that accursed Zaphael.

Kirsty the Selkie bit her lip to hide her glee as the huge bulk of a creature arose from the surf. The Hydra. Eighty feet of huge sea serpent with a bloated oily brown body, nine heads and the worst breath ever recorded. The story of ancient Greek strong man and rampant self-publicist Hercules slaying the mighty beast was a myth, a total crock. He'd turned tail and scarpered, gagging when the creature yawned. But the muscle bound hero was no fool; he hired Vinny Grimes's PR company to spin the story in his favour. It wasn't as if gigantic sea monsters could read the newspapers. Even the most lurid tabloid would go soggy and disintegrate as soon as the paper reached the water.

'There you go, my princess of the dark realms. A fine strong beast to carry you safely to fulfil your heart's desire.'

Demonica could not answer. She had been born in a hellish realm, raised in a fortress where pits of sulphur, cesspits and evil minions' rank armpits were the norm. Yet even she could not stand the Hydra's foul breath, the quintessence of every vile stench the land and sea had ever known. It was all there, all the usual suspects; rotten eggs, smelly socks, mouldy cheese, putrefaction, fetid boiled cabbages, bog silt and 1980s perfumes. And a few less well known ones; boggarts' bellybutton fluff, centaur poo after the creature had been out for a curry, distilled essence of butterbeans, the insoles of macabre butterflies' bovver boots. The demon reeled from the appalling stench.

'Is this all you can offer me?' She railed at the now openly amused Selkie. 'This malodorous travesty of a sea monster?'

The Selkie shrugged feigning nonchalance, in truth she couldn't wait for Demonica to deliver the charmed amulet to Zaphael. 'I'll send her back if you want. But it's a long walk.'

'Her? That ugly thing is a she?'

'Who yer calling ugly, vinegar tits!' sniped one of the Hydra's heads.

'Yeah! You ain't no oil painting yourself, girlfriend!' added another.

'Oi, missus. Ave you looked in a mirror lately!' chipped in a third head.

Demonica raised her hand, before all nine heads insulted her. 'Enough! You have been summoned by the power of the Selkie to do my bidding.'

'Oooooh, get 'er. Lady Muck 'erself,' replied the fourth head.

'Bloody 'ell, she's all maff and nah trousers!' noted the fifth.

'Nah! Miss 'Oity Toity finks she's our boss,' announced the sixth.

The seventh chipped in, 'And look at wot she's not wearing, next to nuffink! Silly slag!'

Sighing, Demonica tried to switch off from the next jibes from the remaining two heads. It was going to be a long journey.

With his horse's feet fetlock deep in a kaleidoscope of colour of a carpet of fallen leaves, King Pravis adjusted the jesses on his fine peasant hawk, its sharp talons dug deep into his thick leather gauntlet.

'An exceedingly fine bird, my Liege.' Ventured the witch hunter as he brazenly pushed his horse forward past the lines of beaters and mounted nobles to join the king.

'Indeed, Strang. I bred her myself.' Pravis proudly stroked the raptor's fine golden brown breast feathers. 'Nothing stoops so fast, so precisely as my beautiful Doris.

But I take it you haven't ridden from the castle to talk about the noble art of falconry?'

Strang took his time, this was a delicate matter. A rash and risky gamble on his part. 'May we ride a little apart from the hunting party, your gracious Majesty? This is not a subject for anyone else's ears.'

Intrigued, the king agreed and yelled a command for the others to halt, before cantering to a nearby glade of conveniently un-enchanted trees. The enchanted ones couldn't stop themselves from eavesdropping and spreading gossip. After all, if you were rooted to the spot for centuries there was sod all else to do.

'What is this all about?' grumbled Pravis, he was looking forward to an exciting morning peasant hunting.

Strang coughed nervously, this could either end his charmed life as a witch hunter or be the start of something far more ambitious. 'You must forgive my impertinence, but a heart in love cannot stop beating loudly...'

The king turned bright puce. 'I have no inclinations that way! I am not an elf! Or a Demon! Or even quite a few of my own noble knights!'

Startled, Strang began to splutter his explanation, 'No, no, no Your Majesty! You misunderstood me. Not that you are not a fine, handsome and noble king. But I am talking about the beauteous Princess Allura. I have fallen head over heels in love with her.'

Calming down, the king shrugged, 'Then marry her! Is that all you wanted to talk to me about?'

An astonished Strang watched as the king impatiently spurred on his horse and galloped back to the hunting party. He was expecting a prolonged show of resistance, anger even from Pravis. After all, he was not royalty nor of an old and respected family. But Strang knew the truth, that efforts to marry Princess Allura off to some prince of a discreetly distant land had come to nothing. Her growing 'condition' was impossible to hide. Marriage - any marriage was clearly welcomed by her humiliated and embarrassed brother. One that clearly hadn't thought this through.

For Strang's marriage to Allura would make him next in line to the throne, once he had disposed of Pravis and Moonraven's bastard, the child due in a few weeks time. Strang's heart swelled with his success. He would become a king and not have had to nearly kill himself screwing a demented demonic princess to gain a crown. He looked forward to his last words to Jed Moonraven, as he placed the noose around the highwayman's neck himself. When he told Moonraven he had a son and would not be alive to save him.

He began to laugh, a strange sound unlike any he had ever made. It seemed that somewhere along his journey to power he had acquired a loud and maniacal laugh. How very odd! He glanced about nervously, had he acquired a deformed but obsessively loyal sidekick yet? No? He sighed with relief but it was only a matter of time.

Shimmering wafts of gossamer minus the silvery bits floated through the trees in the Forest of Mhmin, home of many magical and ethereal creatures. Sunlight dappled the glades and sparkled off the tumbling streams of crystal clear water. Even without the now notorious silvery bits, the woodlands were beautiful, serene and enchanted.

The forest was a separate sovereign state and therefore not subject to the rule of King Pravis. A situation that had never caused any concern. Until now. Worrying reports were filtering through about the new harsh laws in the Land of Goodness and Light. That morning the first refugees had arrived at the woodland edge, mostly Wise Women but there was also a scarecrow. Such an unusual visitor to the forest, it was brought straight to the elven council meeting in the Serene Crystal Gazebo.

'We all have to be registered!' the man of straw wailed, flailing about its floppy straw filled arms. Its face never changed of course, locked forever in one expression. This one had unevenly placed and mismatched eyes and a lopsided jolly grin which was unnerving when coupled with its abject misery. 'You have to tell them what kind of scarecrow you are. They have a list of categories; jolly, jolly but badly made and therefore a little sinister, creepy but possibly harmless or downright evil.'

'Then what happens?' asked a warrior elf called Edrin. The distress caused the scarecrow to flop onto the ground and shudder in terror.

'They burn us! Thrown alive onto a huge, blazing pyre...only those deemed 'jolly' are allowed back to the corn fields. I escaped and fled here but would have ended up in the flames!'

Edrin studied the scarecrow's lopsided grin, yep, this one would have been categorised as jolly but badly made and therefore a little sinister. He helped the wailing creature to its feet and smiled gently. 'Do not be afraid, old chap. You are safe with us. We will protect you.'

But was it? Edrin looked at the serene and elegant faces of the other elves and knew from the shadows in their eyes that they were thinking the same thing. If King Pravis had declared war on magic in his realm, how could he tolerate the Forest of Mhmin so close to its borders? With all the magic fairy snot dispersed, could a small army of elven warriors armed with bows be enough to fend off the army of Goodness and Light? The warrior had another secret fear. Zaff! Unknown to anyone, Edrin had a long term crush on the guitarist, had his posters plastered all over his bedroom. The demon he was secretly in love with was still out there on tour with the band and an obvious target for Pravis's deadly ire. Edrin had to reach him, warn him of the danger. Oh, and of course Cylphie was there too. He felt an unworthy pang of jealousy...how could he ever forget she had all he ever desired.

He needed an urgent excuse to leave the forest, a warrior abandoning his people in a time of danger to save his secret crush would not suffice and Cylphie was officially in exile for her unseemly relationship and causing a riot during the poetry festival. He ran to the nearest coven of Wise Women settling down for a nice cup of tea and a chat after their ordeal.

'Morven? Is the Unwise Woman of Fuggis Mire with you?' he asked, suitably frantic with worry, though in truth it was not a falsehood. Edrin had met her many times in Spangles and chatted over a mug of dandelion and beetroot tea.

The Wise Women shook their heads. 'We had hoped she had reached this sanctuary before us, her hovel and Newe Ayge Shoppe being so close to the Forest of Mhmin.'

One dug out her scrying bowl from her hastily gathered belongings, a proper one made of perfect, clear crystal. 'Oh dear,' she muttered, 'I think our beloved sister Morven is in grave danger. As I speak, men in grey clothing are surrounding her hovel. It looks like a trap!'

'Then I must ride to her defence!' announced Edrin heroically. This was wonderful! He had his excuse to leave the forest to fulfil his secret mission! 'I must travel in great haste...please tell the elven council where I have gone'

Whistling, he summoned up the nearest enchanted unicorn and leaping onto its snow white back, let it rear dramatically, pawing the air with its front hooves, sunlight flashing off the diamonds on its horn, before galloping off in a flurry of gossamer.

'What a lovely lad,' sighed one of the Wise Women. ' So handsome, so heroic.'

'And what a waste,' added another sadly, ' It's always the best looking ones.'

'By Odin's Earwax! What now?' King Pravis had looked forward all morning to a short break from the endless and tedious affairs of state. He understood now why his father had abdicated and cleared off to a secret hideaway on the Costa Lotte. Pravis yearned to return to the simple life of a crown prince, a noble, valorous knight who could travel with the team on jousting tours, go off alone on quests, and roam the land trouncing wrongdoers at will. Now his life was all mind-numbingly complex land laws, treaties and entertaining boring envoys from bizarre and distant lands.

All the frequent banqueting was taking its toll. His gold encrusted red velvet jerkin popped wide open this morning when greeting a diplomat sent from Icelandia, the Glacial Queen of the Frozen Northern Wastes. The envoy assumed it was a customary greeting in the Land of Goodness and Light and tore open her own bodice revealing an un-alluring old grey vest with stains and large moth holes in embarrassing places. Not the highest point of Pravis's diplomatic endeavours.

His expanding girth had prompted Pravis to call together his elite corps of noble Knights and he planned an exhilarating morning of sparring and swordplay plus the merry quips, badinage, back-slapping and ale quaffing that always went with it. They were just lining up to have a 'who has the longest sword' competition when a castle aide came running in urgently seeking the king.

'My Liege, I bring bad news. The peasants are revolting!'

'That's hardly news. They have always been filthy creatures stinking of pig shit and old butterbeans who sleep with their aunties and wear weevil-infested socks on their grubby feet.'

'No, your Majesty, I mean they are really revolting!'

Now Pravis was getting angry. 'Yes I know! They have too many children and swap them for goats and barrels of boggart moonshine, they wipe their noses on their sleeves and poo in the streets, wiping their bottoms with bits of dirty old rag. Which they keep with them till the next time! Unutterably vile!'

The castle aide shrugged, gave up, bowed and took his leave of the king. Let the pompous prat discover for himself that an uprising of peasants was erupting throughout the land, furious that their favourite festival was cancelled and the discovery that all their official village Wise Women had fled in terror. All their carefully crafted decorations had been torn down and burnt by the witch hunter's ruthless minions, bakers ransacked and all the festive Wolfsbane cakes confiscated. Worst of all, with the Wise Women gone, who would birth their babies and cure their aches and pains?

One of Pravis's knights watched the departure of the aide and shook his head in dismay.

'My Lord, what a strange little man. He really had a thing against peasants.'

King Pravis sighed, 'You just can't get the staff these days. Enough of that, I am certain my sword is much longer and broader than yours, Sir Fallus.

In a bizarre coincidence or an outrageously convoluted plot contrivance, Wheatley the Master Baker armed with his lucky bun arrived at the Unwise Woman's New Age hovel at the same time as Edrin the warrior elf to be confronted with a distraught Goth lad wandering desolately through the ruins of their home. He had arrived too late to stop whoever it was from trashing the hovel, smashing all the glittering mobiles and glass bottles of unguents to pieces, sending the guard goats and security toads fleeing in panic. Worst of all there was no sign of Morven.

'Teenage Bog chavs might have caused this but they wouldn't have taken the Unwise Woman.' Robard looked up with tear-streaked eyes, his black kohl eyeliner melting making him look like an anorexic panda. Addressing his former companion on their short-lived and frankly unremarkable Fellowship, he whimpered to Wheatley, 'What is happening? Where is she?'

Wheatley gave the boy a comforting pat on the back, he was a morose pain in the butt but his heart was kind and his loyalty to Morven total and unquestioning. 'Sadly, I fear we are too late. The grey clad minions of the witch hunter must have taken her to Castle Valiant. I have read that nasty bastard Strang's edicts in the Burning Times. They will hang her at dawn!'

'Then you must make great haste to save her!' announced the warrior elf. The others spun around, noticing him for the first time.

'Er ...who exactly are you?' Wheatley queried, not unreasonably.

'I have come directly from the Forest of Mhmin to save our dear friend, the Unwise Woman.' Announced Edrin valiantly.

Wheatley sighed with relief, some good fortune at last. 'Then we need your help Edrin...you are a warrior. I am a baker and this is a...a ...a...'

The warrior elf was torn. Wheatley was right, they would need his elven skill with a bow to shoot down the noose and rescue Morven from the gallows. But his personal urgent mission was to warn his secret demon lover Zaff.

As if reading his mind, Robard spoke to Edrin using the smattering of Elvish he'd learnt since working for the shop. The elf's silver and green silk tabard was covered with Shrike Hell fan badges, all the ones with pictures of Zaff on them.

'Zaphael is the most powerful being in the Land of Goodness and Light. An indestructible immortal. He will be fine. But Morven is in terrible peril. Please help us. Please save her.'

Actually the words came out as 'Zaphael is the greatly potent be at the Soil quality and Enlighten. An indestructible deathless. He will be fine. But Morven is in bed awful peril. Please help ourselves. Please avoid her.'

But Edrin was able to understand the gist. And had no choice but to agree. But how did the Goth lad know about his secret crush? Maybe the boy had hidden powers?

Never had a woman been so well named, thought a distraught Morven the Unwise Woman. How had she been so trusting, so naïve! While the Goth lad was out gathering material for the model scarecrows, a visitor had arrived seeking her help. It was a set up but she hadn't picked up the warning signals. The customer was quiet, furtive and nervous, his averted grey eyes the same pale colour as his plain clothes. A love philtre? No problem she had said and blithely mixed up the ingredients, pulverised ginger biscuits, a dash of goat's cheese, tinned apricot juice and cloves which she poured into a ruby glass bottle with a stopper in the shape of a red wax heart. Very romantic, just what her customers wanted to entrance the object of their affection. She knew the philtre wouldn't actually work, usually the customer's increased confidence was all it took. And she hadn't broken her vow not to do any harm. 'Here you are kind sir, just what the gentleman wanted.'

Not this one. As soon as she handed over the philtre and politely requested payment, he had grabbed her wrist in a vice-like grip and screamed loudly. 'I have proof! This is a witch!'

'Of course I am,' Morven had retorted, trying hard to pull away from her captor, 'it says so on the sign outside. I am fully qualified and licensed!'

'All licenses are revoked by order of the king and the witch hunter. You are now under arrest on the charge of the heinous offence of witchcraft.'

'That's ridiculous! How can it be a crime to be a Wise Woman?'

'I don't make the rules, lady. I just enforce them!'

Now she was incarcerated deep within the dank and dripping dungeons of Castle Valiant, her heart breaking as she now knew her beloved highwayman was here too. Locked somewhere where she could not hear or see him.

Not till the time of their execution. What madness had overtaken that pompous prat Pravis? She had thought him a fool but a harmless enough fool.

'It's that nasty bastard Strang!' whispered a nervous and very tiny voice in the darkness, filtering from the far corner of her cell.

'Oakham Strang? My Jed's ex-partner?'

'The very one!' continued the tiny voice, 'the one that became Princess Demonica's boyfriend. Now he is the witch hunter!'

Morven shuddered. How many times had she offered Strang the hospitability of her hovel, fed him, treated his wounds? Not just a nasty bastard then but a damn ungrateful one too. And who was the other prisoner?

'My friend in adversity, you know much about these sad matters. Who are you and what is your name?'

'Slinglenook the Third. I am one of the Malign Butterflies that awoke from my chrysalis on the wrong side of the border. I belong to the Land of Darkness and Despair. I may be threatening but too small and insignificant for my Demon Prince to rescue me.'

'How did they capture you? You could kick your way out of any net!'

'An evil trap!' sighed the mortified butterfly. 'Flowers covered with superglue. Once my heavy boots touched down on a lupin I was doomed.'

Stifling a little despairing sob, he continued, 'My downfall, I could never resist a lupin.'

Morven could not believe her ears, how low was that nasty bastard Strang prepared to stoop? How many more innocent fluttering insects were needlessly caught in that snare just to capture one Malign Butterfly? Who were only life-threatening when they attacked in swarms.

'At least my small but menacing friend, you have a chance to escape. Hide in the folds of my robes and when I am taken out to meet my fate, you can fly away.'

'Thank you, missus. I will take you up on that.'

Getting more of an evil bastard by the minute Strang knew no plan to take complete control over the Land of Goodness and Light would succeed while there was a full blood demon flying about blasting innocent citizens at will. Zaphael was an uncontrollable and unpredictable force of devilish anarchy, and with Moonraven soon to be dangling crow bait, a potential new glamorous anti-hero for the revolting peasants to rally around. But how was he to rid the kingdom of such a powerful nuisance?

In desperation, Strang seriously considered sending a delegation to the young demon's father, asking for Prince Rafial to sort out his errant flesh and blood. But reason prevailed; being a powerful nuisance was what demons did best. For fun, Rafial would probably inflict another of his monstrous offspring to plague them. Talking of which, Strang shuddered as unwelcome memories of his brief but awful time with Princess Demonica returned to haunt him. He still had deep dents in his backside from her stiletto heels, raking talon scars down his back. And a godawful, garish tattoo on his cock saying 'property of the queen of hell'. Demonica was nothing but ambitious. The tattoo only read 'prequel' now though, his appendage still worn out from his time with the voracious and demanding creature. On cold days it merely said 'pee.'

No human could be safely sent against Zaff. The only defence against the demon was something very holy and fireproof. His research had discovered the Holy Monks of St Asbesto were not immune to fire and protected by their piety as they stoutly claimed. Strang had depopulated the entire monastery testing that bold but ultimately foolish assertion out. Reluctantly he concluded the answer may lie in holiness from a different source. He ordered one of his captives to be brought up from the dungeons. Bjorn Bjornson, Son of Ragnar. The Viking's mother had never fully explained that to his satisfaction.

Out on the razzle to celebrate the birthday of the youngest of their longboat crew, Bjorn was still drunk from the after-riot celebrations following the latest Shrike Hell debacle. Bjorn had been arrested for defiling the town square statue of St Prudia the Devout, though many believed the addition of crossed eyes, a Hitler moustache, frilly crotch-less knickers stolen from a flower fairy and a traffic cone on her head was a vast improvement. The old bag in stone form had glowered down disapprovingly on the town for far too long.

Fixing the errant Norseman with what he hoped was an authoritative, steely glare, Strang began to interrogate his prisoner who was worryingly unable to stand up. Moments later when the Viking was propped up by two stout serfs, he began again, 'What do you know about your people's religion?'

'Bugger all,' was the honest though slurred answer from the Viking, 'I took to raping and pillaging from an early age, had no time for book learning.'

'Damnation,' cursed Strang out loud, 'how else am I to find a way to summon up Throd the Thunderer to rid me of the demon?'

Overhearing the witch hunter's rant, Bjorn piped up cheerily after a spectacular belch, 'No need to do any summoning. Throd can found most days hanging out at the

Knave's Elbow Inn. Addicted to playing dominoes and quaffing their award-winning Olde Serf Sock ale.'

Cylphie could not totally shake off feeling bad about the wake of death and destruction that lay in the mismatched lovers' wake. She was an elf, a being of goodness and light after all. Her time with Zaff, though wildly exciting and thrillingly carnal was inevitably accompanied by many unfortunate piles of ash stinking of brimstone. The sorry remains of anyone who crossed Zaff, pissing him off in any one of a thousand ways, usually involving Cylphie. A harsh fate for often harmless acts of folly.

She did her best to try to tame him in an effort to salvage her own conscience. But with Zaff's hair-trigger reactions and the fact he was a hell-spawned demon, it was always going to be a lost cause.

They lay intertwined in dazed, post coital slumber on the top canopy of a spreading cedar tree, one that was silent, its branches still, pretending to be non-enchanted in order to vicariously ogle at the spectacular and prolonged triple x-rated coupling. Cylphie traced the outline of Zaff's beautiful fallen angel profile with her fingertip.

'Zaaafff...' she murmured.

Nearly asleep, the demon half opened his smouldering come to hell eyes and raised one quizzical eyebrow.

'I know you mean well but I don't get upset by some of the silly, harmless things humans do. Honest.'

Intrigued, Zaff woke up and rested on one elbow. 'Such as what?'

'Well, you know. A cheery wink or playful pat on my bottom. That's what cheeky human males do sometimes. It doesn't mean they ought to be toasted alive.'

Before he could answer, his thoughts were interrupted by a booming sound and general commotion along the forest floor beneath them.

'Oh bugger,' muttered the enchanted cedar blowing his cover.

'Pervert!' muttered Cylphie in disgust.

without knowing why she had never trusted cedars, maybe something to do with the way their cones pointed upwards instead of dangling down like other fir trees.

The booming sound came from a Viking horn, played badly by a very inebriated Norseman, horned helmet askew and wrapped in party streamers and the tangled strings of pink, sparkly balloons with 'Leif Ragnarson is 18 today!'

'Make way, make way - prepare ye all to tremble in awe!' he boomed to the forest creatures.

Zaff growled, the raucous and badly tuned horn was giving him a headache. Knowing what would happen next, an anxious Cylphie took his face in her hands.

'Leave him be, for me? I want to know what I should be in awe of!'

'Aren't I awesome enough for you?' Zaff pretended to sulk, knowing the answer.

'As if you have to ask!' replied Cylphie with a coquettish smile, desperately playing for time, hoping to distract Zaff long enough for the drunken Viking to leave.

The discordant noise of the horn was replaced by thunderous striding, gigantically powerful steps that shook the forest floor and sent the forest's branches swaying and creaking. Wildlife fled in terror, even the hibernating ones who'd overslept or were having a long lie-in.

'Now, that does sound pretty awesome,' admitted an impressed Cylphie.

'Nah! It's pants,' grumbled Zaff.

Noticing the demon and his elven lover for the first time high in the cedar branches, the Viking messenger quailed and wisely ran for his life, pausing only to yell back somewhat recklessly, 'You won't call it pants when Throd the Thunderer gets here to kick your sorry, puny demon backside back to Hell!'

There was a certain inevitability to the resulting pile of ash with only one pink sparkly balloon surviving the roasting, fluttering forlornly skyward in a lone celebration of Leif Ragnarson's birthday.

'Isn't that Throd the Thunderer a Norse God?' Cylphie asked uneasily. Nothing of this world could harm Zaff but a celestial deity was another matter.

Zaff was reassuringly unconcerned. 'Throd the Chunderer would be more apt. And he is only a demi-god. Bores for Valhalla.'

The ground-shaking footsteps neared.

'Or Throd the Blunderer.'

Any worries that Zaff's scornful confidence was misplaced were confirmed at the sight of the demi-god as he arrived at the base of the cedar tree. Mounted on an enormous six legged, flying white ox, extravagantly flaxen-haired Throd was all shining, rippling muscles bulging along his mighty arms, torso and thighs. His only garb was a pair of short dragon leather britches, matching boots with wings, a huge, sharp-studded leather belt of suitably heroic dimensions and a gleaming helmet with the biggest set of horns possible. He dismounted his ox and walked towards the cedar, though with difficulty as his mighty thews were so thickly muscled he had to move in an ungainly waddle. With his legs wide apart, hands on hips, he prepared to address the demon.

Cylphie braced herself for unhelpful laughter, Throd would most likely have a squeaky high voice or be outrageously camp, such was the way of things in this world.

'Zaphael, Prince of Hell, I bring you a challenge!'

Throd's voice was surprisingly deep and booming, so much so it made Brian Blessed's sound fey and retiring.

Zaff leant back against the cedar's tree trunk, crossed one leg and folded his arms. He gave an extravagant yawn of disinterest.

Undeterred, Throd thundered on, 'I have been summoned by the good citizens of the Land of Goodness and Light...'

'You mean that twat King Pravis,' interrupted Zaff with a smirk.

'The good citizens...' Throd repeated with a scowl, 'to rid the land of all evil, all supernatural nuisances, all fiendish blights, all...'

'Yeah, yeah,' interrupted Zaff again, 'we get the picture.'

The demi-god was about to continue when he whirled around in consternation.

'Did you hear that? A sound like a creeping army of crazed anti-matter mites...'

Shrugging, Cylphie and Zaff could see nothing but the forest floor disturbed by Throd's huge winged boots and the mighty ox grazing unconcernedly.

Uneasily, Throd tried to focus on his mission to arrest the demon. As a demi-god, he was fireproof and very strong, perhaps the only being capable of wrestling Zaphael to grovelling submission, a prospect he was looking forward too. It was long overdue time to take one of these arrogant disgraced angels down a peg or two. Lording it over the rest of the immortals just because they used to live in a better postal address than Valhalla and Mount Olympus. 'Used to' being the operative words...

Again the chilling sound. Throd's growing unease was highly amusing to Zaff, still high in the cedar.

'The Land of Goodness and Light will no longer tolerate witches and seers, any magical creatures including enchanted trees and animals.'

The cedar shuddered and went very silent. Cylphie glanced sharply at Zaff, her eyes wide open in shock. Morven! She would be in grave danger. Time to get rid of this oaf, his entertainment value waning rapidly. Peering down, she addressed the now openly jittery demi-god.

'These anti-matter mites, what sound do they make?'

Making a bizarre high buzzing sound, Throd nervously demonstrated the noise of his nemesis. Cylphie turned back to the demon.

'I told you, Zaff hon. That sound wasn't nesting wasps. Far too high pitched.'

His eyes huge with fright, Throd stuttered and stumbled in reply. 'You, you heard it? You? Him? The demon has also heard the sound of *Them*?'

'Must have,' answered Cylphie breezily, 'and very close too.'

'You are right, my beloved,' added Zaff struggling to keep a straight face, 'and getting much closer.'

With ground shaking strides, Throd turned and fled, so afraid he forgot his flying six-legged ox which lumbered after him in surprising and touching loyalty. But not before sighing, big brown eyes rolling heaven wards and shrugging with resignation.

Looking up at Zaff and Cylphie, the mighty beast muttered, 'No such thing as bloody crazed anti-matter mites, the silly sod has forgotten his medication again.'

An amused Zaff laughed as the animal took off in pursuit of his master. Cylphie was too worried about Morven to see the funny side. 'The Unwise Woman needs our help. Let's fly.'

Zaff ran his forked tongue along her spine. 'What's the hurry? While we are up this comfy tree, let's give it something more to ogle at...'

The elf ex-maiden wanted to push him away, this was an urgent and dire situation. His tongue reached the base of her spine and lingered...

Damn him. She was always sparkly elven putty in his strong demonic hands.

'Ok. Ok Zaff. But you'd better make it a real quickie!'

Ffhranghahraad the dragon folded back his impressive wings and sat beside a still pool and pondered his future. He gazed down at his reflection, a glory of glistening green scales with an iridescent shimmer of purple, bronze and dark blue. He was a fine looking, good dragon but his mind was in turmoil. How could this be the land of Goodness and Light when there was so much terror and oppression stalking the population, especially affecting the magical inhabitants? As he flew over the countryside he witnessed the king's militia vigorously backing up the newcomers, the men in grey as they destroyed Wolfsbane decorations, arrested Wise Women, brutally rounded up wizards, scarecrows and druids.

He wanted to interfere but would that make him an evil dragon? He didn't want to be one of those black-hearted monstrosities flying around with gory bits of wood nymph stuck in their teeth. If asked he would have to say he was an ambivalent dragon. He didn't have to wait for long for someone to ask him. A mismatched party of a warrior elf, an apprentice boy and... a...a... baker? Surely therefore the makings of a fellowship arrived to refresh themselves at the pool. They gave a friendly wave and carried on their business.

The dragon singled out the elf warrior, dangerously far from his sanctuary in the Forest of Mhmin. 'You do know what is happening? This is not a good place for one such as you any more.'

With a sad smile of agreement, the elf strolled over to the dragon and began to scratch him behind the forehead horns, a place no dragon of either persuasion could reach.

'Thank you my friend,' sighed the dragon, 'I don't suppose anyone will be able to do that soon. I have no idea what to do or where to go. '

Edrin was adamant, 'You must stay with us, we are a Fellowship on a quest to right a terrible wrong. Our good friend Morven the Unwise Woman will die at dawn in the castle courtyard if we do not rescue her. With your strength, speed and gift of flight we might actually stand a chance!'

The dragon shook his head mournfully, 'That would be an act of rebellion against the king, which would make me an evil dragon. I don't want to be banished to dwell in the Land of Darkness and Despair. It's dark. And despairing. And the evil dragons are mean bullies. I am neither good nor bad. I am Ffhranghahraad the Ambivalent Dragon.'

'Could I call you Frank?'

'Yeah, why not,' replied the dragon with relief. He hated his given name, a nightmare to spell when filling out competition forms. He was a compulsive and avid competition competitor. He had already won several holidays to the Costa Lotte, a speedboat, twenty barrels of finest mead, a toaster and a night out with the delectable Muriel, a famous leading lady. He'd only taken advantage of the mead, being a dragon.

Princess Allura stepped out onto the balcony of her quarters and tried to take some comfort in the sharp early morning sunshine, riot of birdsong and the panoramic view over the Land of Goodness and Light. With difficulty due to her growing bulk, she sat down on a wicker chair in a stone patio stripped of all its once cheerful tubs and hanging baskets of bright and heavily scented flowers. All taken away and destroyed as being too frivolous for a castle by her brother, the king,

Virtually a prisoner confined to her quarters, her pregnancy was an acute embarrassment to the entire household. That lucky bitch of a sister, Princess Charmina, had also taken part in the infamous three in a bed romp with that handsome rogue of a highwayman Jed Moonraven but she had got away with it. Now married off to the diminutive, boss-eyed but filthy rich third son of the Pangolin Emperor of Sharpei, Charmina was out of one prison and straight into another. But with better weather, servants and all the silk cushions she could lie about on.

Allura had no access to her mother which was a blessing and spent her days waiting for the baby to arrive in the company of her servants. If only she could escape but now even walking the steps up to her bedchamber was tiring. Regrets? Allura had plenty. She had enjoyed every minute of the brief, wild, forbidden and pleasure filled encounter with Moonraven but not the result. But at least her hard-to-hide pregnancy did make her unmarriageable to the succession of dim, in-bred or arrogant twats of princes who her brother had paraded her in front of like a prize brood mare. Only to be cruelly dismissed as used goods, soiled. And at least she had known the pleasures of the bedroom, unlike her brother who had sworn a chivalric vow of chastity till he'd married the princess of his dreams, i.e. one that came with sufficient lands and wealth.

She returned to her chambers and sat before a mirror, trying not to notice the sadness in her pretty cornflower blue eyes. Brushing out her rippling waterfall of golden blonde hair, Allura felt the babe kick and she put her hand protectively over her swollen belly. 'You are going to live free, little one. I don't know how but I swear to you I will find a way.'

As always her brother barged into her chambers without knocking, he took advantage of his kingly status at every opportunity and striding through the rooms, walked straight up into her bedchamber.

'Beloved sister, I bring good news. The heinous bastard that violated you has been captured and will hang at dawn alongside his witch mistress. And I found a man of good position who actually wants to marry you even with that rogue's spawn on the way. The wedding ceremony begins at 9pm tonight. Don't be late. I have a banquet to attend at 9.15.'

He turned on his heel and left her quarters leaving Allura in shock. Poor Jed! Poor Morven! And what monstrous suitor had her brother promised her to?

Allura did not have long to wait her answer. Within minutes of her brother's shock announcement she had another unwelcome visitor. Also bursting into her quarters with no announcement stormed a large, burly man with meanest, coldest eyes she had ever seen, eyes like small shards of flint. He was well dressed in noble garb but it looked ill-fitting, uncomfortable as if his clothes were trying to escape from him. She did not blame them.

She did her best to look imperious, though rising to her feet quickly was difficult and ungainly. 'What is this outrage? I am the princess of this realm. How dare you barge into my private chambers!'

The man gave a slight, mocking bow. 'And such pleasant, well appointed chambers,' he leered, ones that are soon to be mine, your high and mightiness. For I am Oakham Strang, the witch hunter. And in a few hours time, your husband.'

This was worse then she could have imagined! Her mind racing, Allura tried her best to push back the fear and panic. She needed to think clearly and speedily. 'Impossible! I am already wed.'

'You lie badly,' sneered Strang. Despite her advanced state of pregnancy, he could see that Allura was pretty. He would enjoy his brief time as a married man.

'I would not have my baby born out of wedlock!' she continued. 'I married Jed Moonraven in a secret ceremony at the little roadside chapel of St Elopia On-the-Runne.'

'Lies! All Lies!' barked Strang.

'I am a royal princess. I do not lie,' answered Allura with her regal poise returning. It was a wild story but hard to disprove.

'And the witnesses?'

'All fled to a life of exile or dead - by your hand. Your terrible purges are wrecking the joy and peace of this land.'

'How convenient,' muttered the witch hunter still unconvinced of her unlikely story.

'But it matters not. I will therefore postpone the wedding until after the execution. Within minutes, you can be a widow then a new bride. One gown will do for both occasions. You had better make it black.'

Allura wanted to slap the arrogant oaf's face, order him out of her chambers but she no longer had any power in Castle Valiant. 'I will never submit to you, you ill-bred peasant!'

Strang laughed, 'You were only too quick to spread your legs for another ill-bred peasant! The only difference was the first one had a charming manner and a handsome face. I am going to enjoy breaking that high and mighty manner of yours, Princess.'

The witch hunter strode out of the princess's chambers without a bow or backward glance, ignoring the flying chamber pot hurled in his direction. For all her fancy breeding and blue blood, Allura was no different to any tavern doxie who preferred Jed's company in bed to his. This time tomorrow, that will all have changed with the sudden jerk of a tightening noose. Forever.

It was the fulfilment of everything he had known would happen to him. Jed spent his last night on earth in heavy chains, in a dank, stinking cell with only a few enchanted slugs as company. They had survived the witch hunter's purges by hiding in the sodden rushes on the filthy cell floor and keeping their mouths shut. If only that damned crossbred colt had. Its foul mouth and bad attitude had alerted the militia as the highwaymen hid in a grove of ordinary silver birches.

Screaming out, 'Oi, you stupid, tin-clad pillocks! You couldn't find an effing whore in an effing bawdy house!' was not the most helpful contribution to Jed's escape plan.

Now Jed was to hang at dawn. It was the price he knew he would have to pay one day for a wild and reckless life of theft on the king's highway, it was just he had hoped he would have been a lot older and slower when they finally caught up with him.

'You will get a large crowd, Moonraven,' piped up one of the slugs, 'and a quick end. All we will get is a jar of salt.'

'Yeah,' added another with a hint of bitterness in its small, slimy voice. 'Plenty of people to affect a last minute rescue. Who would rescue an enchanted slug? No one.'

'Other enchanted slugs?' ventured Jed at a feeble attempt to comfort the creatures.

There was nothing else to do but wait for the dawn. The dungeon had no windows, no last sight of the stars. His mind wandered to Morven. If only she had studied the dark arts, she could have set him free with enchantment. But her vow to harm no one restricted what she could do in her attempt to help him escape. And with no sidekick to rescue him, surely he was doomed. For in truth, there were far more people out there eager to see him swing, the outraged husbands he'd cuckolded, the fathers out for revenge on dishonoured daughters, the nobles he had robbed. And he never redistributed a penny of his ill-gotten wealth to the poor except to innkeepers and whores, so the serfs and peasants would be pissed off with him too. Remorse? Not one scrap. As the wild pirates sailing on those distant shores of the Ocean of Dreams Undreamt would say, a short life but a merry one.

Uproar, discord and fear now stalked the once pleasant, serene and harmonious glades as the Forest of Mhmin had reached crisis point, bursting at the seams with refugees from the Land of Goodness and Light. Now more accurately renamed the Land of Madness and Spite by its persecuted former inhabitants. The Wise Women ran a twenty-four hour comfort station offering counselling and soothing tisanes or warming nettle broth to all the exhausted newcomers that could eat. Spells of support and understanding to those who didn't. Every tree had row after row of displaced piskies and wood gnomes sitting forlornly in their overburdened branches. The normal trees didn't complain but many of the enchanted ones did. Even the enchanted oak log who enjoyed having pert fairy and elf maiden backsides sitting on his face but not fat, flatulent hobnob goblins and dumpy sorcerers.

The still, mirrored pools of crystal clear water were packed to standing room only with water nymphs and all the forest glades were being stripped of all their soft mossy grass by herds of hungry unicorns and enchanted deer.

The Crystal Meeting Gazebo had never been so packed full and un-serene, so much so that a squadron of warrior elves had to be drafted in to keep the peace. But the pandemonium was not without good cause. The elven High Council listened in growing alarm as tale after sorry tale of horrors was related to them.

Devin the Devine, the recently appointed Poet Laureate of the elves raised his hand, used to instant silence and respect; he was shocked when none of the newcomers would shut up and listen to his wise counsel.

'Sit down *Elfis*, no one wants to hear a song or a bloody interminable poem now!' heckled a surly satyr, so desperate for space were the Mhmin inhabitants, for once in his life he had people pressing up close to him, regardless of his rampant flea infestation.

'Yeah!' chirped up a phoenix. 'This is a time for warriors! We must get ready to defend ourselves...not listen to New Age prattle!'

'The elves know they cannot fight back!' stormed a hooded wandering loner. 'None of their elven warriors are up to much anymore, weakened by years of poetry recitals and being serene all the bloody time. And where is the only elf warrior with any cojones? Ridden off to save his poster boy!'

The expected uproar of disapproval did not happen, though the newcomer's unpleasant and unnecessary crudity created a shudder of distaste. Most shrugged with disinterest at such old news and Edrin's only crime in most eyes was perhaps a certain lack of taste in his choice of hopeless crush. But the wandering loner's condemnation was unusual and not in keeping with the free spirit of the Forest of Mhmin. Especially in matters concerning the traditionally uninhibited manner of elven love lives. All eyes turned to the newcomer, who was preparing to rant on.

'No one can protect the forest anymore.'

'We do not need protection,' spluttered an affronted Devin, 'we have magic to look after us. As it has always done!'

'Magic? Magic!' laughed the lone wanderer. 'A dragon-fuelled freak windstorm of dried fairy snot?'

One of the flower fairies had enough of the negative vibe and hauled back the lone wanderer's hood exposing a human. 'A spy!' she shrieked. 'We have been infiltrated by the enemy.'

Squarf stood as proudly as his squat stature could allow. 'I am not a spy nor am I your enemy. I was once a hard done by serf belonging to that prat Prince Pravis. Now he is king and an even greater prat. And since his alliance with nasty bastard Strang, the witch hunter, a danger to us all. I am here to claim asylum.'

'How can we trust you?' shrieked the flower fairy in her normal, calm voice.

'You can't. Not by my words but by my deeds. I will defend the forest to the death. But I would rather not die. Not with the land of Goodness and Light to liberate. The noble and righteous rebellion against Strang and Pravis and their reign of oppression and terror starts here!'

The resultant deafening silence to his rallying call was not what he expected.

'Ok. I get the message. I'll just settle down with a nice hot bowl of bloody nettle soup.

Finding space for fleeing beings wasn't just a problem at the Forest of Mhmin. The steady stream of refugees amassing at his border was also a major headache for Prince Rafial in the dour Land of Darkness and Despair. One solution was simple. To reduce the cowering masses of newcomers to piles of ash stinking of brimstone. Only curiosity held the demon back. Why in Hell would anyone flee to this blighted place? He summoned a quaking underling and ordered him to fetch the prince's favourite accursed unicorn. Rafial decided he wanted to see for himself.

Down in the demonically royal stables, Cuddles the accursed unicorn was about to tuck into a tasty snack of ergot-infested rye bread when his peaceful morning was interrupted by a terrified evil minion.

'Oh no!' it screeched in despair. 'You are turning white!' This was indeed bad news. Cuddles was foaled to an accursed unicorn mare, he should have been born jet black. 'You have not been eating your charcoal, have you?'

'Its yeuch,' pouted the unicorn, 'you try eating that vile, dry muck everyday.'

'I won't be eating anything and nor will you if the prince finds out. We will both be piles of ash stinking of brimstone, things not known for their appetites.'

The minion called for other grovelling sidekicks and planned a desperate solution. One suggested a quick lick of black paint, another a thick coating of tar but nothing would dry fast enough or look convincing enough to fool the shrewd and clever demon prince.

'We are running out of time. What can we do?' cried a well-panicked evil minion, 'The prince wants to ride out now!'

Cuddles wandered out of his stable and looked into a far corner of the barn. 'Quick drying glue...' He muttered, 'Lots of it, all over me.' The minions hastily obliged and while the accursed unicorn was still tacky, he rolled in a swept up pile of cast off fairy snot, the shimmering glitter that had covered all of the Army of Darkness and Despair. Soon all trace of white was obliterated under a dazzling spectacle of glitter. He looked like a four-legged disco ball.

Unconvinced by this ploy and certain his fiery demise was imminent, the evil minion led Cuddles to the impatiently waiting prince in the courtyard.

'What in Hell is that sparkling monstrosity?' bellowed Rafial sending the lackey scurrying, his hands holding his head as if that would stop a lightening flash of fiery death.

'It's me, your choice of steed for the parley, one who was in the front line, your demonic highness. Ready to fight to the death for the honour of the Land of Darkness and Despair, ready to sacrifice all in your service. In doing so, I copped a full load of fairy snot.'

Rafial sighed. It would be unreasonable to zap this brave and loyal creature. Though being unreasonable was a reasonable part of being a demon. 'Get yourself cleaned up. Use dark enchantment, bleach. That stuff advertised by the horrible shouting man. Anything that works.'

Bowing his head in assent, Cuddles watched Rafial storm off to find one of his cowering servants to get an evil black dragon ready for the journey. The accursed unicorn did not have much time left. He had a narrow escape this time but it would not last. He had to flee his comfortable life in the Land of Darkness and Despair and seek a safe haven elsewhere. But with the Land of Goodness and Light fallen into a puritanical madness, where could he go?

Cuddles waited till he could hear the dragon's roar and great downbeat of its huge wings as Prince Rafial took off into the ever-night sky. As soon as every evil minion was out of sight, he attempted to make a furtive exit out of the stable yard but it was hard to be inconspicuous when dazzling like a large, walking yuletide decoration. Light from any flickering torch or gleaming baleful eye caught the glitter and sparkled wildly in the gloom. He might as well have worn a huge neon sign with a big flashing arrow screaming - 'I am escaping from my demonic master!' His hooves were also not designed for sneaking, making a loud clatter on the cobbles, sadly tiptoeing was not a unicorn trait.

Salvation came in the most unlikely form.

'Quick! Over here!'

Cuddles could just make out many small, gruff voices that seemed to be coming from out of the walls. It did not surprise the unicorn; nothing surprised him about Rafial's fortress. Talking walls were small potatoes compared to some of the sights he'd seen since becoming the demon prince's favourite mount. A position he had revelled in until turning back to white. Glittery banshees sporting pink musical sunglasses for a start.

'If you want to live, come over here...Now!' insisted one small, gruff voice.

Cuddles wandered over, glancing up and around the wall - maybe they were the ghosts of past evil minions walled up alive for some transgression. Getting the temperature of Rafial's breakfast of fresh virgin blood wrong or worse still, serving up stale old trollop blood instead. That would earn a walling-in.

'Down here, idiot!' whispered the small gruff voice impatiently.

Crawling from a hidden gap in the wall, came a wizened old gremlin. Or to be more accurate, a wizened old glittery gremlin. Followed by several more, younger and very sparkling specimens. Some may have been female, it was impossible to tell. Gremlins were grotesquely ugly, even by the grim standards of the Land of Darkness and Despair that had gargoyles and gorgons dwelling there. Perhaps, mused Cuddles, it was an inherent trait of creatures whose names began with G to be ugly. No doubt Prince Rafial had a list of them somewhere, gremlins, goblins, gorgons, gulons, gargoyles, griffins, grayhamkooks, gnomes, giants, ghouls....

Cuddles was startled out of his trance-like reverie by a sharp kick on the fetlock by a gremlin.

'You don't have much time, if you want to join our band of escapees, come with us now.'

There was really no option for the accursed unicorn but to agree, peering closely at the gap in the wall, Cuddles could see it was an optical illusion, one too clever for Rafial's evil minions to discover. It was certainly wide enough for a determined and desperate unicorn to squeeze through. Holding his breath, the unicorn wiggled his way through to discover a dark labyrinth of hidden corridors carved deep into the fortress's walls.

'Snotlings!' murmured the older gremlin. 'That's who we reckoned built all this. They were supposed to be the unbelievably stupid, very small, inarticulate slaves of Rafial's cave trolls and evil minions. But all the time, they were secretly hollowing out an escape route after a big dispute over meal breaks and overtime. Or the complete lack of.'

'I've never heard of a snotling,' replied the unicorn, 'let alone seen one.'

'Exactly,' proclaimed the gremlin in triumph, 'and you never will. All successfully escaped their servitude and are living a free and happy life. Somewhere.'

'And that is your proof,' replied Cuddles uneasily, 'the lack of Snotlings? Could they equally have been turned into piles of ash stinking of brimstone? Or have been eaten by ogres?'

'Bugger,' muttered the gremlin as his optimistic theory went down the toilet.

In an uncomfortable silence, as the gremlins hastily questioned their belief system, they went deeper and deeper into the maze of rough-hewn corridors. Cuddles found himself thinking again. Snotlings were supposed to be very small, tunnelling such a large network would have taken them thousands of years. And if the Snotlings had indeed slowly built this labyrinth, what had they done with all the spoil? Walk about the fortress courtyard, slowly shaking rocks and dust from their tiny trouser bottoms while whistling a cheery tune? Found some unearthly creature that ate topsoil and hard core? Before he could come to a conclusion, the party of gremlins stopped at an underground chamber, a meeting place for many other refugees planning to flee the land. It was obvious what connected the miserable looking bunch, including werewolves, vampire bats, gremlins and two-headed snakes. All were completely covered with glitter.

'Welcome to our sorry band of sparkly creatures of the night,' muttered a lone and utterly miserable Drow.

The unicorn felt sorry for him, it must be so hard to be a dark elf when covered in fairy dust. And so far from his own home in the UnderRealm.

'What is your name?' growled the drow in an unfriendly manner.

'Horned Mighty Wielder of Doom.' replied the unicorn truthfully.

'Oh, it's Cuddles then!' guffawed the dark elf with an unpleasant, mocking laugh.

The unicorn chose to ignore the mocking. The Drow clearly had issues. Turning to the others, Cuddles tried to reassure the nervous crowd hiding in the depths of the fortress, 'My master, the prince, said I could use any measure I wanted to return to my former self including dark enchantment, that would apply to all of you too. We don't have to be glittery for ever!'

The Drow stood up and walked menacingly over to Cuddles, waving a long, jagged dagger in front of his face.

'You just don't get it, do you, you long-faced freak.' Drows were notoriously stroppy and judgemental. 'You may be the prince's favourite beast of burden, but you have shit for brains.'

Opening his arms wide in a dramatic gesture, encompassing all the other creatures in hiding, the black clad dark elf proclaimed solemnly, 'We are here because of a common bond, a brotherhood of many creatures bound by one heart, one desire, one need.'

'Which is?' urged Cuddles before the Drow began a long, meandering and over-melodramatic speech, another annoying trait of their kind.

'I was getting to that, prick-head!' snapped the Drow. 'We are here, today, together in hiding in this lonely refuge because we share the same aspiration....'

Cuddles pawed at the ground in impatience, lowering his horn in a threatening manner.

'Ok! I'll skip to the point,' grumbled the Drow, the mangy unicorn was stripping his announcement of all gravitas. 'We are here because we want to stay sparkly. To revel in our new identity as creatures that glitter and shine. We are beautiful, no matter what they say. Words can't break us down.'

The rest of the band of creatures began to hum and join in until Cuddles silenced them with a loud snort.

'That's fine. Live how you want to, that's a good thing. A very good thing, so much so, that I want to join you. But how are we going to escape both the land of Darkness and Despair and the Land of Goodness and Light?'

'We were rather hoping you had the answer,' replied the wizened gremlin.

Edrin's heart leapt as the downbeat of large, powerful wings battered the bog willow grove where the reformed Fellowship had gathered. His knees went weak as Zaff in all his demonic glory alighted with Cylphie holding tightly to his waist. There had been times in the past when just the thought of an autograph would have sent Edrin into a spin. Now he was joining forces and fighting alongside his idol. If only there wasn't the complication of Cylphie, his happiness would be complete.

The rising sun glinted dully of the Hydra's slimy, barnacle-adorned scales and garlands of festering seaweed that, combined with her legendary bad breath, made her journey upstream the talk of the riverside dwellers. She enjoyed the change of scenery but not the annoying rider she had been charged by the Selkie to convey to her heart's desire.

Swiftly if a little clumsily, the Hydra made her way upstream, making light of the sluggish, silt clogged currents of the Fuggis Mire River. Sitting on the beast's broad, slimy back, Demonica did her best to maintain both her dignity and her precarious seat.

'Stop digging in yer 'eels!' snapped one of the Hydra's nine heads.

'Not even Manolos,' quipped another. 'Where did they come from, missus, Bog Chav's R Us?'

Demonica seethed, the creature had been sniping at her throughout the journey. It wouldn't be long, she plotted. Soon she would be restored in all her rightful dark glory as the crown princess, heir to Prince Rafial, supreme ruler of the Land of Darkness and Despair. Once she had rid the world of that insufferable Zaphael. A new vision of conquest and world domination filled her mind, one where her first task would be to make new boots out of Hydra skin. As was finding some way to get back at the Selkie for lumbering her with such a preposterous means of transport.

At least she had the compensation of zapping mocking peasants along the route. Dullard would-be wits yelled taunts at her as she made her stately if unorthodox watery progress through the land, before ending up as piles of ash stinking of brimstone. That show of her power silenced the Hydra for half an hour.

The solemn drum beat pounded out the highwayman's last moments as he was roughly bundled out of the dungeon and up onto the wooden gallows in front of the castle. Solemn until the unseen drummer got bored and began to improvise. Half way into his jazz solo, there was a loud thump, a shrill exclaimed 'ouch!' Then back to the steady sombre beat again.

As the slugs had predicted, Jed Moonraven had drawn a record breaking crowd but the silence that greeted his arrival was bizarre and unnerving. Where were the cheers, the jeers, the witty heckles? The moronic chants of the bog chavs? Where were the weeping love-struck maidens? This was not how he wanted to bow out of this world! As the executioner slowly made ready, Jed studied the faces of the crowd. They were terrified. He had never seen the populace of the Land of Goodness and Light so brow-beaten and defeated. This was the first day of the Pagan

Feast of Wolfsbane. Where were the festive decorations? The jolly sights and sounds of the Wolfsbane Fayre?

As if in answer, nasty bastard Strang, aka The Witch Hunter, strode over with a triumphant grin. Beside him loped a misshapen half-human half-cave troll, cackling and simpering, rubbing his hairy hands in glee. Strang's rise to power was progressing, he had his own sidekick. Probably called Igor. Jed was therefore not surprised at the next development, Strang's maniacal laughter.

'You said you were a nastier bastard then me, highwayman,' Strang crowed, 'but who is about to have their neck broken? Eh? Mwwuaahaha, muaahahaha.'

'At least I am not wearing that dull grey PORN garb, I go to my maker looking dashing and handsome.'

Which was true.

'I have a little surprise for you, Moonraven. Igor, bring out the witch!'

'Noooooo!' Jed cried in horror as his beloved Morven was dragged out to join him on the gallows, held by her captors too far from him to be able to touch for the last time.

'Let her go Strang!' he demanded, 'I deserve to be here, but she is completely innocent of all harm doing.'

'She is a witch by her own confession,' sneered Strang.

'It is not a crime to be a witch!' shouted back Jed, appealing to the strangely silent and sullen crowd. 'Come on folks, don't stand for this! They are murdering a gentle Wise Woman. One who does no harm and births your babies, cures your ailments.'

Momentarily distracted while the witch hunter swatted away at some small but determined fluttering creature that seemed hell-bent on kicking him in the groin, Jed addressed the crowd again.

'I repeat. Since when has it been a crime to be a witch?' retorted Jed, who turned to address the crowd. 'Come on folks, if you want a spectacle, I will be dancing a jig at the end of that rope any minute, but do not let them get away with this travesty, this cruel crime against an innocent woman! Morven has sworn a vow to do no harm.'

Using a pre-arranged secret signal, Strang's grey-clad fanatics, now heavily and malodorously disguised as peasants began to heckle from the crowd.

'She's not a Wise Woman, she is an Unwise Woman!'

'I used her cure for a verruca and my foot turned green!'

'I got bitten by her security toads and now I am covered in warts!'

'I bought a love potion from her and now I am married to my mule!'

'She is a witch! Burn her!'

The last jeer brought a gleam to Strang's eyes. Why hadn't he thought of that? It was a brilliant suggestion. One that would spread such terror, his rule - that is Pravis's rule, would never be challenged.

'Igor, fetch dry kindling and plenty of branches! Muaahahaha!'

Up on the balcony, King Pravis watched the proceedings with mixed feelings. He had no qualms about sending Moonraven to his doom, the man was an unredeemable scoundrel who had dishonoured both his sisters and at some point, stolen from most nobles in the land. But the pretty witch was another matter. He had been peeved with her for her cavalier attitude towards the glitter incident but was that enough to condemn her to burn at the stake?

He carefully studied the faces of the crowds, in the past; an act of grave injustice could spark a rebellion but saw nothing beyond their own fears. His witch hunter had done a fine job in repressing and subduing the population.

On another balcony, the future Mrs Strang watched with horror as kindling and branches were dragged up to the gallows. It was monstrous! An act of unspeakable evil, but what could she do? Her baby was nearly due and she was locked in her rooms.

A furtive Dawn appeared over the horizon. Then the first rays of sunrise gleamed across the land. Time was running out. As the much diminished Fellowship approached Castle Valiant, it was clear that any rescue attempt would be nigh impossible. The witch hunter's grey-uniformed goons, heavily backed up by the king's well-armed militia were searching everyone approaching the castle, weeding out known trouble-makers, like Dawn the Mouthy Harridan and anything vaguely supernatural.

'So,' said Robard, as ever pointing out the obvious, 'that means Frank, Zaff, Cylphie and Edrin are out of the equation. And thanks to your boasting about your lucky bun, you are too well known to slip unnoticed into town.'

'Sod it!' growled Zaff. 'This is a piece of cake, or lucky bun. I'll just have one f◆ⅿ&ᵹing huge barbeque, end of problem.'

'You can't do that!' cried Cylphie in alarm.

'I know, I know... I'll singe the old ladies with the knitted loo roll covers and their fluffy little kittens.'

'What on earth is he talking about?' muttered an alarmed Wheatley, his beloved Morven was about to be executed and they were talking nonsense about loo roll covers.

'And I would have to stop you,' added Frank the Ambivalent dragon, 'because burning up an entire castle full if people is plain evil.'

'Er, excuse me...Demon?' replied Zaff with a wicked grin.

A rustle in the bushes announced the approach of someone. Edrin raised his bow, Zaff prepared to zap, Wheatley readied his lucky bun. A wiry blonde, pale-faced youth wandered out of the bush. 'Looks like it is down to me,' he announced.

'And you are?' ventured Wheatley.

'I am the true apprentice about to discover his hidden identity,' announced a transformed Robard to his astonished fellowship.

'Robard, you are so brave. But what can you do?' queried Cylphie, changing out of her rock chick garb behind the protective screen of Zaff's outspread wings. Not that anyone would dare peek, the price of an eyeful of the delightful elf ex-maiden was too high with the demon being such a jealous lover. She had changed into her 'elf in disguise as a young male human traveller' garb. Still utterly unconvincing. 'And I will come with you' she added, ignoring Zaff's furious glare of protest.

'I'm a poet, not a fighter,' the lad replied, 'but there is nothing so powerful than a nasty rumour. I will start a Chinese whisper that will terrify the crowds, cause pandemonium and Zaff and Frank can swoop down and rescue Morven and Jed.'

The baker bit back the unworthy temptation to whisper 'Just rescue Morven.' It was nothing personal, just that damned awful poetry.

The crowd waited in a tense, horrified but subdued silence with only rivulets of tears running unchecked down many faces as the solemn drum roll began. Strang stepped forward and snatched the noose from the executioner's grasp. 'I want the pleasure of sending this scoundrel on his not-so-merry way.' He draped it over Jed's neck and tightened it with a hard jerk, a premonition of what was to come.

'I'd like to say it was a pleasure riding the highways all those years with you. But I am not. You were a vain and reckless fool that wouldn't have survived five minutes without me. But no one sings songs in taverns about me, no one will weep at my demise.'

'What can I say?' muttered the highwayman. 'Some of us were born to be handsome anti-heroes others to be ugly nasty bastard sidekicks.'

Strang sneered, it was true. But he would be the nasty bastard sidekick who became king of the Land of Goodness and Light while Jed would become forgotten crow bait swinging on some remote gibbet.

'I will wait so that you can watch your witch die in the flames before I dispatch you. And look up at that balcony. See that pretty princess, she is about to drop your bastard whelp. After I marry her tonight.'

'I'll see you in Hell, Strang,' growled a distraught Jed, 'but let Morven go. She has done no harm.'

'Fetch the kindling!' shouted the witch hunter, doing his best to ignore the ripple of growing horror in the crowd, his minions planted within the masses were not doing their job properly. Where was the hysterical baying from the mob? Where were the jeers and howling to burn the witch?

At the edge of the crowd, Robard and Cylphie felt the tension and growing alarm in the crowd intensify at the sight of approaching lit torches. It was perfect. They split up and walked in opposite directions at the back of the crowd.

'Aaaaarrghhh! The Plague! Someone has Fungus Badger Plague!' shouted Robard at the top of his voice, his years of acting training with the mummers brought his well-projected and realistic panic soaring above the heads of the crowds.

'Oh Noooooo!' screamed Cylphie. 'A Fungus Badger is loose in the crowd! It has the Plague...Run for your lives!'

Robard's cunning plan, not actually that dissimilar to Cylphie's successful scheme to empty the auditorium at Burpington-Not-on-Sea worked beyond their expectations. Within seconds, total pandemonium broke out, the terrified crowds fleeing the courtyard in any way they could, some taking advantage of the ever-present convenient swinging ropes, a few got shot out of catapults, there were even a couple of pole vaulters leaping the castle walls. But most just legged it.

So appalled at the prospect of Fungus Badger plague, they hardly noticed the downbeat of two sets of massive wings as Frank and Zaff swept low and fast above their heads. Curbing the desire to incinerate the whole castle, Zaff alighted on the gallows and cut the prisoners free, feeble attempts at firing arrows at him bounced harmlessly off his wings.

'Tell your dragon to rescue Morven. I have a score to settle with Strang and Pravis,' Jed yelled at the demon who surprisingly complied without an argument with his alpha male rival in the Fellowship.

'I love you!' cried the Unwise Woman throwing her arms around Jed's neck, before climbing on board the dragon's scaly neck. 'But don't risk your life looking for revenge, they are not worth it!'

'Bugger that!' snarled Jed, slapping the dragon's rump to send it on its way.

'Ouch!' snapped Frank. 'I felt that!'

'Ouch,' moaned Jed, nursing his bruised hand, 'So did I!'

'I suggest if you want to run Pravis through, just get on with it. Strang has bolted, I'll find him,' added Zaff.

'Thank you, but leave him to me,' warned the highwayman, 'vengeance is mine!'

'Help!' shouted Princess Allura, 'While you lot do all that macho posturing, I am in danger up here. I beg you; get me out of this madhouse!'

Frank flew up to fetch the princess, while Zaff dropped Edrin and the highwayman on Pravis's royal balcony before seeking out Strang. Down below them, the courtyard was nearly empty; Robard and Cylphie's Fungus Badger plague had even sent the witch hunter's minions scurrying away. It was a glorious victory for lack of common sense and mindless hysteria.

Jed Moonraven whispered a brief command in the warrior elf's ear, causing Edrin to smile broadly, bow and run deep into the castle, his bow raised for action. Jed then calmly walked into the royal chambers alone.

Though furious that Zaff had gone after the nasty bastard, the highwayman could only hope the demon would keep Strang alive long enough for him to exact his own and rightful revenge. Being turned into a pile of ash stinking of brimstone was far too kind a fate for that treacherous and homicidal animal.

Jed did his best to concentrate on the matter in hand, the king. He found Pravis not cowering but hastily trying to buckle himself into his suit of armour, calling in vain for his serf, Squarf. So caught up in extricating himself from a jumble of unbuckled cuirasses and greaves, he did not notice Jed's silent and swift approach.

'What is the worst thing I can do to you Pravis?' growled a furious Jed, his knife pressing deeply into the king's throat. How easy it would be to end this miserable worm's life with one swift pass of the knife.

Moonraven was no stranger to cold-blooded killing. The highwayman had earned his date with the hangman, his beloved Morven had not.

'Nothing!' gasped Pravis. 'I will die at your hands a great and noble king. You will always be a murdering low-life scoundrel. A common thief. A violator of innocent women!'

Jed laughed without a shred of humour. 'That again! It really bugs you I have had both your sisters!'

That settled the king's fate. 'I am going to let you live, seething over my conquests, knowing I had both your sisters writhing in pleasure beneath me, calling out my name over and over again. That I had your miserable life in my hands and I spared you. And one more thing.'

The highwayman grinned and signalled to Edrin, now waiting by the door. The warrior elf stood aside to let in an irate woman with a peculiar blank face like a startled and badly ageing wax doll. One hand on her hip, the other wagging furiously, she stormed over to the king and began to hit and poke him. Jed and Edrin walked out to the balcony to await Zaff and Frank, horrified squeals of protest ringing in their ears....

'Mother! Ouch! I am sorry! I will be your good little soldier...Ouch! Ouch! I promise!'

With no time to watch the touching family reunion, Zaff and Edrin flew off the balcony and fly high into the sky soon followed by Jed nervously hanging onto Frank's scaly neck. They soared through the azure morning air anxiously searching for the rest of the Fellowship. Queen Hemelda's wrath would delay the king ordering out the militia in pursuit, but not for long.

They found them heading at full speed for the Bog of Fuggis Mire. Morven knew every inch of the dangerous swamp and could cross it quickly, while their pursuers would soon be mired down, hopelessly lost, preyed on by hungry boggarts and pelted with tin cans by the bog chavs. If the quick sand didn't get them first. Wheatley drove a stolen light landau pulled by a team of fine fast thoroughbreds, a well-sprung vehicle that would lessen the jolt to the heavily pregnant princess, carefully tended by Morven. Cylphie rode the highwayman's swift grey mare, ignoring the whingeing protests of her spoiled brat of a colt who had to carry a rider for the first time, the Goth boy, Robard.

As they reached a crossroads, Zaff recognised another fleeing horse drawn cart galloping away from the land of Goodness and Light. It contained his fellow band members Lennie, Tofus and Desmond, minus roadies, groupies or any of their gear. A sure sign that they were seriously spooked and were fleeing under threat.

In a tumult of huge wings and subsequent downdraught, the demon flew to the ground and landed in front of the band's cart, causing their already panicked horses to rear in fright.

'Nice one Zaff old mate,' seethed Lennie struggling to control the terrified beasts. 'Always with the theatrical entrances!

The sound of tiny agitated voices coming from the floor of the farm cart triggered Edrin's curiosity. Glancing down he made out a crowd of enchanted shrews, piskies, brownies and a wood sprite all jumbled together in a miserable huddle on the cart's rough wooden floor. Something else was resting in a small wooden casket beneath the driving seat, something believed nocturnal. Also under the seat was a book, no one knew who it belonged to or how it got there but as it was doing no harm, the fugitives left it alone.

'A warrior elf! We are saved!' squeaked a piskie, leaping up and down with delight. 'We tried to get back to the Forest of Mhmin but it was too far. These oafish but kindly humans helped us escape.'

'But now we don't have to endure their crude language and vile body functions for a second longer,' chirped up the wood sprite, 'we have you to take us home!'

Edrin shook his head. 'Sorry to disappoint you. I am in exile too. I am with a Fellowship on a quest to seek justice for all the persecuted fey folk of the Land of Goodness and Light.'

'Pox!' cursed one of the enchanted shrews taking note of Edrin's many badges. 'Pox, pox and pus-filled boils! Trust us to meet up with the one warrior elf with a thing about a rock star.'

Before Edrin could react to another shocking revelation that his secret might be known, there was a furious scuffle and shouting match behind him.

Zaff, his eyes dangerously angry and lit by flames, faced up to Jed Moonraven who had both pistols aimed at the demon's head.

'Moron! Human waste of skin! You had that twat Pravis right where you wanted him and you let him live? What kind of notorious criminal are you? Pathetic, that's what you are!'

Oblivious to how close he was to be being turned into a pile of ash stinking of brimstone, Jed's eyes narrowed in cold fury as he cocked both pistols.

'There are things worse then death, demon. But how would you know? You are just a permanently stoned immortal, a monster casually snuffing out innocent life as the whim takes you.'

'So?'

'So, as an intelligent human, I can make more sophisticated choices.'

'Robbing unarmed women travelling the land in coaches of their valuables. Leaving a fanatical leader alive and free. A madman who is burning scarecrows and witches and supergluing butterflies. His fate? To be told off by his mother. Soo sophisticated!'

'So, the winged wonder would reduce him to yet another pile of ash stinking of brimstone?'

'F◆♍&ing right I would!'

'Environmental vandal!'

'Wuss!'

'Arrogant show off!'

'Pussy!'

'And who let that nasty bastard Witch Hunter Strang escape, eh?'

'Who said I let him escape!' replied the demon with a knowing wink.

Over in the landau, Morven watched the argument in shock and alarm, Jed was being a suicidal idiot taking on a full blood demon with a short fuse. But the princess was in distress, the Unwise Woman needed to tend to her. She turned to Wheatley, her lovely green eyes tear-filled and pleading.

'Gentle baker, can you be as brave as you are kindly and diffuse that silly macho scrap before my beloved but downright stupid Jed gets turned to toast!'

The day before Wheatley would have had mixed feelings, Jed turned to a pile of ash stinking of brimstone would have left him clear to woo Morven. But now he knew she would never stop loving her highwayman even if the rogue was dead. And besides, he was becoming increasingly enamoured of the lovely Princess Allura - and surprisingly at the thought of the babe on the way, even though it was not his.

The baker took his life in his hands and with one hand deep in his pocket, holding his lucky bun tightly, strolled manfully over to the sparring pair.

'Hey guys, way, waaay too much testosterone flying about. You are frightening the ladies. We are all on the same side, remember?'

'Bog off baker,' snarled Jed.

'Yeah, f◆♍&; off back to your buns before I overcook them!' sneered Zaff.

Maybe this was his hidden destiny at last, to have the courage to stand up to these warring males, face them down and diffuse the dangerous confrontation to save the disintegrating Fellowship. He stood up to them in a surge of pride, his head held high, arms folded resolutely.

'That takes some cojones,' admitted Zaff.

'Or downright stupidity,' muttered Jed.

'Ok, whatever. I'm cool,' grumbled Zaff

'And I agree to differ about what to do with Pravis,' remarked Jed, uncocking the pistols and stepping back.

As the two swaggeringly macho aggressors stalked off, Wheatley felt his knees give way, far from standing his ground, he had been rooted to the spot in sheer terror, his face frozen in one expression. One look at Zaff's blazing eyes and Jed's pistols had destroyed any sense of destiny fulfilled. He returned to Morven and the princess on wobbly legs, needing a strong drink. All that was on offer was one of the Unwise Woman's alcoholic cordials, a liqueur made from fermented crushed dandelion clocks, purified marrowfat peas and liquefied lemon meringue pie. A lively little brew. Wheatley knocked it back in one; he'd worry about the taste later.

It did not take a great deal of persuasion for the remnants of Shrike Hell to agree to join the Fellowship in their escape from the Land of Goodness and Light. Though the row between their lead guitarist and the highwayman had unnerved them, what other choice could they make? Three heavy metal rockers and a handful of small beings against a fanatic army! But they may well have harboured second thoughts as another furious row broke out, this time among the elves.

'It was kind of Zaff to rescue you Edrin but now you are here, just get on this mare and let me be with my boyfriend!'

'I am perfectly happy flying with Zaff, thank you. You can stay on the horse.'

'Demons do not date elves!' insisted Edrin.

'This one does!' declared Cylphie.

The demon laughed at the escalating battle, it seemed he had another elf admirer, the devil in him decided to stir things up a bit. Zaff strolled over to the Goth boy and held out his hand. 'Fancy a change of transportation from that bony, noisome creature?'

Without a second's hesitation, Robard gratefully leapt off the colt and with a whoop of exhilaration felt the cool air rush past his body as he experienced flight for the first time.

'Zaff!' Cried Cylphie and Edrin in unison.

In the other cart, the princess gave out a loud yelp of pain. 'Boys and girls,' announced the Unwise Woman, 'could you please pack in this unseemly squabbling. We must be ready to greet the newest and smallest member of our Fellowship.'

Night fell gently with a glorious deepening purple sky with the stars appearing out one by one as if coming out for a theatre curtain call. Beneath the twinkling sky, the exhausted Fellowship made camp on a tree-lined island of dry land deep within mile after mile of stinking, foul ooze. Surely, they reasoned, even the most fanatic of the witch hunter's minions wouldn't try to cross the Bog in the dark? Especially as boggarts hungry for human flesh had good nocturnal vision and darkness brought the added threat of will-o-the wisps. They couldn't do much being mostly mist but they could knock a full grown horse unconscious with their methane breath. And they were perilously sarcastic.

Morven made sure the new mother and baby boy were settled, pleased to see Wheatley's arms protectively around Allura's shoulder, his eyes glowing with astonishment and adoration of the newborn babe. The Unwise Woman suspected he had discovered something more wonderful than cakes and buns. Perhaps even his true hidden destiny at last. It was exactly what the princess needed, a good man who would stand by her and the baby and look after them both.

Jed would be teary-eyed and sentimental over his son for about half an hour, then the wanderlust would send him fleeing into the night. He had had plenty of practise, siring kids with many a bawdy tavern wench across the country. A few she had even helped bring into the world. Not for the first time had loving the highwayman felt like a cruel curse. Unwise by name and unwise by nature, Morven glanced at her lover as he sat beneath a tree, tricorne hat pulled down low over his lean face, covering those twinkling dark blue eyes that promised so much. Her heart twisted at how close she had been to losing him. Wistfully, she envied the princess, not for her title and family wealth but her discovery of a decent, honest and faithful man.

Against all reason, she also envied Cylphie. Curled up next to Zaff, laughing and chatting quietly, there was no doubt in the Unwise Woman's mind that there was genuine love growing between them beyond their initial unbridled physical attraction. Something beautiful and unexpected.

Frank the ambivalent and insomniac dragon kept watch while the rest of the Fellowship fell one by one into a deep sleep. Soon the little glade resounded with snoring, some high pitched and tiny, some deep and rumbling. Who would have thought a twelve inch high wood sprite could sound like apocalyptical thunder while asleep. The dragon kept himself alert with a particularly tricky crossword to win a year's supply of washing-up liquid. A task made more difficult by the difficulty all dragons shared with spelling.

Zaff spent most of the night awake with his wings protectively wrapped around a slumbering Cylphie. But he still had a score to settle. Gently, he extricated his wings and wrapped her in a warm blanket, hoping she would sleep on undisturbed. Since he took up with the beautiful elf, he felt different, strange. He found himself thinking about her all the time, hated being away from her. His heart beat faster whenever she smiled at him which was often. He had no name for this odd feeling but he liked it. Zaff kissed her forehead, pleased as she smiled and murmured his name in her sleep.

Quietly as he could, he took to the air and flew low and swiftly over the dark clad landscape. As he swooped down to the spreading leafy canopy of a magnificent old oak tree, it raised a branch in greeting.

'You are a sight for sore eyes, Zaff. I was about to forget my promise to you and dump the fool onto the ground.'

'Giving you aggravation?'

'An earful. I didn't know there were so many swearwords in the human language!'

Zaff laughed, 'Then it is a good thing our prisoner isn't a demon. We have millions!'

Deeply entangled within the enchanted mighty oak's branches was an irate Witch Hunter Strang, unable to move and covered with leaves and pigeon poo. Zaff roughly pulled him free and after thanking the oak, took off into the sky with a wildly struggling Strang kicking the air and punching at his abductor.

'I'd pack that up if I were you human,' snarled the demon, even in the unlikely event you survive a drop of two hundred feet, you won't walk away from being a pile of stinking cinders.'

'What are you going to do with me? What infernal torture have you planned?'

'No torture! Just a nice friendly reunion!'

Zaff landed on a wide riverbank after throwing the witch hunter to the ground from a height of ten feet, thoroughly bruising and winding him. So much so that he could only splutter with shock and dismay at the sight of a familiar pair of high stiletto-heeled black patent boots approach across the grass.

'Hi sis! I brought you a little present, just to show some brotherly love.'

'My errant boyfriend! How thoughtful, Zaphael,' purred a delighted Demonica. Double the revenge was twice as sweet. She strode away from the dozing Hydra and put her foot firmly on Strang's neck. 'I'll deal with you later,' she snarled before turning her face back to her half-brother with a sickly smile. 'I too have a peace offering, a precious amulet.'

Warily Zaff watched as she produced a silver medallion in the shape of an oyster shell from a velvet pouch, it had great power, he could feel the waves of energy emanating from the large black pearl set in the centre. Not harmful energy but it made him strangely compelled, a strident desire to go to the sea. He hated anything being in control of his life and backed away with his hands raised. 'Sorry Mons, but the whole medallion look would wreck my image. So uncool.'

'Please, do not be so rash, my dearest brother. You do not have to wear it. But it does have great sentimental value to me. I want you to have it.'

'Let me see how it looks on you first.' Zaff uttered, not hiding the warning threat in his voice. 'It would be a shame to give away something that flatters your beauty.'

A furious Demonica was at a loss, was the charmed amulet's lethal power only attuned to Zaff or could it destroy all demons? Could she risk wearing it or give the game away by refusing? Before she could answer, her brother strode forward and snatching the amulet from her grasp, placed it over her head. 'There, I thought so, it looks great, flatters your black eyes.'

Demonica was unharmed, the spell was indeed only meant for that wretched Zaphael. Her hand went to remove the amulet but paused. Powerful and compelling images of the sea filled her head. It was so beautiful, so alluring, so very desirable. She wanted to go back, *had* to go back to find the Selkie again. To be with her forever...and ever...

Back within the hidden labyrinth in the bowels of Rafial's fortress, an escape plan was taking shape. Well, not so much of an escape plan as a saunter out and hope for the best plan. The alternative was to stay cooped up in the labyrinth forever, though Cuddles was certain he couldn't last another minute without running the mouthy and opinionated Drow through with his horn.

The unicorn had been instructed to seek out a dark enchantment cure. So he reasoned if anyone stopped the glittery tribe as they marched through the Land of Darkness and Despair, all they had to say was that they were following the prince's orders and were seeking out a Necromancer or Dark Mage to cure them. Simple. Except of course if they actually did meet a Necromancer or Dark Mage. Luckily, ahem, coincidentally, there was a popular and well-attended four night conference of Practioners of the Dark Arts at the other side of the Principality. Every evil sorcerer, enchanter, mage and wannabee would be there, jostling to be seen and show off their powers. Subsequently, the number of talking toads in the area would suddenly rise. There would never be another opportunity for the glitteries to scarper en masse and in plain sight.

Cuddles' great ploy to cross the Land of Malice and Spite was just as simplistic, they would travel only at night to avoid most humans and if stopped would say they were on their way to audition for a new mummer's group, re-enacting the great battle between the two lands. They would play the defeated Army of Darkness and Despair.

If they miraculously survived such an epic trek across two hostile territories, they were determined to live happily and sparklingly ever after. But where?

(Yep ....A blatant sequel set up)

The disgruntled ex-serf Squarf had lived in the horribly overcrowded and inevitably quarrelsome Forest of Mhmin for as long as he could stand. Which was three, long miserable days. He couldn't decide what was worse; the endless diet of nettle soup and a vile broth of similar dour vegetation. No meat was ever consumed in the forest for fear of eating someone's non-talking auntie. The overcrowding? Trying to sleep wedged in between a snoring, flatulent satyr and several restless wood gnomes was no fun. Just his normal bad luck, why else couldn't he find a cosy spot snuggled close to some cheeky flower fairies or beautiful elf maidens? Even a water nymph would be better company - they looked good though they made damp bed companions.

Squarf was tired, cold and hungry. But where else could he go? By abandoning his master, the king, he was officially an outlaw but he missed the comforts of castle life. Being kicked around the kingdom by Pravis was irksome but the perks made up for it. His comfy straw pallet pitched outside the royal kennels, the tasty banquet scraps the king's hounds had left uneaten. It had been horrible and humiliating to be locked up in a dungeon after the battle that never was to save Pravis's face, but Squarf had got over it. It had not been all bad, he'd found some jars of homemade marmalade under the filthy straw, left over from when the dungeons had been tea rooms. And made friends with a couple of jolly enchanted slugs.

Being in service was all he knew but he could not bear to see the terrible changes in the land of Goodness and Light. He was angry at losing the fun of celebrating the Pagan Feast of Wolfsbane. But the final straw was the heinous crime of trying to burn the delightful and innocent Morven at the stake! So what that her eccentric salves and potions didn't work...at least they caused no harm. What an outrage!

He was no hero in waiting, no apprentice with a hidden destiny. But a wrongdoing needed to be righted. Luckily others thought so too. By the end of his third day in the forest, Squarf had acquired allies albeit not the most promising ones, a cloud of still glitter-covered evil mosquitoes left behind by the fast retreating Army of Darkness and Despair. Two leprechauns confusingly both called Oisin and an enchanted duck. It was a start.

Rested, the little group had time to reflect on their future. As a rosy sunrise woke them from their slumbers, Morven wondered what were they? Explorers, exiles, a Fellowship searching for help restoring balance and justice to the Land of Goodness and Light? She could not make up her mind exactly what they were and what they would do next. Only that fate had drawn them together and they needed to escape.

Under the shelter of a stand of bog oak was her man, a notorious highwayman joined by a master baker armed with a lucky bun, a genuine teenage apprentice, two elves both in love with the same demon. Also a couple of human musicians from a heavy metal band and runaway princess with her newborn baby boy to protect and care for.

Also waiting to see what direction fate would take them was a bad-tempered mare and her most appalling brat of a Pooka/cursed unicorn/horse hybrid. An ambivalent dragon. A cart load of diminutive enchanted creatures including an evil butterfly in bovver boots. A mysterious and silent thing in a wooden casket-like box. Oh, and a couple of ghostly vapours that had just wafted in and silently joined them.

The weight of responsibility fell heavy on her young shoulders, most were here because of her. She was a witch, a healer, midwife and guardian of the wisdom of the earth and now she must accept her role as a Wise Woman and not a seller of New Age trinkets, salves and love potions.

With the two alpha males finally and amicably reconciled, Jed and Zaff walked to the top of a hill and surveyed the bright, mist-clad unknown landscape stretching before them. In the distance towered the Mountains of Adventures Yet Untold and beyond them, there was a vast

Ocean of Dreams Undreamt. It was daunting, exciting and downright terrifying. They had all heard of the legends - of the terrifying orange-faced Allo Vera harridans, the tribes of Too Tall Gnomes, all born with huge chips on their shoulders and many more hideous monstrosities. And magical edifices like the Non-Existent Towels of Obsidian. Which was universally believed to be a typing error.

'You could always go back down to Hell, Zaff. You don't have to stick with us mere mortals.'

'F◆♍&; that!' laughed Zaff. 'Where's the fun in living in a sulphurous cesspit filled with the languishing eternally wailing souls of the damned. The stench blocks up my sinuses and the endless wailing and gnashing of teeth gives me a perpetual headache. Sorry, old chap, look like you are stuck with me!'

He wanted to add that he couldn't bear to be away from Cylphie but that would have sounded a bit sappy for a demon to confess to the rakish Moonraven..

Jed grinned, relieved. Whatever adventures, dangers and insanity awaited them, having the powerful demon with them gave them a chance of surviving. He looked back at the two most precious things in his life he knew he didn't deserve. His wondrous, buxom Morven and the newborn babe sleeping in Allura's arms. His son. And he knew that staying alive and keeping them safe had never been so important.

(And yes, yet another blatant sequel setup.)

Morven The Unwise Woman pretended to be sorting her bag of salves and checking her supply of headache making powders...her top sellers, popular with women wanting to avoid sex with unpleasant partners. She caught Jed's misty-eyed glance towards her and the baby and dismissed it as self-indulgence. The first whiff of a lucrative bit of thievery or provocative flash of a shapely ankle and they wouldn't see him for dust. Time to grow up, time to cut him free from her heart and kick him out of her bed for good.

No! Not now! Jed sauntered towards her, tricorne hat at a rakish angle highlighting the smile that was guaranteed to turn her legs to water. She tried to stiffen against his arm around her waist, turn her head away from his kiss, shut her ears to his loud whisper...'There's a mossy bank behind that mireberry bush with our names on it...'

It was no use. All her good intentions to change dissolved to nothing as she allowed herself to be led by the hand towards the thicket.

She truly was the Unwise Woman of Fuggis Mire.

Aftermath

Even deeper in their hidden cave, the secret cell of St Epiligia Pedants continued to plot their increasingly fiendish plan of protest and resistance, their 'spectacular' to force the stubborn, blinkered world to finally see sense. Their deepest, darkest, most sincere desire and personal belief system all hinged on knowing that everything everywhere was infinitely flawed and that it was the entire point of their existence to seek out flaws where no flaws had been sought before – and correct them.

But as yet no action had been formalised, that was the problem with pedants. Every aspect of every suggestion had to be picked over and pulled to pieces over some slight inaccuracy in speech or fact. For example the phase 'blown to smithereens' uttered by one plotter caused much angst and discussion. What exactly was a smithereen? How many pieces of debris consisted of a smithereen? What was the words true origin? Was it a corruption of old

Irish or old English with an Anglo/Irish diminutive addition?

The good folk of the Land of Goodness and Light were able to sleep safely in their beds for weeks due to that one utterance.

There was nothing for it but to consult the pedants' sacred tome, which could settle the 'smithereen' debate once and for all. The Book, the repository of all precisely inscribed definitions and knowledge. When they could find it, for at some time during the misty oceans of the past, it had mysteriously disappeared.

This had been and still was a complete disaster for the pedants. For The Book was destined to be kept in a secret hallowed room, guarded by what would become the uppermost hierarchic echelon of their organization. All its syntactical errors, points of conflicting text, and spelling mistakes must be read, studied, corrected and discussed with loving pedantry by those who would become known as the St Epiligia Guardian Readers. Forever and ever. Anem.

Also available from Endaxi Press

Summer Shorts compiled by Sheena Ignatia
Featuring a story by Raven Dane

Ever wanted somebody fun and full of laughs to take with you
on holiday? Here are a whole gang of holiday companions to share
a joke with. Better still you can stick them in your suitcase and
don't have to buy them drinks.

And if you aren't going on holiday these writers will bring
sunshine into your dullest days.

Summer Shorts – a book for all seasons.

Writer & artist Stevyn Colgan said, *"I now have the perfect book
for my holiday this year. The stories are funny, pithy, and just the
right length to keep me smiling between dips in the pool. If the
weather this Summer is as enjoyable as this book I'll be a very
happy camper."*

Miranda Dickinson - Best selling author said, *"Summer Shorts is a
dazzling array of stories and poems - the perfect holiday read. I
loved it!"*

BAFTA award winning writer Kevin Cecil said, *"A lovely selection
of fun pieces, like Haribo for the eyes. Pack it."*

Summer Shorts ISBN: 978-1-907375-39-2
Available from http://www.endaxipress.com and all good
bookshops

Lightning Source UK Ltd.
Milton Keynes UK
05 September 2010

159422UK00001BA/38/P